Charity

A Dip into Donation Paradise

Charity

Charity

A Dip into Donation Paradise

By

Simon Bramhall &

Fionn Murphy

Scalpel Stories

ISBN: 978-1-9161-9151-8

Already published
by Simon Bramhall and Fionn Murphy
Trick or Treat?

Disclaimer
Charity is a work of fiction. All characters in this publication are fictitious and any resemblance to real persons, living or dead, is purely coincidental.

www.scalpelstories.com

DEDICATION

This book is dedicated to all those who volunteer in charity shops, to all those they help and to all those who complete CSOs.

Charity

CONTENTS

Charity

ACKNOWLEDGMENTS

We both owe so much to so many. Thank you.
Huge thanks are due to our families: Fiona, Jack, George and Doug for Simon; Nick, Alipops, Pippa, James, Alexis, Shirley and Ian for Fionn.
Thank you to all those who have advised, proof read, commented and supported, especially Jo, Julie, Jenna, Shayna, Jo, Estelle and Lynne.
And very special thanks to Simon, without whom Fionn would not be here and to Fionn, from Simon, for helping keep him sane.

Charity

Chapter One
Our Door Is Always Open

"It's closed."

"Leave it outside then."

"But what if someone takes it?"

"So? What's it to us? We don't want it. Anyway, we're not the first. Look. Someone's already left stuff there."

She looked at the doorstep, festooned with torn bin bags and a soiled quilt, piled up untidily against the double-glazed door.

"You sure it can't be traced back to us? What if someone sees us?" She looked around at the deserted street, slumbering still, defiantly clinging to the last moments of rest. Not even the litter was moving.

"They won't. Just shut up and dump it."

"What if it moves?"

"For God's sake, just put it down and get back in the car."

They drove off, he at the wheel, foot down, without a backward glance. She would have liked to, but did not dare.

The tramp did not stir. Too early, and it had been a long night – not so much cold, even though it was close to freezing, as full of interruptions and police sirens. He liked this doorway but had had to work hard to get it. Now the others knew it was his domain. Every morning his cardboard mattress was carefully folded and stored in the alley where the bins were kept - not the recycling ones, so no one ever removed the precious flattened boxes. More than a disposal operative's worth to cart off undesignated rubbish. If it wasn't in the right colour bin it stayed. His boxes were quite safe and on friendly terms with the blue general waste bins which hid them from sight, sheltered them from the worst of the rain and enjoyed their daytime company. The alley could be boring, the view was limited and most life was simply passing through. There were the dogs of course; bloody nuisance, peeing up against them and sniffing around. So intrusive. Such bad manners.

In his doorway, Corpy snored. The street was reaching into the day, a full body stretch, the artery of the city centre pulsing into action. He gave a loud snore, full blooded in three parts, as if swallowing himself. The last vestige of sleep before the onset of consciousness and the need to move on, or away from the door at least, before Her arrival. Corpy turned and unfolded himself; languidly straightened out his legs inside his sleeping bag. Kipping hunched up against the wall in the corner of the doorway was safe; he had learned that in the army. Not comfortable but kept you warm and you soon got used to it; always face to the wall, arms tight, legs up to the chest, completely covered. Disguised. Just a heap of detritus in a corner, of no interest to anyone. Don't draw attention; stay low; don't move. Incognito. Safe. Choose your moment. He could hear the instructor, on and on and on, a mantra in his head. But it had helped when they drove over the Taliban IED and he had been left at the side of the road.

Still a while before She arrived. Time enough for him to fully wake up, take stock of his position and reconnoitre. He would fold away the cardboard as always - army habits die hard - and secrete it in the alley. No need to carry that with him all day. Travel light, move fast. Everything that mattered would be meticulously folded and stacked inside his kit bag which went wherever he did. He did a rain check. Dry, chilly but the prospect of sun. One of those sunglasses and mittens days. Might try and get a shower and wash through some socks and pants. His standards were high; cleanliness mattered. Dry socks equaled healthy feet. Save the launderette for a wet cold day when he wanted to be off the street. His army pension was meagre but enough to sustain this life: the one he had chosen. Or was it the other life that he had rejected? Who cared?

His attention turned to the black bin bag on the other side of the doorway. New, shiny, smooth, very black, smelling still of the roll from which it had been snatched. Plasticky, an odour of domesticity, the smell from under the kitchen sink, bleach and washing up liquid. The past. He'd have that bag: essential for keeping things dry and clean. It was only half full, if that. Easy to empty and who knew, there might be things of use inside? It had been donated to a charity shop so why shouldn't he help himself to those things discarded by others? Wasn't he a charitable case? He extracted himself from his sleeping bag, rolled it up tight and put his old army issue belt around it, heaving at the buckle to make it the bundle even smaller. Then he would wrap it in the new bin liner. Belt and braces. Ha! His pun amused, but not enough to make him smile.

Crawling over to the other side of the doorway - inset double doors, double glazed, dark within, dated tile floor under the badly painted porch area which he regarded as home - he started to unpick the bag's loosely knotted top. Then stopped, a film paused mid-movement, frozen in the moment. Below his hands the bin liner was starting to shift and speak.

It was early but She was ready for work. She always was. It was always better to be in the shop before anyone else; gave her a head start on the day as well as the moral high ground. It meant she could do the float and check the till roll from yesterday, keep on top of the banking and there would be no one to sneak up behind her when she was opening the safe and find out the combination. No danger of her password being discovered when she turned on the aging desktop in the office. Prying eyes led to breaches in security, fraud, identity theft, all sorts of dishonesty. Apart from her deputy manager - and that was another story – all the workers were volunteers but no one was beyond reproach. Sad, but true. She shook her head sadly at the middle ageing woman in the full-length hall mirror. Who, apart from herself, could she trust these days? Time for another trip to the hairdresser she noticed, frowning ruefully at the dark roots sneering back at her. Once they had been darker but now the grey was beginning to impact. Oh well, perhaps not quite so much peroxide would be required this time; better not to be too blonde or people might think she was going white.

According to the Mail on Sunday white was classy, the new black; grey was 'in', to be embraced and celebrated. Poppycock. It was just old. She would ask about having some colour along with the highlights, earth colours for interest and allure, perhaps a hint of pink? Her gaze turned to the figure standing in front of her and all the satisfied anticipation of the new hair colour liquified and flowed away. That outfit did absolutely nothing for her. It had looked alright when she tried it on in the shop but here it just made her seem, well, heavy. Not fat. Never fat. Women in their late fifties always carried a little extra weight. Did she have time to change? A glance at her cubic zirconia encrusted watch told her not. She had to go. Sucking in her stomach and averting her gaze to her face, she bared her teeth to check for rogue lipstick smudges, licked her right index finger with which she smoothed and shaped her threaded eyebrows, reached for her handbag and jacket from the row of hooks on the wall alongside the mirror and let herself out of the front door.

In the doorway the bin liner was getting louder and livelier. Corpy's hands were held aloft, apart, as if in supplication to the Gods while he stared at the ministrations of the plastic bag before him. It seemed to be trying to walk. Its voice was high pitched and penetrating. Curbing the instinct to slam his booted feet and fists into it, he retreated as the bag advanced towards him until he was once more huddled in his corner. Nowhere else to run. Fight or flight. He reached out one hand - oh so slowly - and prodded the blackness at his feet. It yielded and his tentative finger sank into pulpy softness, which immediately fixed and went silent.

Nothing happened. Now what? It was a standoff. Then the voice in his head told him what to do: his friend, always there. Take the initiative. Assume control of the situation it said. Make them afraid. Uncertain. What will you do next? Unsettle them.

He reached out with his left hand and began to tease the knot undone, a movement at a time. Fluid and careful, soothing, like stroking a baby's head. His right hand gripped his SA80. He could feel it, solid and cool against his thigh. Inside the bag nothing was moving. Slowly he released the last tie of the knot and began to pull the crumpled edges apart, a crease at a time. Poised. Taut. Ready for action.

The explosion caught him by surprise. Flesh and fur erupted from the dark interior and four legs were deposited in his lap. Above them was a wiry body and a head with folded ears, wide molten brown eyes above a bearded nose. A little damp from confinement in sealed plastic where breath had turned to moisture but apparently none the worse for the experience. In fact, the small dog seemed invigorated. Energised. Oblivious to its appointment with death and now simply happy to be in fresh air - street air, city air, any air. It shook itself vigorously, dispelled the past and looked at Corpy as if to say,

"Well. Here I am. Now what?"

He stared back. What the hell was he supposed to do? He had never had a dog. Knew nothing about them. Was not sure if he even liked them very much. And why had someone dumped one in his doorway? He did not even know what type of dog it was or even its sex, although that was easily sorted. A quick glance at its undercarriage told him he was definitely dealing with a male, no doubt about that, and somewhat beyond the puppy stage judging by its undoubted assets. You did not have to be a vet to work that one out. It did not seem very old though but quite friendly, almost sociable. No collar but just a flattened band of hair around its neck and a neat inch long cut on its right shoulder, still open, which had oozed blood that was now blackening and sticking the nearby hair into spiky lumps. Its head was like a shoe box, a hairy brick with a beard that drizzled around its mouth and the sloppy tongue that pulsated and dripped enthusiastically too close to his own face.

What did they eat? Was it trained? He realised with a shudder that he was asking the kind of questions that suggested he might not get rid of it and that shocked him. At the same moment he recognised that his right hand was no longer gripping metal. At some point he had put down his weapon and had no idea when. But now, time was against him. She would be arriving any minute and he had to be gone. No choice but to get up and go, leave the dog and scarper. He stood up, grabbed the black plastic and his kit, picked up the cardboard for its daily sojourn with the green bins and set off for day care alley. The dog followed, cheerfully, trotting amiably alongside his new best friend.

She parked the car, a second-hand but only just {6 months old, unexpectedly deceased traffic warden's Nissan Micra) in the loading area behind the shop. Hers was a designated spot, clearly marked. She had seen to that on her first day. 'VHS Manager Only'. What the volunteers did with their vehicles she had no idea, but there was a perfectly good public car park further down the street at very reasonable rates. When asked about parking by new staff she always suggested that they use public transport: so eco-friendly, or what about cycling? She was sure she could find a sheltered spot for a bicycle. She wasn't, but as almost all the volunteers were elderly and verging on the infirm, cycling was never really an option. Anyway, they had bus passes. Of course, for her the car was a necessity: meetings to attend, confidential paperwork, her presence in the shop in all weathers all year round. She was permanent; salaried; it was different. So was Candy, but that was another matter. Carefully shutting and locking the car door then checking the lock, just to be sure (you couldn't trust anyone these days, even outside a charity shop) she picked up her handbag, a rather garish pink and yellow Radley still with the little dog tagging from the zip which had come into the shop a few months ago and which she discreetly put aside in the office as 'designer'. That and vintage were always of interest to their customers but pricing them was so tricky. Too little and they were a giveaway; too much and no one would buy. Unable to put a number on the handbag she had made a symbolic donation straight into the till and kept it for her own personal use. Tag side out.

It was always surprising what was donated. You simply never knew what might come in, arrive on the doorstep or materialise overnight on the doorstep like cast-off manna. With that in mind she unlocked the dingy back door and let herself into the sorting area at the back of the shop. The smell no longer bothered her. Dried sweat, ingrained dirt, stale air, mustiness, sorrow and neglect, wrapped in futile aerosol attempts to sanitize and sweeten. She walked straight through to the front door, flicking on lights as she passed, heels clacking on the hard floor. Squinting through the glass of the front entrance she noted with satisfaction that the doorstep was clear – a little dusty from the street perhaps but no collections of other people's detritus dumped overnight. Thank heavens the sign she had put up, large and prominent, was beginning to take effect. It had taken weeks of discussion to choose the wording. What she wanted to say was “Don’t chuck your rubbish on my doorstep for anyone to come and help themselves, however awful it is” but in the end had conceded to the polite but impersonal “No donations to be left overnight. Thank you.” and underneath in much smaller letters, “Your donation matters to us. We want to keep it safe. Please bring it inside when we are open.”

She peered suspiciously through the double-glazed doors, looking for trouble. Street quiet, not much traffic, no vagrants or beggars (weren’t they the same?) Nothing to bother about. Slightly disappointed she turned and click-clacked back towards the office.

Five minutes later he could be seen peering into the shop. Lights on so she must be there already. Wasn’t she always? But no sign of life. What should he do? She knew he would be there, didn’t she? How could he tell her? There was a doorbell but he did not like to use it in case she was busy; she hated being interrupted and had so much important work to do that it wasn’t fair. She needed the peace and quiet. It was marvellous how she used the computer - could print things and photocopy as well! Amazing. So clever. Perhaps if he tapped on the glass, she would hear but not be cross about being disturbed. Colin began to sweat. What would he do if she did not hear him? How would he get in? He wiped his brow. Inhaled and tapped very lightly on the door. Soft finger ends paddling in water, barely a ripple on the surface. He waited.

She checked her watch against the time on the computer and frowned. Five to nine. Where was he? She would have to open up and man the till herself. It was just the two of them on the shop floor this morning for the first hour which was manageable as the shop tended to be quiet first thing. Otherwise she could not possibly leave Colin alone behind the counter. Irritation in every pencil heel step she clattered back to the shop floor and positioned herself at the till where she furtively dredged a small key from beneath her blouse. It hung on a long chain around her neck down to her cleavage where it lived, warm and cosy, coming up for air only when it had a date with the till. Safe. Impregnable. Had she realised just how safe, Davinia might not have felt so satisfied.

The soft knocking at the door startled her. She froze, key in till.

Immobile. Turned her head carefully without moving her arms and saw Colin peering through the glass at her, waving eagerly and pointing to the door handle. He was mouthing something that she could not hear but no change there; Colin often spoke but most of the time no one had any idea what he was talking about. Repressing a sigh and smiling over-brightly she unlocked the door and held it open, wearing her best 'how lovely to see you remember I am in charge' face.

"Colin. Come in. Have you just arrived? Problem with your transport? It's not like you to be late."

Colin blushed and sweated a little more.

"I was here."

"But it's nearly opening time. Where were you?"

"On the doorstep."

"I didn't hear the bell."

"I didn't ring it."

She looked through him into the week ahead and waited for some sort of explanation. It did not come.

"Shall I put out the open sign, Davinia?"

"Yes. Excellent, Colin. Thank you. I'm just sorting out the till."

"Oh. Can I watch?"

"Well, yes, if you want to. But there's not much to see." Even Davinia was thrown. Colin was keen, usually reliable and very popular with some of the older customers but wanting to watch the machinations of turning on the till, inserting the float and closing the cash drawer was a new one on her.

"It's all so complicated" he wondered, awestruck as the drawer pinged shut. "I don't know how you do it."

She hoped he did not see her shake her head while her eyebrows soared up to meet her hairline.

"Don't forget your lanyard, Colin. You can't be on the shop floor without it you know. Company policy."

"Oh yes, I know. It's in my pocket. So that I know where it is."

The eyebrows stayed aloft but now the face was turned towards him.

"Shall I put it on?"

"Yes please, Colin."

"Now?"

"Yes."

"It's so that people know who I am isn't it?"

Yes. And proves that you are an official volunteer for the Veteran's Homeless Society."

"Serving those who have served".

"That's exactly right, Colin. That's what we do. Raise money to help veterans in any way we can."

There was a pause. Colin was thinking.

"Davinia?"

"Yes?"

"Veterans are old soldiers, right?"

"They're all types of military personnel, Colin, not just from the army but yes, lots of them were soldiers."

"So why do they call them vets?"

It was going to be a long day.

Colin had stationed himself behind the counter and was beaming beatifically across the empty shop floor, Lord of all he surveyed but never touched unless it was to put it in carrier bag - a source of great stress. Customers who wanted carriers were required to part with 5p for the privilege of a VHS emblazoned receptacle. They had to pay; it was The Law. That's what he had been told to tell them that if they quibbled but it distressed him. Asking for money for a carrier bag! And they were a charity! It did not seem right, especially when they just threw the bag away afterwards. Candy had told him to tell them to recycle to save the planet but all of them were walking or came by car so did not have bicycles. And what did that have to do with the carrier bags? It was very complicated but he loved working there, meeting people, doing his bit for the old soldiers, helping Davinia and Candy. He liked the other regular volunteers too. There weren't many of them but everyone was so friendly although sometimes they wanted to be behind the counter, but that was His Job. He was learning how to do the till and one day might even be able to do Gift Aid. So exciting, although the responsibility often kept him awake at night. Sometimes, he did not know how he coped with His Job and The Shop and the demands of his tropical fish. And now Swiss Railway Journeys was showing on the television.

The click of pencil heels brought him to attention. Davinia! She looked marvellous. She always looked marvellous. Smart, sophisticated with lipstick and high heels, she never wore trousers. Candy said that was because her hips were as wide as her legs were long, but that did not make sense. Davinia wore dresses mostly, a real lady. Skirts and blouses restricted her movement apparently so dresses were best – more slimming, Candy said, but Davinia wasn't fat so that did not make sense either. Standing in the doorway Davinia looked like one of those framed pictures in the photographer's window, a photograph made to look like a painting. Really beautiful. His smile split his face. Davinia was consulting her watch, the one with all the diamonds.

"She's late. Again."

"Who?"

"The Community Service girl."

Colin had to think for minute.

"The other one's here. The old bloke."

"Oh, him. Yes. Why do we have to put up with them?" It was a rhetorical question and Davinia did not expect an answer, but Colin did not know that.

"Because there's no one else."

"You'd think after what she's done, she'd at least be on time. Community Service is meant to be a punishment. Not that we look at it that way" she added hastily turning her attention to Colin, who had not noticed.

"Colin."

"Yes?" in his best anything I can do for you Davinia, consider it done, even if I have to die doing it tone.

"You're wearing your shell suit again. We've talked about this."

A small boy chastised, mortified, so anxious to please, such a hopeless failure.

"But it's so comfortable."

"Something smarter next time please. Think of our image." His smile fixed itself to his face which crumpled into it as his eyes moistened. Now it was Davinia who did not notice. "Couldn't they do their Community Service painting benches or something? Isn't that what footballers do?"

Colin did not like to argue but he was hurt. "It's winter. I expect they want to be inside." Then, "it's cold."

"Well they're staying in the back. This is a high-class charity shop and I don't want them on the shop floor. Especially her. She's a distraction." Having been defeated, surrendered and lost the will to fight, Colin searched for something to say and eventually resorted to his favourite topic of conversation, the epicentre of his waking and too often, sleeping existence.

"He's good on the till." A reluctant accolade, but admiring and heartfelt. "'Cos he's used to fancy hospital equipment I expect." There had to be an explanation; no one could possibly work it without some sort of prior training or expertise. And there was so much machinery in a hospital. He knew. He'd been in one.

Davinia decided to move the day on.

"Is Alex in the stockroom?"

Colin's smile became flexible again now that he was back on safe ground. He knew the answer to this one and knew he was right, so no one could tell him off.

"Mr Whiteley? Yes. Sorting."

"I'll go and check on him." The framed image turned its back and made to move off into far perspective but suddenly stopped and faced the figure in the foreground. "Let's keep the door closed today, Colin. As you said, it's cold, and heat costs money." Vindication; a brief moment of victory but then consternation verging on panic. Colin's smile vanished.

"How'll people know we're open if the door's shut? They might think we're closed."

"Put the 'Open – keeping warm' sign up. On the door. Inside but facing out. So that people can see it. Can you do that for me, Colin? Thank you."

And she was gone, lips pursed, heels clicking, eyes narrowed, in pursuit of Alex.

Chapter Two
Serving the Community

Alex Whiteley, senior consultant surgeon did not want to be there. He was in the sorting room under duress: serving time by serving others, even though he had already been serving them for the best part of thirty-five years in the NHS. His crime had been to over-serve someone on whom he was operating, to save their life, in that he had been found guilty of inscribing his initials on the donor liver he had just inserted in the patient on the table before him. Obviously, without their consent. Alex accepted that he had done wrong; crossed a line; abused his privileged position as a surgeon but no harm had been done and the patient went on to live a full and healthy life. However, Alex had to be punished and be seen to be punished. The media insisted on it. So here he was, paying his debt to society in the form of a substantial fine (or woefully lenient depending on which paper you read) and working hundreds of unpaid hours sorting out donations to the Veteran's Homeless Society. He also had the added responsibility of steaming, brushing and cleaning the aforementioned donations to remove every trace of their pre-loved existence so that they appeared on the shop floor crisp, fragrant and enticing.

"They need to be irresistible" Davinia had said. "So that people just have to buy them; can't live without them. We must turn needs into wants." Or was it the other way around? She could never quite remember but no matter, it amounted to the same thing. She knew; she had done an online course in Business Administration at Madison University, Gulfport, Mississippi and had the diploma to prove it. Although the qualification was from an American institution, business was the same the world over, as she had told them in her interview. They had been most impressed, especially with the certificate itself which she had removed from its frame and taken with her to prove her accreditation. No lying on her CV! She had heard that some people invented qualifications and embellished their experience but she was not one of those. "What you see is what you get", she had told them. And clearly, they liked what they saw and she got the job.

That was five years ago and the difference in the shop under her management was "exactly what they had hoped for" she had been told at her most recent appraisal. They were "delighted" with her performance. Takings were up, morale was rising, their standing in the local community was high and getting higher. The local branch of Rotary had even awarded them their coveted Outstanding Contribution to The Local Community Medal for their input to the life and image of the town. And all since Davinia had taken over the shop. Senior managerial faith in Davinia at Head Office was absolute. Even though she had been the only applicant for the position, she would undoubtably have been the first choice even if she had not been the only choice. She was marvellous. Understood what was wanted and how it was wanted without argument. Ran the shop without any problems; conformed, followed orders, submitted the (tedious but necessary) weekly analysis of the type/amount/condition/price of all clothes sold without complaint, unlike the other managers who never stopped griping. She met targets and even got on well with the Regional Manager, who descended regularly once a week - supposedly unannounced but always by arrangement on a Friday - to check the stock and appearance of the shop floor. She managed her staff effectively and charmingly; one of them even seemed to be quite in love with her.

Alex was struggling to come to terms with the arcane system of sorting and distributing clothes. He could remove and replace a human liver thereby restoring a person's life and future in a little over four hours, if all went well, but the convoluted VHS system of sorting donations had him stumped. Davinia had explained it to him and Shelley, his partner in rehabilitation, on their first day at the beginning of the week. It was now Wednesday and still he could not get his head round it. He and his wife, Lisa, had studied the hastily written instructions he had been given by a frustrated Davinia which read like a flat pack Sudoku.

"It's ridiculous!" Lisa had said. "How can it be so complicated? And this has to be done every time it moves on? That's crazy!"

"Unpack, steam, hang, brush, date label, display, bag, transfer, repeat." Alex was invoking the mantra under his breath.

"One more go then we'll call it a day. Christ. I'd rather be in A&E on a Saturday night." He reached for another glass of red. "Right." Geared for action, fortified, he started again. "Clothes arrive at Source A. Unpack, steam, hang, brush, date label, display, but if they don't sell are bagged and transferred to store B which does same, then sends to store C, ditto to store D and so on until the clothes either a) sell b) disintegrate from so much cleaning or c) are deemed unsuitable for human consumption so are sent to North Shields where they are flogged off at rock bottom prices. And if they don't sell there, the last hurrah, they are sent for recycling God knows where, the final resting place. And that's just the distribution. We haven't even started on the in-shop labelling and coding system. Or the fate of goods donated directly to stores. Or those with dirt marks, threads, burn marks, holes …"

"red wine stains" muttered Lisa.

"… which go straight to North Shields".

"Where is North Shields?"

"I'd have to Google it."

Davinia was super cheerful, always a bad sign.

"Good morning Alex! How are we this morning? Ready for action?" She beamed as she scrutinised the pile of donations he had started lifting out of a bin liner and which were now being laid out on the table like corpses for an autopsy. "Are we sure we know what we are doing?" The beam cast its rays over him like an oxyacetylene torch. "Not quite the table you are used to I'm afraid!" She wasn't and she wanted him to know it. She was in charge here and it would do him no harm to be reminded of it. Frequently. He had arrived on Monday wearing a suit. A suit! Who did he think he was? And not just any old suit, but one of the expensive Italian range from M&S with the silk linings - she was in retail, she knew these things. No tie, admittedly, which both irked and satisfied. If he wanted to make the right impression then he should have put one on - he could have removed it later - but if he wanted to dress down and fit in with them, mere mortals, why wear any part of a suit at all? Obviously, she had said nothing but he had got the message and she noticed with almost approval that he was in jeans and a casual shirt today. With a T shirt underneath. Sensible. The steaming made everything so hot that any clothes were an encumbrance and he might have been better off in shorts, except that it was freezing outside. He was wearing trainers today instead of those polished black lace ups which showed up water stains so badly. They appeared to have developed vitiligo by closing time on Monday and were probably ruined. She smiled even more broadly.

"Good morning, Davinia. In great form, thank you. Looking forward to another day in donation paradise ..."

The smile never faltered but the eyes narrowed. Be charitable, give him the benefit of the doubt; he's paying his debt to society. She became saintly.

"...steaming and brushing out the detritus of someone else's discarded life."

Saintliness tested, smile concrete solid, she did not react. But did not ignore; it would all be written verbatim in the report for his Probation Officer. The silence hung around them like chemical air freshener. "Plenty to do then" she added brightly. "Any sign of your co-worker yet?"

"The lovely Shelley? Outside. Having a quick one." ... "Cigarette" he added to clear up any misunderstanding. Davinia's face cleared.

"So, she's here. She should be inside, working." Then it clouded.

"What's she smoking?"

Alex peered at her over his glasses much as he would over a sterile mask at a theatre nurse who had handed him the wrong surgical instrument. Much to her disgust, Davinia flinched, but retaliated.

"She'd better put the ends in the bin, that's all I can say. Not drop them all over the floor. I hope she's wearing something more appropriate today."

They both examined the steaming equipment basking beside them, listening to its wet gasps and steamy breath, a slumbering overweight dragon of ancient lineage and uncertain temperament. 'Appropriate' might mean anything from tropical army kit or a mankini to a thong, assuming that full nudity was unacceptable.

"Which reminds me," Davinia said. "We need to discuss the type of clothes being put out on the shop floor. The Regional Manager was upset last week to find a lightweight dress on sale. More suitable for summer than this time of year. It's November so it's cold weather clothes we should be promoting at the moment." Alex nodded sagely. He wanted to say that winter was coming but did not trust himself.

"Winter's coming." she said. "Remind me to show you the cellar."

"Davinia! Davinia!" It was Colin. "I can't get the till to work!"

Saintly Davinia sighed, donned martyrdom and headed out towards the shop floor and Colin's escalating hysteria.

As soon as she had left the stockroom the back door was pushed fully open and Shelley appeared.

"Where's the witch?" she hissed.

"Shop floor. Colin. Till crisis." Alex replied. "Leave the door open, it's getting hot in here."

"Bloody freezing outside" muttered Shelley but came in nevertheless. "She notice I'm late?" Alex grinned. Of course she had; this was Davinia they were talking about. Shelley shrugged two bony tattooed shoulders poking out of a wide-necked sweater. As much as neck and shoulders were exposed, arms and hands were covered. The sweater slopped down over her buttocks nearly as far as the hem of the skirt skimming the top of her thighs. Gravity in action; the sweater helpless in its grip, descending to the earth. At least she was wearing leggings – or were they tights? Alex had no idea, but was glad she would not freeze to death. Not yet, anyway. He liked Shelley. Her openness and honesty were refreshing; whatcha see is whatcha get she had told him when they were introduced and it seemed true. Hard to believe she had been convicted of shop lifting and was doing her Community Service in a charity shop 'to learn how to empathise with those she had victimised'. So far, it was not working, largely because of Davinia.

"I told her you were here but having a cigarette outside."

"She believe you?"

"I think so. If you find her outside checking for fag ends, you'll know she has."

"Thanks, Al. I owe you." Shelley pulled up her sagging sleeves revealing more tattoos scrolling up her arms. "Right," she said. "What we doin' today?"

Alex laughed. They did the same thing every day and it was only Wednesday. The question was entirely superfluous and they both knew it. It was astonishing. Polar opposites in every conceivable way they were totally united in their antagonism to Davinia. No mean achievement on her part. Perhaps she could be hired out as a solution to international conflict: the one thing to unite opposing parties into a truce based a dislike of the enemy being greater than their dislike for each other. Sleeves rolled, ready for action, Shelley, bird-skinny black-legged in her pelmet skirt and Doc Martens looked like something that had itself arrived at the shop in a bin bag. An exotic animal with vibrant hair and mismatched earrings swinging exuberantly from lobes festooned with inky fingers from the tattoos creeping up her neck and yet she still somehow assumed the demeanour of a char lady, mopped and ready to go. Alex laughed again and felt very old. She pulled her left sleeve up above the elbow and lifted up her arm so that he could see the soft flesh of the underarm, pink and tender, covered in cling film.

"Got a new tattoo. Whad'ya think?" He peered at it closely. Impossible to make out what it was under the creased polythene and crusting incisions.

"It looks sore".

"Yeah. That's normal." The sleeve came down again. "Gotta keep it clean" she said, reaching for an unopened bag of donations. "God. I hope these aren't like the last lot. How do people live like that?"

On the shop floor, saintliness was being sorely tried. Davinia had explained to Colin how the till worked so many times she now felt like a budget airline stewardess giving the safety demonstration at the start of yet another short haul flight. Smile, engage the audience, use clear actions to accompany simple verbal instructions with props as appropriate, smile a little more, look encouraging, then hope for the best. For Colin it was new every time: exciting, in close proximity to the lovely Davinia, inspirational and important. Almost overwhelming. He would love to be able to remember how to do it but it was all so complicated; so much to think about at the same time; so much that could go wrong. But Davinia would put it right. She was marvellous.

"We'll go through it again, Colin, from the start. Obviously, the till is already on so all you have to do is enter the price of the garment …"

"On the price tag?"

"That's right. Exactly as it's written on the price tag, which you will find…?

"Inside the clothes, where the labels are."

"Excellent. Exactly right. So…" here she steered his attention towards the keypad on the electronic till. This was where it invariably started to go wrong. Slowly, carefully, actions to correspond with words, she went through it again,

"Number of pounds, decimal point, number of pence." Colin was about to speak but Davinia cut him off at the pass. They had been here before. "And if there's no pence you just press the number of pounds and then the decimal point. Then press the Transaction button – that's right, the square one with Transaction written on it and the amount will register. No, no decimal point after the pence. Only one decimal point in each transaction Colin, and always after the pounds. … Only pence and no pounds? Well, yes, that's different and there's no decimal point at all. I know, it's confusing but all you do then is put in the number of pence, for example 50, like this, and no decimal point, and then press Transaction. Yes. The till will know that it's just pence and that there's no decimal point. No, it won't think you've forgotten it." Davinia clinging onto saintliness now with desperation, praying for an oxygen mask to fall from an overhead locker and bring relief. "So, the next part."

Colin inhaled deeply. This was the really difficult bit. He could remember that much about it.

"After the Transaction button enter the amount of money the customer has given you – yes, in exactly the same way, including the decimal point and – this is the important part - press Sale. That's right, the green button with, you've got it, Sale written on. Then the till will do the work for you and calculate the amount of change, if any, you need to give the customer. And when you press Sale, the till drawer will automatically open. It is clever, isn't it? Then all you have to do is look on the screen – it is like a little television, yes, - and the amount will come up so then all you have to do is take the change out of the drawer and give it to the customer. ...Well, if there's no change to give, then don't give them any. Yes, they'll understand. Then they take their purchase, yes. ... Don't forget to give them their receipt which pops out of the till when the drawer closes. What? Well, obviously, you know that they've paid the money, but the receipt is their proof of purchase in case they want to return something. Or change it." She avoided the 'so that we know they aren't a shop lifter' for the time being. A moment's silence. She knew what was coming.

"Yes, carrier bags do have to be paid for, Colin, you know that. Not my rule and if I had my way, they'd be free but we have to abide by the law so they cost 5p each. I know how tricky it makes things for you so I have an idea. Instead of putting the money in the till we'll just ask the customer to put 5p in the VHS donation tin on the counter, here. That's right, through the little slit in the top. Well, if they don't have the exact change ask them to put in whatever they can. No, no it doesn't matter if it's more than 5. It's all in a good cause and will compensate for those who don't have any change at all. Any questions? My goodness, look at the time! Important phone call to make! I'll be in my office if you want me. Gift Aid? Call Alex.... What? Yes, I know he's not allowed on the shop floor but he can if it's to help with the till. Yes, and debit cards. But not her. Don't let her anywhere near it."

Chapter Three
The Community

On the street, Corpy was struggling. Not the usual kind of struggle of blending in with the background, keeping warm, trying to stay clean, boredom: life in the trenches without the shelling, but struggling to avoid the attention of everyone who wanted to meet his dog.

"He's not mine" he had started off by saying but had now given up. Clearly no one believed him, least of all the dog, forever amiable and well behaved. Never left his side; met those who approached him with graciousness and charm but stuck tenaciously to Corpy, even when he tried to sneak away unnoticed. He had tried telling him to go away, to piss off, go home, find someone else, but the dog just smiled and continued to follow, paw to heel. Unshakeable. Furtive too, Corpy noticed, in a slyly benign way. Watched; listened, but quietly, surreptitiously, as if logging the info for future reference. Brains behind the smile. He liked that. His mates on the street were amused and intrigued. Where had he come from? When? How? They could not believe the 'how'. Were outraged.

"Dumped? On the doorstep? In a bin bag?" "But who'd do such a thing?" They were shocked and immediately, the dog became one of them, a member of the dispossessed army in the heart of the city outside society.

"Whad'ya call him?"

"Whad'ya mean he ain't gotta name? Gotta have a name."

This was true. Corpy knew it but also knew that by giving him a name he was forming a relationship and that was not what he wanted. He did not do relationships, not since the army anyway, and probably before if he was honest. Somewhere in his past was a wife and a daughter, and another woman whom he had not married, all of whom he had consciously abandoned. He was always sorry he had hurt them but it was better this way. The last thing he wanted was a dog. How the hell would he feed it? Hard enough to feed himself.

"Yer not thinking this through, mate" one of the displaced told him as they were sitting on the pavement, backs to the wall out of the wind enjoying the pale sun. "'Ee'll feed himself, and you too if yer canny. Look how everyone likes 'im. All you 'ave to do is sit somewhere public - discreet, mind - not in people's faces, they don't like that - and let the dog do the work. People'll give money for a dog if it looks 'ungry. Not for you, but for the dog. Tell them you're an old soldier, which is true, then make up some shit about 'im being a sniffer dog you brought back from Afghan or a stray you rescued there. Somefing like that. They'll love it."

"I'm not begging!" Now Corpy was outraged.

"Can yer afford to keep 'im if you don't?"

"I don't know that I want to keep him at all."

The dog gazed at him, hurt but understanding, eternally forgiving.

"Don't think yer've got much choice, mate" his friend said. "'E's not goin' anywhere. Gotta have a name."

Man and dog exchanged a long unblinking stare. It was Corpy who looked away first. The dog gazed at him contentedly.

"Rupert," Corpy finally announced.

"Rupert? Yer can't call the poor bastard Rupert!"

"I can and I will. After the guy that picked me up off the roadside, Second Lieutenant Rupert Horrocks. But I'll call him Roop, or maybe Troop. Whad'ya think?"

"Troop's ok. Fits with you as a Corporal."

Troop appeared quite satisfied with his new name. Corpy had the disturbing feeling that it was not he who had chosen the name at all, but the dog, but that was absurd. As long as he knew who was in charge, they would get along fine.

"'E needs a collar. The PDSA place will 'elp you out with that and fix that 'ole in 'is shoulder."

Corpy wanted to know what it was.

"'E was chipped but some git cut it out so 'e couldn't be traced, poor little bastard. There are some real psychos out there."

They sat in the sun for a little while longer, the three of them, enjoying the meagre warmth.

"Where's this PDSA place then?" asked Corpy.

It was getting hotter in the stockroom. Windowless, they had the back door open to try and relieve the pressure but the steam was building and the walls were weeping. Alex had stripped down to his T shirt and trousers and was contemplating removing shoes and socks so that the sweat had a clear run down his legs to the floor. Shelley had removed the oversized sweater to reveal an undersized cami top which did not reach the top of the skirt that hardly reached the top of her thighs. Yet she still looked hot. Her midriff was shiny and the piercing in her belly button had begun to glisten and droop. The tattoos clothing her arms and shoulders seemed darker somehow; overbaked, a matching pair for her black clad legs. Underneath its cling film the new tattoo had become red, angry and wet so she had removed the protective covering, freeing the wound to breathe.

"Not much longer now" Alex said encouragingly. "Just this pile then we can turn this bloody thing off and cool down."

"But then we've got all the sorting to do for the next lot" Shelley muttered as menacingly as the serpent climbing up her left arm into her ear. She had said it was a tribute to *Hamlet*, her favourite Shakespeare play which had astounded Alex. Just when you thought you were getting to know someone, they proved you had no idea what went on in their minds and lives. He wondered if all her tats had literary connections. And then, what she had been shop lifting. The complete works of Shakespeare? He looked at her with new respect.

The sorting system for clothes on the shop floor was as arcane, if not even more laborious, than the inter-shop distribution network. What irritated most was that all the tags on clothes passed on to them from other stores had to be removed before hanging and steaming. New tags with the current date and size had to be put on and then either

Davina or Candy would price them and they would be put out on the shop floor for exactly fourteen days.

"No more, no less, unless they've sold of course" Davinia had emphasised.

Alex had made himself very unpopular.

"If they were transported still on their hangers, on rails in the van instead of stuffed into bags, then most of this hanging and steaming wouldn't be necessary" he had suggested. Davinia had stared at him, incredulous.

"This is your first day, Mr Whiteley" she had said. Then added, "And what would we do for coat hangers in the shop if they're all in the van?"

Alex had had sense enough not to answer and the torment continued. Only when the steaming of yesterday's pile was over and the garments were cooling into shape would the day improve until the Promethean steaming began again the following morning. He resolved to spend his lunch hour shopping, in the next room, to see if he could find a pair of hiker's trousers that would unzip at the knee. But then he remembered that at this time of year all summer and lightweight gear was bundled up into ever more black plastic and carted off down to the cellar, usually by Colin, where it was left to mould and mushroom until Summer arrived on 1 May, whatever the weather.

"What's the carbon footprint of all this?" Lisa had asked. It was not something he had thought about before but now he wondered more and more.

"Lady Macbeth'll be bringing in today's victims this afternoon I s'pose" Shelley muttered darkly at the prospect of the arrival at their feet of everything 14 days old from the shop floor. "Plucked untimely." Alex had no idea what she was talking about but got the gist. Really, the girl was astonishing.

"Is it me?" she had said on their first day. He had turned around to see her wearing a leather corset with long red evening gloves that reached up to her elbow. Her eyes had all but disappeared behind the black satin mask over the top half of her face and in her hands, she was holding a leather whip and a pair of handcuffs: a diminutive Dominatrix in Doc Martens and, on that occasion, yellow and black stripy tights. His howl of laughter had brought Davinia running into the room, abandoning the hapless Colin to the terrors of the till while she investigated the suspicious noise.

"Whatever is going on?" she had begun then stopped, on arrival, with shock. Shattered.

"They were in the donations you asked us to sort" Shelley had said, unbidden, pointing with the whip to the carrier bag, "that came in today. Do you often get things like this?" Davinia ignored the question and tried hard to reconcile them with the image of the middle-aged woman with the pearl stud earrings in Jaeger who had deposited the bag that morning with a smile and Gift Aid. When Shelley had removed the offending articles, Davinia stuffed them back into the bag and assigned the whole lot for recycling, then sought temporary refuge in the sanctity of her office to restore her decorum with coffee and a Danish. Sod the weekly weigh in; she'd had a dreadful experience and needed the sugar.

Steaming over and donation sorting in progress, Alex and Shelley were working their Community Service way through a collection of enormous clothes.

"They're all homemade" Shelley observed, turning one of them inside out to examine the seams and find a label that was not there. "Someone's gone to a lot of trouble. Look, all the seams are overstitched and they're really generous, not like bought clothes." Not having a clue what she was talking about, Alex was marvelling at the sheer amount of fabric involved.

"It's massive. There are yards of it." Shelley was of a generation that thought in metres but the conclusion was the same. "Whoever wore it must have been gigantic."

"Or still is," she was saying when Davinia had materialised in the doorway.

"We do not refer to our donors like that" she said. "It is not our policy to comment on the physique or appearance of any of our clients. We respect all shapes and sizes in this organisation. Items such as that belong in our Curvy Customer section which is extremely popular. Not everyone is a size 10." This was aimed at Shelley, who was definitely no more than that and probably less. The barb struck, but did not injure. Davinia pivoted and pincered on her high heels and clacked away as if to make a point with their pencil tips.

"Cankles" Shelley hissed. If Davinia heard she did not respond. Alex only understood when Lisa explained about cankles that evening over dinner.

"Never mind" he had said to Shelley as Davinia flounced out. "We've got Candy tomorrow." "Yeah". Shelley brightened. "Lady Macbeth's day off…she's back on Friday?"

"So I believe. When the regional manager comes in."

"I thought he was supposed to be arrive unexpectedly and catch us with our knickers down. She said he always arrived unannounced."

"Every Friday apparently. According to Colin."

"Then it must be right." Was she being sarcastic? Alex thought not, because that was exactly the sort of thing that Colin did know, that and everything to do with the care of tropical fish. She was wearing her sweater again but now rolled one sleeve right up above the elbow to examine her newest inking.

"That looks painful." Alex the medical man. Concerned. "Does it itch?" She nodded. "It ought to be covered; let's get you a plaster or something. It means disturbing Davinia in her lair I'm afraid, but needs must. D'you want me to go?"

"No. Pleasure's all mine." Now that was unmistakably sarcastic. Alex wondered if he should feel sympathy for the lovely Davinia, who had no idea what was about to happen.

The door to her office was shut even though she had said it was always open – Company Policy – so Shelley gave it large when she rapped on it with her knuckles. Not waiting for an invitation, she was halfway into the room as Davinia was bidding her "Enter!"

"Shelley!" Shock or just an unpleasant surprise, it was hard to say, but the smile switched on and settled round her mouth like Botox. "What can I do for you?"

"Plaster. For my arm." Shelley stuck out the tattoo sleeve with the inflamed addition which was looking very sorry for itself indeed; angry, red, violently moist. "Please."

Shelley pulled away from the skinny limb and sniffed above the immoveable smile. "Plasters cost money" she said, thinking 'it serves you right for being such a barbarian', "and it will have to be recorded in the injuries book. We can't give out medical dressings without explaining why. Accountability. Insurance requirement. Company …"

"Policy" they both said together. The smile never budged; the teeth moved like actors inside a proscenium arch.

"What size plaster do you want? A small one would let the air in better than a big one."

And be cheaper they both thought together.

"Definitely a big one. To keep it clean." Shelley grinned and showed her teeth. Dentures drawn, smile to smile combat. Personal. But Davinia had the First Aid box, her trump card so victory would be hers.

"No. A small one. To let the air in. Stand there and I'll get you one." She opened one of the drawers in the desk upon which the arthritic computer languished and took out a small key, with which she opened a locked drawer on the other side of the same desk. From this she withdrew the green emergency first aid box with the white cross and lifted the lid. Inside was the injuries book, which she opened and in which she wrote, carefully, the date, the injury and the treatment required – none.

"Sign here please, Shelley. Then you can have the dressing."

"I need to read it first." A sigh, the book was turned to the patient and Davinia waited, pen in hand, for Shelley to finish reading.

"You'll notice I've said that the injury was self-inflicted, off the premises" Davinia explained, "for the insurance. VHS accepts no responsibility should you attempt to claim. Sign, here … that's it. …Thank you. … Your plaster." Game and set to Davinia, but not the match. Not yet. Shelley regaled Alex with the skirmish.

"But what happens in a real emergency? If there's no one around to open unlock the drawer? What are we supposed to do then?" His outrage almost matched his disbelief.

At exactly five minutes to five, Colin glued his attention to the clock on the wall opposite the counter and began counting down. Important to be punctual and precise: Davinia had said so and he would never let her down. As the clock hit the hour, he was standing behind the door ready to remove the 'Open - keeping warm' sign and replace it with one that said 'Closed.' Just that, straight to the point; end of. Not opening for anybody. Davinia would lock the door but he would stay there until she arrived, just in case Somebody tried to get in. He felt like James Bond as he turned to the sound of heels on tiles and watched Davinia approaching, key in hand.

"Ready to go Colin? I'll lock the door behind you. The others have gone already. Couldn't wait to get out of the door. I don't know. What's the world coming to?" He could not think of anything to say so slid out of the door she held open for him and smiled as helpfully as he could.

"See you on Friday then" she said. The smile collapsed.

"Oh. Yes. Tomorrow's your day off."

"Yes. Bye Colin." He was outside the locked door and she was already disappearing into the back of the shop.

"Bye Davinia. Have a nice day tomorrow." He peered through the glass at her receding backside and sighed. "Marvellous" he whispered and headed off down the street towards his tropical fish and a cheese sandwich in front of Swiss Railway Journeys on the telly.

Davinia turned off the lights on the shop floor as she passed through into the sorting room and headed straight for the table where Alex and Shelley had sorted out the donations for sacrificial cleansing the next morning. Some were on hangers, relaxing and straightening before the rigours of the morrow, others draped in piles over the back of chairs or hard surfaces as if waiting to be racked. The secret was to look for expensive fabric, tailoring and most of all, labels. Designer were the best but there was a whole tranche of desirable names that although not high end, had enough cachet to make them sought after: M&S Autograph, LK Bennet, Boden. Next was too common and Per Una too frilly; flouncy rather than fitted - over-trendy for women of a certain age but not trendy enough for those who were younger. She would know exactly what she was looking for when she found it … and there it was. A blouse, silk, grey and white, tiny pearly buttons all the way down the front and on the cuffs. A Whistles classic. Perfect, with the Kate Middleton factor to boot. It was already on a hanger and needed only to be hung in her bathroom overnight to be ready to wear. Anything else? Pair of tailored trousers or skirt to go with it? … No. Nothing, but there was a Monsoon dress. She mused. Monsoon used to be a dead cert but recently had become a little too boho for her target market – over bold colours and too much bling. This was understated though, quite classy. She'd risk it. Carefully folding both garments, without hangers, she put them into her Radley bag, picked up her coat and car keys and left the shop by the back door, turning off the remaining lights as she went.

On the street outside, Corpy and Troop were waiting. They had positioned themselves on the opposite side of the road where they could see the activity in the shop but were not conspicuous. Corpy had learned by careful observation that Davinia's departure occurred in stages. First the shop floor went dark but light was still visible at the back - probably her office or something. She never went straight home but pottered about for sometimes up to an hour. Only when all light had been extinguished was it safe to assume that she was leaving, but even then, it was necessary to wait. She was parked in the alley behind and he did not want to be seen collecting his cardboard mattress from behind the bins. Only after fifteen minutes did he dare to venture across the road towards home. This time however, for the first time, he had company. Troop trotted beside him, wearing a PDSA issue collar, reeking of flea repellent and none the worse for the stiches in his shoulder and the enforced worming tablet he had been obliged to swallow. "He's an Airedale," the vet had said. "Quite young, about a year old I should say and pedigree. I can't imagine why someone should want to get rid of him; he'll have been expensive. Nice dogs, Airedales. Loyal and intelligent." The vet's nurse had also fed him and given Corpy a bag of dog biscuits. He wondered if he could develop a taste for them; it would ease the problem of how to feed them both. Chips were not a long-term solution.

He retrieved the cardboard as Troop stood quietly in front of the bins, head tipped slightly to one side. Always watching. They settled themselves in the Veteran's Society doorway, a little earlier than Corpy's usual hour but he wanted an early night; it had been an eventful day. Hopefully it would not rain but if it did, at least he had Troop's bin liner for added protection. Corpy wrapped himself in his sleeping bag and curled up into his corner, back to the wall so that he could keep an eye out for the enemy, hand firmly gripped around the cold steel of his SA80 propped up against his side. Troop lay down over his feet. As Corpy drifted into sleep, the dog stayed awake. Perfectly still, eyes half open, the hairs above them occasionally twitching. Corpy slept; his body slackened, his hand released its grip on the gun and all the time, Troop watched.

Chapter Four
Davinia's Day Off

When it started raining Troop had remained on Corpy's feet but tucked his body further into the doorway to stay dry. He was still soaked by the time dawn creaked wearily out of bed but it had taken a little longer than if he had stayed where he was. Corpy awoke and was surprised to find that he was stretched out and had obviously been fully asleep. He reached for his SA80 but found only softness and the aroma of wet dog. So, Troop and he lay sedately together in the doorway like an old married couple. There was no hurry this morning. It was Thursday. Her day off. The Other One would be in charge and she never arrived more than two minutes before the shop was due to open. The chap would be waiting outside, wearing a track suit or what looked like gardening clothes because no one bothered much on a Thursday. Very often the door did not open until five or ten past nine and had been known to close as early as 4.45 pm.

They both peered out at the rain. Corpy was perplexed. Usually on days like this he headed for the library or launderette if he was in funds, but he could not do that with a dog in tow. And that was clearly what was happening; Troop had made that obvious. They could not go to the covered market or the mall, not that Corpy went there much anyway – too conspicuous. It made him uncomfortable and shabby in the presence of so much well-lit affluence although the toilets were clean, spacious and available. He could shave there and it was possible to have a discreet strip wash if you chose your time right. Not today though. Or any other day unless Troop could be persuaded to sit outside and wait. They would have to go underneath the arches until it dried up. They and all the rest of the shifting population. At least it would be dry(ish) and they could stay warm(ish) beside the fires in the oil drums. There would be chat, yesterday's newspaper and a cup of tea with a sandwich from the Sally Army. Yes, and he could introduce Troop to his compatriots. Corpy did not drink, do drugs, smoke or judge but now he had a dog. Everyone had a weakness he thought ruefully and wondered, again, how he was going to feed his habit.

"Come on, mate" he said and shocked himself. Since when had Troop become his 'mate', his buddy? "We'll think of something."

Colin and Candy arrived at the same time, both at the front door. Candy did not drive; she Nordic walked, wearing hiking boots under a midi length skirt that flapped but did not impede. Sturdy calves in woollen tights supported the dripping kagoule-clad whole topped by a wholesome face under a hand crocheted hat covering a waterfall of hair that rippled all the way down her back. Originally chestnut and lustrous it was now uniformly hennaed and wilted but its length was glorious. Today it was hanging loose, ridged from tight, overnight plaits newly brushed but now coagulating in the rain.

"Morning, Colin" she breezed, handing him her Nordic walking poles as she swung one arm out of her backpack and began rummaging in the outer pockets for the key. "It's here somewhere. Always is! In we go, out of the rain." A "thank you" as she retrieved her poles and marched across the shop floor to the office.

"Are we open, Candy? … Shall I put out the signs? … Are we 'Open - keeping warm', or 'Open', or 'Open – keeping dry?' … Candy? Candy?"

"Yes, Colin. I'll do the till in a minute."

Colin stood mournfully by the still closed double glazed doors. To open or not to open? He decided to stand there and open the door for customers himself. Then he could explain that yes, they were open even though the door was closed, but he wasn't quite sure why, but that he'd know soon. And then he could tell them. He knew the

Community Service people had to go around to the back so he wouldn't have to explain it all to them. Davinia did not want them being seen to enter by the main entrance, like customers. Especially her. He wondered if he should get a tattoo. It was his day off tomorrow and he had planned to go to Aquarium World; there was often a delivery of exotic weed on Fridays. He sighed and studied the rain outside. It was never the same on Davinia's day off. He wondered what was she doing now. A well-earned lie-in probably; she worked so hard. Marvellous.

Shelley and Alex were girding themselves for the daily steaming. She was staring at a pile of clothes that had been donated to the shop yesterday, unpacked and lay as supplicants for a ritual cleansing.

"God. I hope they're clean this time. Ugh. How can people take sheets straight off the bed and send them here when they're crusty?"

"It's when the steaming releases the urine smell that gets me" Alex responded, trying to sound flippant.

"More than the banana onesie covered in dried barf?"

"I work in a hospital. I'm used to puke."

"Makes me glad I'm a shop lifter." A spilt second. "Was".

"What did you … lift … if you don't mind me asking?"

Shelley shrugged. "Depends." Books mostly. Not bestsellers though, they're crap. Waterstones is best. Not enough staff."

Candy appeared in the doorway but came no further.

"Everything OK? Good. Call if you want me. You'll help Colin with the till if he needs it won't you, Alex? Thanks." And was gone.

Far from lying in bed, Davinia was up betimes, showered and dressed. Thursdays were her busiest day, certainly in terms of sales. This was the day she posted on eBay and the day that time ran out for the previous weeks' items. Every evening she monitored their progress, loving the chi-ching of the cash register whenever a sale was made. When she first started, she had posted a whole variety of items with limited success but had now refined her market. It was fascinating - so different to the shop but the one common denominator was that everyone wanted a bargain. Something for as close to nothing as possible. Making a profit was much harder than people thought and all depended on the price you had paid, or not, for the auction items. Really, people could be so stingy. She had watched a perfectly good pure new wool/silk mix Hobbs dress creep up by pence until it reached its reserve price and so she was obliged to sell. And then it went no further. Honestly, she had virtually given it away. At least buyers paid their own p&p and she had learned to recycle jiffy bags to save packaging costs; the 10p included in their payment for packing was, frankly, derisory.

Clothes were best. There had been an unfortunate incident in her early days of trading when a customer disputed the condition of a rather sweet Capo Di Monte figurine. Said a finger was missing. Of course, it was a try on. Davinia knew it was perfect when she parcelled it up in a mountain of bubble wrap and it was not her fault if the courier was a hooligan. However, she had been forced to refund the money or else lose her excellent seller rating, insisting that the ornament remain with its new owner as a gesture of goodwill. No skin off her nose, as it had come from the shop and cost her nothing, but that was not the point and since then she had left bric a brac well alone. No, clothes were safer and she was becoming quite an expert on knowing what would produce the kind of profit she wanted. She had the laptop to prove it. Whistles blouse and Monsoon dress tastefully displayed and photographed from at least 5 angles, labels photographed in close up, details of items filled in, she thought for a moment as she composed her mini sales pitch. It was her policy to be scrupulously honest about the condition of the garments and to make a point of drawing attention to even the most minute defect - created trust in customers and saved all sorts of unpleasantness if anything went wrong. The blouse was absolutely perfect but the dress had a very slight mark on the inside neck seam which she carefully photographed, over enlarged and documented, pointing out that it would not show when worn but that it was only right that a potential buyer should know absolutely everything about the garment, good and bad. Then she clicked the mouse and both garments were up for auction. Now all she had to do was wait for the others to come home, as it were, and watch the growth of her PayPal account. It would soon be time to make another transfer into her ISA.

It was still raining. To absorb the expanding puddle inside the door where muddy feet had taken refuge on the dated tiles, Colin had laid out a flattened cardboard box which was now soggy and soft. Should he replace it? A bigger one maybe? But that would mean leaving the till unattended when there were customers on the shop floor and he knew that he could not do that. Davinia had said so. He had found the cardboard beside the bins in the alley behind the shop but he couldn't possibly abandon the till to get some more. Then there were the umbrellas. People were supposed to leave them inside the door to drip onto the cardboard but some didn't. What was he supposed to do? He could make a sign, but where would he put it? He hoped it would stop raining then the problem would go away and he could relax. What was it he had been told to do when he felt stressed? That's right – think about something nice. He closed his eyes and focused on the image of his tropical fish in their pink back-lit tanks in his living room. That transported him to the anticipated trip to Aquarium World the next day and the discovery of a new variety of exotic weed or even a fish. Could he possibly dig a pond and move into the Koi Carp world?

"Are you the manager?" Three, two, one, back in the shop.

"Me?"

"Yes. You."

"No. I'm Colin. I'm a volunteer. Look." Colin held out his lanyard at the end of its blue ribbon for the benefit of the customer, a man, wet, holding a plastic carrier bag in his hand. "It's my day off tomorrow." The man ignored the lanyard and the comment.

"I want to see the manager."

"We don't have one. We have a manageress. But she's not here today."

"Then you'll have to do. I have a complaint. Was it you who sold these to my mother?"

He dumped the dripping carrier bag onto the counter. Rain water slid off it into tiny puddles which expanded rapidly as he rummaged inside to retrieve its contents which he slammed down, spreading the water ever further. Colin was distressed. Should he wipe the surface dry now or later, and with what? Two DVDs in their cases lay between the combatants, gaudy, slim, stranded in a refund no man's land. He looked at the DVDs. Yes, he thought he might have sold them last week. Must have been him; the till was His Job. Perhaps there was something wrong with the quality - the sound or they did not work properly? No, nothing like that apparently.

"My mother watched them. Both."

Colin beamed. "They're good, aren't they? My mum loved them." The man stared at him, transfixed.

"Your mother watched these films?" Colin nodded; felt confident and expansive. If the man wanted to complain about a couple of DVDs, that was easy to deal with. He became chattier, leaned against the counter, relaxing.

"Oh yes. She's watched them lots of times. *Beauty and the Beast* is her favourite but she liked *Little Women* too. Said it was just like the book."

"The book?" Colin nodded again, more vigorously, with great enthusiasm by way of answer. The man stared harder, directly at Colin's smile. Colin was warming to this chap. Obviously looks after his mum he was thinking. Maybe Colin could recommend some other films for her. *The Sound of Music* always went down well.

"I don't know what to say" the man said, astonished. "How old is she?"

Now it was Colin's turn to be surprised but he was happy to chat if that's what the customer wanted. Davinia had said how important it was to engage with the customers, to make them feel welcome and valued.

"Mum? Ninety next birthday."

"She must be very open minded." Colin considered for a moment. He had never thought about it but yes, now you came to think of it, his mum was easy going, especially for an old lady with arthritis but she didn't complain, not all the time. He nodded, pensively, before replying

"She likes *EastEnders*."

The man stared even harder. Perhaps he was short sighted? Colin beamed more widely so that he would be sure to see how friendly he was.

"Have you watched these DVDs?"

"Yes, but I thought they were a bit boring." The man goggled. Clearly needed glasses or contact lenses. There was an optician in the high street. Should Colin say something?

"You don't look the type." Colin's stomach lurched – heaved – he felt sick. Davinia had been right! Oh, why didn't he listen and do as he was told? She had told him to dress more smartly and he was still wearing his shell suit, the one he had on yesterday because he knew it was her day off and he thought it wouldn't matter and now, here was this man who was complaining about his clothes and saying he did not look the type who should be working in a charity shop and not just any old charity shop, but Davinia's, which was high class and she was always so smart. Colin's face shrivelled with shame.

"The clothes? Yes. She told me off about that."

"The clothes?"

"Yes. Not smart enough."

"Your mum said that?"

"No. Davinia."

"Davinia?"

"The manageress. You won't tell her, will you? She's very professional. Wears lipstick. Used to be an accountant and a hairdresser and a ballet dancer and she knows everything about hospitals because she worked in one for a very important consultant who said she was marvellous and she is and …"

"I'd like to speak to her then, as soon as possible. Someone so professional will share my concern about a charity shop selling pornographic DVDs inside Walt Disney covers. It's disgusting."

"Candy! … Candy!" Colin's falsetto cry of fear ricocheted around the whole shop. Even Alex and Shelley stopped to listen.

The break in the steaming was a welcome moment before the torture continued. Shelley took that moment to stand by the open door and wipe her forehead. The new tattoo was angry and red through its fresh layer of cling film on her lifted arm, Alex noticed. The plaster of yesterday had been too small and had stuck to the edges of the design which had been tugged and torn when the dressing had been removed. It was still impossible to work out what the tattoo actually was and he did not like to ask.

"So whatcha in for then, Al?" Shelley asked, after peering out of the door. "It's peeing down out there but at least it's not hot" she added.

"Do you mean my Community Service?"

"Yeah. Your crime against humanity."

Alex hesitated. But there was no point in avoiding the issue so he told her, not in great detail but enough to make her move back into the room to hear him more clearly. He was embarrassed; he had been an idiot, out of control and now he was paying the price. He said so, a man in his fifties confessing his sins to a skinny, pierced girl-woman covered in tattoos. How would she react? Reactions were something he had come to fear. For all his years in the NHS, dealing with patients, he had realised that he actually did not know people at all; they were totally unpredictable. That was why he and Lisa had gone to ground, preferring to be with only Dave, their dog, and themselves.

When Shelley screamed with laughter he was absolutely stunned.

"You mean you put your initials on someone's liver? That's awesome. God, if I'd known I could've got you to do my tattoo! Youd've made a better job of it, being a doctor than that so-called artist I went to. Hey! You're an artist! Who signed his work! Brilliant." Shoulders rocking with mirth she high fived him. Fortunately, he knew what to do and they slapped hands, mid-air. Partnership; sealed. Alex allowed himself to smile. Shelley was intrigued; he'd seemed so boring. More to him than met the eye that was for sure.

"Who's your P.O?" she asked, genuinely interested.

"P.O?"

"Probation Officer."

"Oh. Nerinda. She never uses her last name. It's always just Nerinda."

"Yeah. Me too. It's so that we can 'engage' with her. Think of her as our friend rather than our P.O. … She's OK. I've had worse." Alex did not know what to say. He was out of his depth. Oh, for an emergency three-way 'piggy-back' organ transplant to get him back into his comfort zone. Shelley however, was perfectly at home. This guy was alright she had decided; she liked him. Shame he wasn't thirty years younger but on the other hand, older men were safe and respectful and had manners. Married of course, which was even better. They could be friends; no complications. Bet he's got a dog she thought; something feisty. Not cats, he's not the type and his wife'll be nice - grounded. Yeah, Alex was okay.

"Whad'ya think of Candy? she asked

Alex did not know what to think.

"I haven't seen enough of her to say. When Davinia's here she's nowhere to be seen and apparently, it's the same when Davinia's not here, so I don't know. Maybe she's not here at all? We just think she is."

"Nah, she's in the office doing yoga. I heard the ohmming." Now it was Alex's turn to laugh.

"I hope she takes her boots off or she'll do herself an injury." Shelley sniggered and wagged her finger at him, matron ticking off a small boy with dirty knees,

"C'mon Al. Back to it! The steaming must go on. Pretend it's Davinia you're cleaning and it'll be easier."

Davinia had had a most successful morning. Most of her auction items posted the previous Thursday had sold. Once payment came in, she would sort out postage and dispatch and everything would be sent off tomorrow. She would drop them into the post office in her lunch break. They knew her there and were never very pleased to see her; said that lunchtimes were their busiest periods and couldn't she bring all her parcels at a quieter time? Well, she had told them what she thought of that. A shop manageress could not just leave work and undertake important business to suit the staff in a high street post office; she had responsibilities and it was her lunch hour to do with as she wished. If she chose to spend it not eating and drinking but working, that was her choice. So rather than complaining, wouldn't it be better if they just got on with the job and reduced the queue that way?

She would do all the printing in one go later. In the meantime, she would write the first weekly Community Service report on Alex and Shelley for their probation officer. Technically it was not due until close of play on Friday but three days was more than enough to accurately assess what they were like. He was no trouble: routine, predictable. A little superior but nothing she couldn't handle. The girl, however, was more difficult. Attitude. Tacky. Insolent. A Piece of Work. Davinia was looking forward to writing about that one. She sat down in front of her laptop with a cup of coffee and a box of low-calorie snack bars.

It had arrived. The inevitable. Colin's Nemesis – Gift Aid. What was he going to do? The lady was very nice and said she was happy to wait but Colin's anxiety was rising. He could feel it in his knees. It would be the stomach next, and then his heart. He might die! Eyes closed; think nice thoughts, breathe evenly, hold onto something secure. He gripped the till with both hands imagining his Guppies and Black Mollies but it did not help. All he saw was Gift Aid. When he opened his eyes, he noticed that the lady was glancing at her watch and had shifted her handbag into her other hand as she picked up her not quite unfolded fold-up umbrella which was dripping on the floor in front of the counter. Water on the floor! For people to slip and fall on. And hurt themselves. Health and Safety! Oh, what would Davinia do? What would she say? The Health and Safety of my customers is everything to me is what she would say and he - he! - was putting them at risk. Colin feel the panic crawling up his thighs. He could not call Candy, not again. She had been very embarrassed about the DVDs. The customer eventually accepted that it was not deliberate and had been given not just a refund, but his choice of replacement films that he assured them he would, personally, and at great inconvenience, inspect himself, in order to avoid exposing his mother to any more distress. She had been terribly shocked apparently: kept talking about the experience and had been too traumatised to turn the DVD machine off so had been obliged to watch them all the way through. Dreadful; simply dreadful. He did not know how she would ever recover. Candy had recommended something called a flower remedy to soothe the lady's body and healing crystals to soothe her soul. Her chakras, whatever they were, were out of balance and had to be realigned. Healing crystals would put her right; Lapis Lazuli was perfect for restoring an air of calm and tranquillity apparently, but the man did not seem impressed. Colin had given him a free carrier bag; well, he had not charged him for it. No, he would pay the 5p into the tin himself. The least he could do.

When the man had gone Candy had taken the offending items with her into the office: confiscated, she said, to prevent further problems. Colin had had to remove all the DVDs from the shelf and stack them in the corridor outside the office. They could not go in the stockroom because of all the steam and heat.

"They'll all have to be checked" Candy had said. "Davinia will sort that out when she gets back" and had disappeared into the office to write an incident report where she Was Not to Be Disturbed. What should Colin do? Then, thank God! He remembered.

"Alex! Alex! It's a Gift Aid!"

The lady, still waiting but noticeably less patiently, followed Colin's entreaty and gaze in the direction of the emptiness at the back of the shop. Nothing happened.

"Alex! It's a Gift Aid!" Not so much an entreaty now, but the anguished final request of a condemned man. "Alex!"

Salvation. A sweaty middle-aged man in a damp T shirt and flaccid jeans appeared through a doorway and emerged into the light of the shop floor, blinking slightly to divert the drops of sweat running from forehead into eyes.

"Can I help?"

"Alex!" Thank the Lord. Saved! Colin smiling beatifically at his saviour; reprieved at the last moment. "It's a Gift Aid" he explained, soggy with relief.

"No problem."

No problem? The man was a miracle. Colin was in awe as he watched Alex manoeuvre the till and process the transaction as if to the manner born. It took about three minutes - he timed it. The lady and her umbrella departed and in one stroke, Colin was relieved not only of the dreaded Gift Aid but also the problem of more water accumulating on the floor.

"Alex." he began, suffused with gratitude and wonder, but was interrupted by an almighty crash. Huge. It began with a slump and then became a crescendo of metal, soft thuds, hissing, a groan or two and then silence, interspersed by what sounded like a percussion of metal coat hangers tinkling a tearful finale.

"Shelley!" Alex leapt from behind the counter and sprinted towards the noise. It became more of a steeple chase as he hurled himself over the DVDs in the corridor, clearing most of them, then swung himself into the stockroom where Shelley was lying, comatose, on the sticky floor, cradled in a metal nest; embedded in the ironing board, iron, flex, coat hangers and bulging bin liners with half cleaned clothes steaming gently around her like hot flannels in an Indian restaurant.

She looked like a fledging that has failed to fly. Alex knelt down beside her and picked up her wrist.

"Call an ambulance. Shelley's ill."

Colin was horrified. He had never done such a thing in his life! What would he say? Fortunately, Candy had materialised in the doorway and immediately dematerialised into the office to make the call. She had a mobile of course, but that was also in the office so she might as well use the VHS line and save her battery. Mustn't forget to put it on charge when she'd rung the emergency services, she reminded herself. But then she reappeared in the stockroom.

"Are you sure we need an ambulance? Maybe she's just fainted; it's quite warm in here. Try this." She offered her flower remedy to Alex. "Two drops on this occasion, I think. Strong, I know, but justified. One drop is usually all it takes but she does seem to be rather out of it."

"Just call a f…" he checked himself…. "an ambulance."

"What shall I say is wrong?"

"Tell them it's an emergency. The patient is unconscious. Blood pressure's low, pulse is fast, temperature's high. Suspected sepsis caused by infected cellulitis around a tattoo. And tell them, yes, I am a doctor, and I do know what I'm talking about, and they need to get a move on."

Candy looked blank.

"Sepsis?"

"Blood poisoning."

Her heavy boots thundered to the phone.

At home, Davinia was enjoying herself. It was not a long report and just the first of many, but it was important to set the right tone. She chose her words carefully: succinct and pithy. Direct, revealing insight and intelligence. Nerinda was one of the better Probation Officers and always appreciated the quality of Davinia's writing. Just because it was a report that was no excuse for poor style. Davinia prided herself on her literary skills and had plans to write professionally one day: something romantic and sensuous, but tasteful, not like that shades of grey book which had appalled her. So repetitive! It was just finding the time.

They regularly had Community Service 'volunteers' in the shop, largely because head office promoted a rehabilitation of offenders within society scheme, and because they made up the numbers: there were never enough ordinary volunteers. Not that they ever had real criminals of course, who had been in prison, just those convicted of petty crimes or on suspended sentences. Motoring offences were the most common, drink driving, that sort of thing. Alex and Shelley were exceptions in that they rather broke the mould of their usual candidates. She did not really understand quite what he had done; Nerinda had said that it was an unusual situation but that he was, absolutely and categorically, of no danger to the public. Shelley was no more than a petty thief; you only had to look at her to see that. And thank heavens for email. So much more efficient than those ghastly paper forms and so much easier to correct and amend one's words before flinging it off into the ether and forgetting about it.

"Mr Whiteley," she wrote, "has made a good initial impression. He is punctual and hard-working and is learning to adapt to the methods and demands of the VHS system. He appears to be making an effort to conform and please and I recommend that we overlook the arrogance displayed on his first day. I believe that he now understands that we have our own way of doing things and that it is he who must adjust, not us.

Miss Walton is, unfortunately, less compliant and has yet to prove her commitment to work. Her attitude leaves much to be desired and this is reflected in her manner and appearance. She has been asked to dress more modestly but has yet to do so and persists in displaying her many tattoos: most unprofessional. She makes little effort to engage with other staff, has an air of insolence about her and has yet to show any signs of insight or reflection about why she is doing Community Service. Of course, it is early days and I hope that she will eventually settle down, mature, show remorse and become a team player. We will, as always, give her all the support and encouragement she needs as we do with all those who join us as part of their rehabilitation into society."

She paused over the keyboard. What else to say? Probably nothing. Let Nerinda work it out. Besides, Shelley had not actually said or done anything disrespectful or rude, it was just her attitude. And her tattoos, but Davinia could not say that. No, she would leave it at that; there was always next week. She dated the report the next day, Friday, copied in head office and scheduled it to be sent at 9.00 am so that Nerinda would receive it in plenty of time. Davinia was nothing if not efficient and Reg the Regional Manager would be calling in first thing, as he always did. Theirs was a special relationship and she liked to be able to give him her full attention which was why she insisted that Friday was Colin's day off; Candy manned the till. Then she closed the screen and clicked into her eBay account.

Corpy and Troop saw the ambulance arrive at the shop and then depart a few minutes later. Quite a crowd had gathered around the blue lights, red lights, open doors and green paramedics with their bags and equipment beetling in and out of the charity shop, followed by the excitement of a girl with tattooed arms being wheeled out on the gurney and taken off at speed accompanied by an older man in jeans. Man and dog were seated in a deep-set doorway mostly out of the rain, opposite the shop at a tangent so that they could see most of the street but were not overly conspicuous. Even so, Corpy had been overwhelmed by the attention they had received. From complete strangers! People who would normally walk straight past, deliberately unseeing, suddenly preoccupied with the zip on their handbag or the sky or something in the distance they had just spotted; anything rather than see a beggar. Now, however, they all seemed to want to stop. And talk. To ask about Troop. It seemed that it was the sign that had caught their imagination; that and the dog.

Corpy was no beggar and woe betide anyone who thought otherwise, but he had to feed Troop. So, he decided to tell the truth. With a black whiteboard marker borrowed from the PDSA receptionist he had turned one of his flattened cardboard boxes into a notice that was now propped, slightly damply but still extant, against Troop as he lay demurely on the ground on another piece of cardboard. The sign read,

Dog Food Only. Please. Thank you.

That was it. However, it seemed no one quite believed it.

"You don't want money? Really? Just dog food?"

"Yep. For the dog. I can look after myself but not both of us so, I'm asking for help."

What had resulted was almost embarrassing. He had been inundated with dog food: tins, chews, packets of biscuits, treats, more tins, sachets, sacks of dried food not to mention several bowls, collars, leads, toys, tin openers, a couple of blankets and, extraordinarily, a huge golfing umbrella under which they now sat. It was becoming difficult to know where to put everything. The tins were piled up behind him built up into a kind of wall against which he leant, barricaded on both sides by the other accumulated wealth of a day on the pavement. They had acquired enough food to keep Troop going for weeks; their problem now was to where to store it.

Chapter Five
Colin's Day Off

Corpy and Troop had spent a comfortable night on their doorstep. They were glad of the blankets donated to them the day before as all the cardboard boxes behind the bins had gone; one for his sign, Corpy knew, but he had no idea what had happened to the rest. Never mind. At least it had stopped raining. He could stockpile Troop's provisions out of sight and sticky fingers behind the bins until he found somewhere better and they would spend the day sourcing more boxes. The umbrella and the blankets they would carry with them - far too precious to leave unattended. Filled with a sense of purpose and Troop with Pedigree Premium for the discerning dog, they trotted off, well before She arrived, in pursuit of coffee and cardboard. Corpy had a plan. They headed off in the direction of the PDSA Dispensary. He forgot to pick up his SA80.

Davinia had dressed with especial care and was even earlier than usual, as Corpy had anticipated. She liked to brush off any leaves or litter from the doorstep before the arrival of Reg. 'Reg the Reeg.' as she liked to tease him. Sweet that his name should be so like his job title. Regional Manager carried some weight in the VHS organisation so Davinia liked to keep him on side, not that that was difficult. He obviously found her attractive and her shop met all its targets and beyond, as well as outperforming many of the others. All down to her skilful man management Reg said and her practice of leading by example.

"It all comes from the top" she liked to say. "Get that right and the rest will follow." Yes, she and Reg were an excellent team and she had high hopes that when the time came for him to move up, or on, or retire early, or whatever, her application would be looked upon more than favourably. No sign of Candy yet. Really, she was so unprofessional. All that hair and those clothes! Didn't she ever look in the mirror? She meant well, of course, with all that yoga and New Age nonsense but would never progress beyond deputy manageress. No ambition. Far too fey and well, frankly, scruffy ever to be senior management. Destined to be forever someone else's second in command she thought as she threaded her pencil heel way through the corridor from the back of the shop to the front. She did not notice the DVDs stacked untidily against the wall until they grazed her shins. What the hell…? Her first thought was for her tights – new on that morning. If they were snagged or laddered, she always carried a spare pair in her Radley but that was not the point. What were they doing there? Grim faced she marched onto the shop floor. Lights on, full, the destruction was obvious. An empty space! A whole shelf! With nothing - nothing - on it. And the Regional Manager due any moment. She glanced at the clock in panic. A quarter to nine. Fifteen minutes to rectify the damage. Thank God she kept a cool head in a crisis and could heal the breach as it were. Books and bric a brac would do it. Some rather loud pottery had come in a few days ago; clumsy heavy hand-made stuff with uneven glaze, the sort of thing that Candy would buy, that would fill the gap; she would find some books about crafts or creative urges or some such guff to display with them. Tell Reg it was a promotion; crafts, hobbies, that sort of thing - promoting local interests and skills. Serving the community! Smiling now with immense self-satisfaction she headed into the shop's nether regions to perform her magic. Only when Reg had gone would she investigate; DVDGate as she now thought of it.

Shelley had slept well but nevertheless, she still felt sleepy. She was awoken by bright lights and someone in blue slopping something down onto the table next to her bed. The table was like a trolley on little wheels and was twisted round over her prone body near her chin so that as she lay with her head propped up uncomfortably on the pillows, she found she was eye to eye with a cup and saucer. Tepid (Health and Safety) milky tea was the last thing she actually wanted but there was no way of getting rid of it so she gave in and drank it. Her arms were restricted, one by the tube pinned into the back of her hand tying her to a bag of something clear and wet which dripped monotonously into her body, the other arm barely able to reach above the table to lift the cup. Fortunately, a fair amount spilled into the saucer then a little more dribbled onto the white sheet so that by the time it reached her mouth, there was hardly any left.

"Feeling better?" The body in blue had a voice. "Nice cup of tea first thing always does the trick. You look perkier this morning. Doctors will see you when they do their ward round and tell you what's happening but you're on my list to go home so that's good news. What d'you want for breakfast? I've got Weetabix and toast… Nothing? Oh well, up to you. 'Nother cup of tea? No? Sure? Well, I'll bring one anyway in case you change your mind. Oh, you've had a bit of a spill. Never mind. Clean sheets for the next one. Bathroom's in the corridor. The drip? Take it with you…Yes, the whole thing. It's on wheels. Bell's behind you if you need anything but it might take a while. It's busy this morning. Every morning. Haha! I'm Precious. Enjoy your breakfast."

Blue voice had gone leaving nothing but tepid tea. Then Shelley remembered what had happened and where she was. It was Friday, nearly the end of the first week in the charity shop and she was already hospitalised. If it wasn't so surreal it would be funny.

Davinia was not amused. It had gone nine. Candy was on the shop floor, meditating upright behind the counter with her hands pressed in supplication at her heart centre, lost in mindfulness but nevertheless, ready to namaste anyone who entered. Davinia was standing, legs akimbo, hands on hips to help her balance on the vertiginous heels she was wearing in honour of Reg's visit. She had positioned herself by the back entrance: all the more prepared to pounce on Shelley when she finally deigned to put in an appearance.

"Well, where is she? Don't tell me she's smoking outside because we both know she isn't. She's late. Again." She stared vehemently at her watch, at Alex, then back to the watch's relentless movement towards the quarter past mark. "This will have to go on her report, of course" she added sorrowfully, in her well-rehearsed 'I am so disappointed but it's no more than I expected' tone.

"She's in hospital."

Davinia thought she had misheard.

"What?"

"Yesterday. Collapsed. Too much steaming." Alex spoke like a telegram. He was enjoying this but was still ready to catch her if she fell off her shoes.

"Hospital?"

Alex nodded. "Yes. An emergency admission by ambulance. She was unconscious; we had to act quickly."

"Unconscious? In my shop?"

"I'm afraid so."

"In front of the customers?"

"In the back, not on the shop floor." As if that mattered. He was annoyed. "You haven't asked what happened to her. If she is alright."

"No, sorry. Is she?" Davinia had been caught unawares and was now abashed; she must look as if she cared and in a way she did, and Reg would be arriving any minute and… then she felt sick. The email copied to head office! Hell. It would have gone by now; would be sitting like an incendiary in someone's inbox and no way of getting it back. Nerinda didn't matter but head office… "Why wasn't I told?" she barked.

"You weren't here."

"That's not the point, I should have been informed. Who made the decision to call an ambulance?"

"I did. … I'm a doctor." Yes, she knew that perfectly well, thank you. What mattered now was curtailing the damage, managing the paperwork, raising her profile in a positive light. Reg's visit was inconvenient but could be useful to that end; she wondered if he had plans for lunch. Oh, and she had to find out what had happened to the silly bitch and how long she would be in hospital. She would need all the details when she made her report to Health and Safety, who would have to be told and who always asked the most ridiculous questions. Why did they always assume that it was the workplace to blame? Actually…

"Thank you, Alex for such prompt action. Thank goodness you were here. Now, tell me exactly happened to poor Shelley. What made her collapse?"

She felt a great deal better when she found she could throw the blame onto the new tattoo not the ancient steamer. Of course, it was Shelley's fault. She knew it would be and that made things so much easier. No need to take Reg for lunch now either. Keep the money in the PayPal account.

The doctor on the ward round was well fit, Shelley decided. A bit short perhaps - another three or four centimetres and he'd be the perfect height, but slim in an athletic way. He'd said his name was Eduardo which immediately made him interesting and he had an accent - nothing heavy but sort of Mediterranean or maybe South American? Hard to tell but she liked it. Suggestive of heat and lush vegetation. He could take her pulse anytime. He'd also addressed her as Miss Walton and asked if he could call her Shelley which he said with a kind of creaminess which made her think of buttered toast, dripping, warm, salivating. And he had admired her tattoos.

"We have filled you full of intravenous antibiotics, Shelley" he was saying "to sort out the infection but you must keep your new tattoo clean and dry and complete the course of antibiotic pills we will give you when you leave. You must finish the course; we do not want to see you back here again, do we?" God! That smile. She would seriously consider not taking any of the tablets. "You have a wonderful collection of tattoos. But perhaps enough now, already? No?"

"Maybe."

If you say so. But I might have to have at least one more, for you, Eduardo. You're an experience I want to remember. She sighed and gazed after him as he moved on to his next patient. She wondered whether she might not have been one of the medical students following in his sexy wake if she had not dropped out of school.

To Davinia's surprise and huge relief, Reg was not unduly bothered by what had happened. She had explained in detail and he had metaphorically shrugged his shoulders.

"Her fault. She knew what to expect but had the tattoo done anyway so she's liable. Don't worry about it." She told him about the email. "But you weren't here so what's the problem? How could you know? So, what that you dated it for today? Just being efficient. Not a problem. Lots of bottled water on tap" (hearty laugh) "when she's back and breaks when she wants them, within reason of course. Does she have to steam? Couldn't she go on the till?"

"She's here for shop-lifting!"

"Okay, not on the till then. But not steaming – let the other one do it while she sorts and hangs. Let her dress for the heat. Bikini if necessary. No-one'll see her. Just so long as she's wearing her lanyard. Company policy. Right, let's have a look at this shop floor of yours."

She followed him out of the office. He was short, swarthy and skinny, a true Forest of Dean man with the characteristic narrow pixie-esque eyes slanting up towards the tops of hirsute ears. He also had dark Dean-man hair; Reg's was straight and constantly fell into his eyes so that he was forever flicking his head to see out of his fringe which always looked untidy and oily, even when freshly washed. He wore his suits, perfectly respectable on the hanger, like a Harry Potter house elf. Nothing seemed to fit but bagged, morosely, creased and shapeless on his thin frame as if clinging on to it for fear of falling off and being left behind. He also had an unfortunate habit of rubbing one side of his groin when talking. Most disconcerting if you weren't expecting it. Davinia had learned to ignore his hands and to concentrate on his face when he spoke to her. That was not always easy either as he chain-smoked and reeked of cigarettes and strong black coffee through bad teeth. However, he was the regional manager and her boss, and she never forgot it.

"That chap Colin not in today?"

Davinia was surprised. Since when was Reg interested in the likes of Colin? From the time he had met him about a year ago, when there had been that dreadful debacle about the till and Colin had over-rung a perfectly simple transaction by £30,000 because he had put the decimal point in the wrong place, she had endeavoured to keep him out of Reg's way. At first Colin had wanted to have the same day off as Davinia but she had told him she couldn't manage without his expertise when she was away so he had agreed to Fridays and, to date, there had been no further embarrassments when Reg was on the premises.

"He just the same?"

"Just the same," she answered.

"Always talking about tropical fish?"

"Hmm." Davinia nodded regretfully.

"Still doing five days a week including Saturdays?"

She nodded. Oh yes, five long days. Every week.

"Consistent then?"

"Very. Never changes."

Now Reg nodded and moved over to the bric a brac.

"Nice display" he said looking at the pottery. "Good idea." He added, thoughtfully, rubbing his groin. "I think I'll pass that on to the other shops."

Colin decided to treat himself and get the bus to Aquarium World. It wasn't that far a walk from the three-bedroom 1930s semi-detached he called home, but it was cold, the days were short and getting shorter and he wanted to spend as much quality time there as he could. Bidding a fond farewell with the promise of exciting new weed to his fish, serene and oblivious in the tanks that lined the living room, he walked down the avenue to the main road at the end and took refuge in the bus stop, where he studied his watch, anxiously. His bus pass was only valid after 9.30. He could afford the full fare but would much rather pay only 50p; he had a state pension and a pension from the Post Office (when it was the GPO, oh happy days) where he had worked in the sorting office since he left school at sixteen so money was not a problem, but entry into the Koi Carp world did not come cheap. It would involve a significant outlay. For a time, he had seriously considered keeping marine tropical fish but the problem of maintaining water quality was enormous - critical for the health of the fish and likely to cause him great stress. He felt it was beyond him, especially if he was working five days a week in The Shop. It had come down to an agonising choice between marine fish and the Veteran's Help Society but in the end, there was no doubt in his mind. He could not possibly let Davinia down. The Shop must come first. Koi Carp might be a compromise, if he could manage to dig a pond in the back garden. His dilemma now was what best to line it with?

As he boarded the bus, he felt a thrill of excitement. The frisson of anticipation of the unknown; what he might discover, whether there would be new weed, the daunting prospect of costing Koi Carp and, oh, possibly, the joy of being able to watch new species of fish and maybe, maybe, buy one. Colin clutched his purse and his expectations as tightly as his bus pass. There would be so much to tell Mother when he made his weekly visit to her in The Home.

He wandered, mesmerised through the hallowed tank-lined halls. Dimly lit, like his own living room, the fluorescent light of the back-lit tanks suffused the atmosphere with watery softness, illuminating endless movement combined with perpetual bubbles and burps from the aeration in the tanks, where weeds shivered and beautiful creatures swayed and darted. Enraptured, absorbed, he did not notice the lady until he trod on her foot.

"Oi. Watch where you put your size nines."

He was mortified and overcome. Colin did not often speak to women; never in fact, unless safely positioned behind the counter in the company of The Till, and never alone. Here, unprotected and exposed, he was completely at a loss. Apologise, yes, obviously, but talk to her? What would he say? What if she wanted to make Conversation?

"It's alright" she said, seizing the initiative and rendering him utterly helpless. "No harm done. I'll live… Nice fish."

Colin's heart leapt. He could talk about fish! They were positioned in front of a tank of Neons, common enough but endlessly fascinating and gorgeous with their hairpin movements and reflective stripes. Moments of fractured light igniting and flashing before them.

"I've got some of those" he offered, as much of a peace offering as an opening gambit.

"Very nice. You're a connoisseur, are you?"

"Oh no, I don't vote. But I do like fish. Tropical fish I mean. And marine but I'm thinking about Koi Carp instead."

"Are you now? Well, that is interesting." She had stressed the 'is' and Colin was enthralled. She liked fish! And, she was beautiful. Very like Davinia but perhaps a little shorter and a little plumper, not that Davinia was in any way heavy but she had a spongy softness that he very much admired. Springy, like a freshly baked roll. "I'm Barb." She said, holding out her hand. “Barbara by birth, but everyone calls me Barb.”

“Colin” he gushed, amazed and thrilled. Was he dreaming? No, he held out his hand towards hers and she grasped it; he could feel her fleshy fingers and the hardness of the rings on most of them as she squeezed.

“Nice to meet you, Colin. Well, I think you owe me a cup of coffee and a piece of cake for standing on my foot, don’t you? There’s a nice café here. Let’s go there and get something to eat then we can sit down and have a nice cosy chat.”

She led; he followed, utterly captivated. Enraptured, all thoughts of fish forgotten.

Where did the morning go? Colin had never experienced anything like it. Barb was fascinating. She did not have tropical fish, as yet, but was seriously considering getting some and now that she had been able to talk to an obvious expert, felt much more confident about the prospect. No, she was a complete beginner - a tadpole she said and they had laughed and laughed. Of course, Colin would be delighted to help her. Nothing he would like better, and he meant it. She was intrigued about his work in the charity shop and, it seemed to him, impressed, especially when he told her that he was in charge of The Till and would soon be doing Gift Aid. Then, if all went well, he would be authorised to give refunds and after that? Well, who knew? Did she live far away? Near the Forest of Dean. Oh, that was quite a distance. His disappointment must have shown because she said she would make a special effort to get to Aquarium World (lovely place wasn’t it?) again next Friday, as that was his day off. It seemed her nephew travelled for work so she was sure he could drop her off for the morning as he had done today. She was meeting him for lunch. Oh, my goodness! Was that the time? She would have to get her skates on (skate was a fish wasn’t it? How they laughed!) She mustn’t keep him waiting. Where had the time gone? She hadn’t had such a lovely morning, in oh, ever so long.

“May I walk you to your nephew’s car?” Colin offered, astounded at his own temerity.

“Bless you, dear, but no. It’s cold out. You stay here and sort out those Koi Carp you've told me all about. So exciting. Same place, same time next week?" Yes, most definitely. No, he wouldn't be late; Colin resolved to get an early bus and to hell with the full fare. He watched Barb as she went through the automatic glass doors and disappeared into the distant car park where a smart blue car, almost new by the look of it and very swish, was waiting. She got into the front passenger seat and was gone.

Colin sighed with immense happiness. When the waitress came to clear Barb's mug and plate, he asked her to leave them on the table, just for the time being. She did not mind; said she'd be back later; did he want another coffee? No, he was fine, thank you. He just wanted to look.

So, he sat for another half an hour staring wistfully, disbelievingly at the place where Barb had been sitting, the plate she eaten from and the mug from which she sipped her drink. Colin was in love.

"How'd it go?" Reg asked as Barb put on her seat belt and he slowly drove the car out of the car park and out onto the main road that led to the motorway.

"Like a dream. Same place same time next Friday. We're in business."

Shelley was discharged just before lunch which she thought was a pity, as she had ordered the vegetarian option on one of those dinky little menu choice forms that Precious had handed around the evening before. Not that Shelley could remember all that much about it, but she had recoiled from the liver and onions that had been given to her as the choice of her bed's previous occupant. Now she was hungry and wished she had had some breakfast. She had a paper bag containing a course of antibiotics and clean dressings for the tattoo, which did not hurt and was looking a great deal less inflamed. It was even becoming vaguely identifiable. What was supposed to be rose coming into bloom - the new Shelley putting her shop lifting career behind he and moving on into more legitimate enterprises, as yet undetermined – was now more flower and less incendiary jellyfish. She wondered what Alex would make of it. Thank God he had remembered her bag and jumper when he had accompanied her in the ambulance or she would have been completely stuffed. As it was, she was freezing. She pulled the top of her sloppy sweater up over her shoulders and wondered where to go.

Davinia had seen Reg off with a sense of relief not normally felt, but this Friday had turned out to be something of a terrible exception. Candy's incident report on Shelley was useless: scanty, colloquial and sentimental. It would have to be completely re-written. They were understaffed; Alex was steaming alone in the stockroom, doing his best but woefully behind, Candy was tied to the till and she, Davinia, their leader, had onerous managerial responsibilities that indisputably confined her to the office. It was a nightmare. There was no one to remove the two-week old stock from the shop floor, to replenish the racks, to retrieve empty hangers (why did people have to take the clothes off them when they took them to the till? Did they think the hangers removed themselves into the stockroom?) Then all the clothes had to be constantly checked so that they were facing in the same direction (fronts to the left) with hanger hooks all facing away from the customer (Health and Safety) and the clothes arranged properly, hanging straight in serried rows (Company Policy). Customers were so untidy. Careless. They replaced clothes all higgledy-piggledy or not even at all, just draped them over the bar of the hanger. Some were just abandoned in the changing room, inside out, upside down, hangerless, second-hand skins in pursuit of a host. Really! She put it down to poor upbringing and entitlement; and the internet. So much of it these days.

None of the other volunteers had been able to come in and help out. She had called and asked, almost begged, but no. Too short notice they had said, to a woman. Had to get ready for the weekend, going to the dentist, making lunch, not even answering at all in two cases. Good job they were just volunteers or she would have given them verbal warnings, the whole bloody lot of them. Three strikes and you're out. And then she recalled with a lurch of the stomach that she would have to email Nerinda and update her with the Shelley saga. She hoped to God that Alex had not already been in touch with the Probation Officer. That would be really awkward but just the sort of officious thing that someone like him would do. No wonder the NHS was in such trouble. She shut her office door with vigour. No one would dare to disturb her now.

"Hi Al!"
Alex was shocked.
"Shelley! What the hell are you doing here? Why aren't you at home?"
"You've never been to my house. Thought I might as well come in. Gotta make up my hours anyway."
"Here, sit down. How are you?"
He lifted several bulging black bin liners off an ancient chair and pulled it out for her, then stood back to examine the out-patient.
"How do you feel?"
"Fine. Really. Much better."
"Headache? Pain? Itching?" No, none of those. "May I see?" Yeah, of course. She rolled up her sleeve to show him the offending inking but he refused to allow her to remove the dressing. "No. Keep it on and do exactly what they told you in the hospital. Keep it clean and dry, yes? And finish the course of antibiotics? That's important, Shelley, to prevent reinfection. Paracetamol if you have a temperature?"
"Yeah, yeah. Whatever." But she knew she would do it and she knew he knew. She grinned. "How'd lady Macbeth take it?"
He grinned back. "Horrified! Completely floored!"
"Yes!" Shelley punched the air and they high-fived. "I'll go and tell her I'm here. That'll make her day."

Let's take Dave for a walk. We'll have a glass of something in The Barrels. They take dogs there don't they? Lisa nodded and Alex went to look for Dave's lead. It was a cold evening but dry and the streets were well lit. Christmas was still over a month away but the onslaught of festive come hither and buy had begun as soon as Halloween had passed and the clocks changed. Alex was convinced that the change to winter time was entirely to suit the promotional whims of Christmas retailers but Lisa had accused him of becoming a grumpy old man. She loved the twinkly lights, the bling, the glitter - all the glorious excess. The annual battle of the fairy lights had yet to take place and as usual he would protest and she would win.
"Pretty isn't it?" she said by way of an opening gambit and Alex

pretended that Dave was pulling on his lead to avoid replying. Dave ignored him. He never pulled. Goldendoodles had more self-respect. Besides, he was a strong. If he'd pulled then Alex would have known about it.

"Let's go down the High Street." Alex led and Lisa followed where the pavement was narrow then walked side by side as it broadened out. "Come on, I'll show you the charity shop. Candy was complaining that the Christmas window display still hasn't been done but Davinia has had other things on her mind." They sniggered. Alex had told Lisa all about the Shelley debacle. Apparently Davinia had gone pure white when Shelley knocked on the door to her hallowed portals and invaded her space. Then she had turned very red and tried to move the computer screen to one side so that Shelley could not see what was on it, but as it was an ancient desk top it was too cumbersome to shift so an unseemly tussle had ensued, which the computer monitor had won. So Davinia had shifted herself to conceal the screen, all the time with a rictus smile and bared teeth as she welcomed Shelley back into the fold and repeated how delighted she was to see that she was back on her feet and looking so well. She was to take it easy, for a few days, and not get too hot. Could wear summer clothing if she chose as long as she kept her lanyard on and stayed off the shop floor. Staff there should always be appropriately dressed: Company Policy. Talking of which, how was her injury? Davinia could not bring herself to say 'tattoo'.

Alex and Lisa were laughing as they approached the Veteran's Help Society premises. Suddenly Lisa stopped.

"There's something there. On the doorstep. Look!"

They went nearer, tentatively, creeping along the pavement. Dave growled and definitely did not pull; all three inched their way forward together. Whatever was on the doorstep did not move. Or react. Remained solid and still, black in the reflected light from other shop windows. Behind it, there was only darkness where Davinia had turned off the lights.

"What is it?"

As if to reply there was a low murmur from the doorstep. A growl that died almost as soon as it started and then silence.

"Not so much as a what, but a who, I think" said Alex, straightening up and holding Dave on a very short lead as he lurked behind Alex's legs.

Troop could bear it no longer. He was a dog, after all, and dogs had rights. This was his territory and uninvited boarders had to be repelled. Other people he could tolerate, especially if Corpy seemed to approve, but canine assailants were strictly off limits and had to be dealt with. His claws struggled for purchase on the slippery cardboard but not enough to diminish the enthusiasm of his onslaught as he launched himself at Dave. Who moved not a muscle but stood, immobile, petrified, as Troop, hackles in ranks ready for the charge, sniffed his nether regions with deep intent. Dave gave a low growl – more a vibration than a sound but it was enough. Troop circled Dave one last time then stood, short and defiant before him and they eyed each other. Lisa, Alex and Corpy waited. Watched. Stand off on a doorstep. Corpy had no experience of canine military operations and wondered if he should intervene. But then, for the same reason decided to sit back in his corner and be ready for action, whatever that was. The SA80 was in his grasp, cold, reassuring. Face and body were a stone; emotionless, as cold as his weapon. He never looked at the two people at the end of the strange dog's lead and they never looked at him. All eyes were on the dogs between them.

Nothing happened.

Then Troop's tail moved. Almost not at all at first, but increasingly it became, unmistakably, a wag. A full bodied, side to side sign of acceptance, greeting and friendship. Diplomatic incident over; crisis averted, peace in our time. Now it was all up to Dave. Who needed no second bidding. He had been terrified by this untidy interloper inspecting his privates and checking him out like a piece of meat in that shop in which he was never allowed but had to wait outside, unattainable heaven. It was a wonder he had not been squeezed to check for freshness. Well, he would reciprocate for form's sake but he already knew that they would be friends and he knew that the stranger knew, so his tail also became mobile and all the humans watching the dance macabre relaxed and heaved a collective sigh of relief. And as always happens when strangers with dogs meet, the owners follow suit, making cautiously polite conversation instead of sniffing crotches and then, if the going was good, developing it to introduce non-pet related content, like the weather. It usually took time but Corpy was new to the game, and this was his doorstep.

"Nice dog." Alex opened the batting. An easy one.

"He's lovely." Lisa was crouching on the pavement beside Troop caressing his ears. Dave was outraged but kept it to himself, discretion being the better part of valour and also knowing he would have her full attention as soon as they moved on.

"I know you." Corpy spoke, taking the initiative, on the offensive. Always the offensive – take control, keep them guessing. He had addressed Alex who was gratifyingly floored.

"Me?"

"You work here."

"I do. Well, for a while. Volunteering, you know."

No, Corpy did not know. He had enlisted and was committed; paid to die. His study of Alex's face was so intense and unwavering that Alex wanted to scratch his discomfort.

"You started on Monday." Make him know that I know, that I have the advantage. Knowledge is power. Corpy in control.

"Yes." Alex had no idea what type of combat he had apparently entered into but appeasement would be his policy. He said nothing else. See what happened next and be ready to retreat at any moment. Lisa had distracted the military back up; Troop was putty in her hands and now lying on his back in the doorstep having tummy tickles. Dave was a picture of canine saintliness and fortitude.

"Why d'you always come in the back way?" Corpy had changed tactic and caught Alex unaware but it was a master stroke. Davinia: common ground.

"She – Davinia – the manageress – prefers it that way."

"Ah." So that was her name, Corpy thought. He knew she was in charge but it was always good to have identification details. The two men eyed each other, much as their dogs had done. Meanwhile, Lisa had been looking about the doorstep as she attended to Troop and making deductions.

"Is this where you sleep?" she asked. Alex was shocked; the thought had never occurred to him.

"Yes. Home sweet home." Corpy swivelled his eyes down and over Troop to look into Lisa's, on the same level.

"Every night?"

"Pretty much."

"I've never seen you" Alex interjected.

"Always gone by the time She gets here" Corpy replied, briskly.

"Ah." Now it was Alex's turn to understand. "Against Company Policy I expect."

They grinned. Bonded. Davinia diplomacy had done it again.

"That's what she said when she found me here. Tried to tell her I was a veteran but she didn't buy it."

"And are you?" Lisa asked.

Corpy nodded and, prompted by Lisa, was astonished to find himself telling them about his deployment in Afghanistan. Not in great detail but more than he had ever told anyone else, especially the counsellor the army had provided on his return to the UK whom he had singularly mistrusted. Who knew what would be reported back about him? He made light of the IED and said nothing of the nightmares and the flashbacks and the SA80 he carried in his head. What he did describe in detail was the arrival of Troop. Lisa and Alex were appalled. Troop looked suitably crestfallen as his story was told, perking up at the point that he and Corpy had become one and wagging his tail approvingly at the account of the charity of the street.

"Is there anything we can do to help?" Lisa asked. Corpy thought for a minute; Troop watched. No, not for him, the dog seemed to say; he had everything he needed, thank you but Corpy might want something. Yes, he did.

"Something to read'd be nice. It can get a bit boring during the day." Alex leapt into action.

"No problem. What do you like? I know someone who knows all about books and she'll find you something I'm sure."

"Not crap. Something with depth. But light to carry. George Orwell, Aldous Huxley, that kind of thing. Not military." For the second time in as many days Alex realised that people were unexpected; full of surprises. He would have been hard pressed to spell Huxley, never mind read it. He wondered if he had been in the NHS too long.

"We must do something to help" he said to Lisa as they walked home.

"Yes. If that's what he wants" she answered and Alex was surprised all over again.

Chapter Six
Saturday

Saturdays were busy; all hands to the deck days led by Captain Davinia who liked to think of herself steering her vessel, a little leaky in places, crew occasionally mutinous but ultimately compliant and nothing she could not handle. Volunteers, of course, were not ideal. Lacked commitment and recoiled from real work. They seemed to think it was a social occasion, a place to chat and gossip, an opportunity to be the first to check out the stock. One of them, who would remain nameless but Davinia knew exactly what she was up to, carried her husband's measurements about her person at all times 'just in case' something nice came in. He was a large man - huge - and preternaturally needy. She was diminutive and pretty pointless because she could not reach any of the higher shelves and got vertigo on ladders. He got upset if she did not bring him a 'present' when she returned home so she spent most of her day ferreting through the lower racks in pursuit of outsized trousers or vests; he especially liked those. Davinia had not met him and had no wish to do so; she had seen the size of the vests and tracksuit trousers when they arrived in the shop. Volunteers were so … sloppy: just did not seem to understand the concept of dedicated action; arrived late without apology or shame - honestly did not seem to care or if they did, completely failed to understand the difficulties they created. She was an excellent manager, everyone said so, but she had to have something to manage. They thought nothing of slipping out to do a spot of shopping or taking an extended coffee break because they had met someone they knew and stopped for a catch up; took days off without notice, disappeared on endless holidays and cruises or absconded in the name of family. That's why the Community Service people were so useful; they had to do as they were told. So, in theory, did Candy but somehow that never quite seemed to happen. Davinia had never worked out why. Candy was there but not there, as it were, busy and occupied but impossible to quantify. Yet Davinia was not able to explain why, especially in written appraisals when there were so many ridiculous rules about what you could and could not say.

Colin could not wait to get into work. Saturdays were always so exciting but now he had such news. He had met a lady! Would be meeting her again! Did that make her his 'lady friend'? The very idea made him go fuzzy at the edges. He, Colin, had a lady friend, called Barb who shared his love of tropical fish and looked a bit like Davinia and wore make up and liked cake and wanted to see him next Friday. It was a dream. And when he arrived at the front door, wonder of wonders, Davinia was there on the shop floor and saw him even before he knocked so he did not have to wait to be let in, and she noticed that he was wearing his best slacks and a shirt and real polyester tie under the sweater Mother had knitted for him before her hands had seized up. He wanted to sing.

Davinia assumed a 5 out of 10 rictus smile when she saw Colin hovering on the doorstep. At least he was always on time and thank God he wasn't wearing that terrible shell suit although the sweater seemed to be of the same era, need washing and had frilly cuffs. And, oh dear God, it looked hand knitted.

"Good morning, Colin". The words writhed from behind her rigid smile-clenched teeth. Colin beamed.

"Hello! I've got lots to tell you, Davinia." He rolled the name around his mouth and glowed.

"Jolly good, Colin. Nice day off? Till's all ready to go. Mind the drawer, it's a bit sticky this morning. Unlock the door at 9.00. I'll be in my office." She was gone, leaving only her parting words "It's an

'Open - Keeping Warm day" floating in her Shalimar scented wake.

Colin's disappointment was only temporary. Plenty of time during the day to tell Davinia his news and she was so busy: so much to do, so much responsibility. However, his enthusiasm was somewhat tempered by the news about the till drawer. What did she mean by sticky? Was it dirty? No. He examined it carefully, bending over for a closer view and then running his finger over its smoothness. No problem there. Perhaps it was sticky inside. He positioned himself behind the counter, ready, waiting, lanyard face-side out ready for inspection. Then he remembered he had to open the door. The sign explaining the closed door was already hanging on the back of the door so all he had to do was turn it round. Feeling daring he performed a complicated manoeuvre: twisting the sign the right way around while unlocking the door and pulling it ajar for confirmation of its unlocked status. He was inspired - the Power of Love. He skipped to one side to shut the door and saunter manfully back to the till but found that his lanyard had become entangled with the shut door. He was trapped, pinioned by the closed door, his neck on one side, the lanyard on the other. As he unleashed himself, he pretended to be peering out into the street, checking for miscreants and robbers.

Corpy and Troop were on their way to the PDSA Dispensary. Their plan had been formulated and finalised overnight. They would need assistance, maybe a van, but Corpy was confident it would work although it had to be implemented quickly. His mates could not be expected to stand guard for long; they had themselves to look after. He and Troop felt invigorated and motivated. Suddenly he stopped. What was happening to him? Troop was a dog. How could he feel invigorated and motivated by a plan that was purely of Corpy's devising? Man and dog studied each other, in the middle of the pavement, oblivious to the people flowing around them as water avoiding a rock in a shallow stream. Troop wagged his tail encouragingly, grinned and gave Corpy a look of such innocence that the man was disarmed, dismissed his suspicions as ludicrous and resumed his position of master. Troop grinned to himself and trotted beside the man, quietly steering him along the pavement.

In the stock room Alex was telling Shelley about the chap he had met on the doorstep the night before.

"You mean he lives there? With his dog?"

"Yes. Calls it his home."

Shelley was silent for a moment.

"And he's a veteran?" Alex nodded. "A veteran living outside the Veteran's Help Society shop?" Alex nodded again. "That sucks. Why doesn't he come in? He could live in here for God's sake … if he could find room. Even the cellar'd be better than outside." Alex looked at her. "Alright, maybe not. But you know what I mean." Yes, he did,

"It's against…" Alex began

"…Company Policy?" Shelley finished; a question to which they both knew the answer. "Isn't there anything we can do?" she asked.

Apparently not but Alex did tell her about Corpy's reading list. Could she help? Yes, she absolutely could. As soon as they had a break - she would say she was getting hot so Davinia could not argue - then she would check out the book shelves and find something suitable. It would be a pleasure; nothing she liked better than looking at books. It meant being on the shop floor in sight of the public but she'd play it cool so Davinia'd never know. Just like old times in Waterstones. She grinned.

"I'll pay for them" Alex said.

"No, you bloody won't" she said. "This one's on VHS. I'll ask Candy who's bound to say yes. Or I'll find books that are defaced so can't be sold." She winked. Alex resolved to turn a blind eye and put the appropriate payment into the donation tin on the counter. He changed the subject and they got back to work.

"Anything good come in today?" Shelley wanted to know. Anything to delay the onslaught of the inevitable steaming. Alex was suspiciously extracting the contents of a particularly creased green garden waste bag; he did not want a repetition of the vomit-encrusted banana costume despite his medical grade familiarity with the rejected half-ingested abdominal contents of strangers.

"Not so far. This might be good for the vintage rail." Shelley shrieked. Alex was holding up a shell suit, bat-winged, lurid, large and smelling of cigarettes.

"Oh my God! It's so gross! Did you wear things like that Al?"

"Regrettably, yes. Everyone did." It was a lame excuse but true of so many. "I was slimmer in those days" he added as if to minimise the damage.

"More hair?" Shelley sniggered.

"Enough to mousse and scrunch." She shrieked again and he joined in, remembering the Wham days and momentarily regretting that he had not gone more down the punk route as he continued emptying the plastic sack.

"What's that?"

Alex was holding up a man's black T-shirt, with yellow insignia. It had obviously been worn and needed a wash but was in good condition, not faded, twisted out of shape or frayed. The lettering was uncracked and vivid on the front, a huge yellow and black LZ with Knebworth written underneath. Alex had a look of wonderment on his face.

"Al?"

"It's a T shirt."

"Yeah, right, Al, could've worked that out. And your point is?"

"It's a Led Zeppelin."

"More 1980s nostalgia fest?"

"No. Earlier. Iconic rock band. This is worth money." Shelley looked at him as if he had finally lost the plot. She was a child of the noughties, a snowflake. To her the unwashed hairy enthusiasm for heavy metal was a historical blip, the time before. She lived in a world of the internet, Fit Bits, You Tube and Now. Music was eclectic and instant, on demand, the swipe of a screen. Of course, she knew all about Rock, who didn't? But you could buy any number of similar T shirts on eBay or from internet dealers at rock (Ha! She smirked) bottom prices and in better condition. What was the big deal? She said as much but Alex shook his head.

"I'm pretty sure this is an original, a one off. Look at the back." Alex turned it round and held it out by the sleeves so that Shelley could examine what was imprinted on it, which meant nothing to her. Alex explained, patiently, reliving the days of his elder brothers who had both been fanatical Rockers. Those days were long gone; one was now a lawyer and the other ran a successful bespoke kitchen and bathroom refurbishment company specialising in high-end hand-crafted eco-friendly installations which had made him a fortune. Neither of them had much hair and their vinyl collections had long since gone, probably to a charity shop if his mother had had anything to do with it.

"This is a back stage pass T shirt from Knebworth. 1979. It'll have been worn by one of the crew or maybe even the one of the band. Who knows? That makes it valuable in itself but the point is, there are hardly any of these. Only the stage crew will have had them. It's a rarity and it's in good condition." Shelley understood the scarcity factor but was still puzzled.

"What's Knebworth?"

"Good morning. How are we? Lots to do I see." It was Davinia. "Feeling better, Shelley? I shall be able to tell Nerinda that you're back and only have a few hours to make up which is good news for us all, isn't it? I do so want to be able to give her a positive report about your progress. And you too, Alex, of course. What's that?"

For the second time that morning Alex said that it was a T shirt. Davinia gave him a withering look, rolled the tip of her tongue over her lips as if testing the flavour of her lipstick and pretended not to have heard. Clearly his arrogance had not yet been curbed; Nerinda would have to know. Was he being insolent? It was impossible to tell so she would give him the benefit of the doubt, this time. She flared her nostrils as she twisted one pencil heel from side to side as if drilling a hole through a small furry object and began a discourse on the necessity of season appropriate stock. Alex and Shelley listened, glassy eyed.

"...so pack it up for storage if it's worth keeping. Oh!" Davinia was looking at the offending article, still held outstretched by Alex as if he was about to slip it over the head of a giant baby waiting to be dressed. "We don't sell anything with logos on."

"Against Company Policy?" Shelley asked sweetly. Davinia was pleasantly surprised. Perhaps the girl was learning after all. She nodded assent and smiled, tight lipped, tepid but open to the possibility of warmth.

"There are collectors for this kind of memorabilia. It might be worth something." Alex had spoken and a cold front promptly descended as Davinia glared at him. Now he was undoubtably being impertinent if not actually insolent. Challenging her authority as well as her expertise. Really, the audacity of the man was breath taking and not to be endured. She gave him her tightest smile and told him that, no, she did not think so. It was T shirt and should be put for immediate recycling so that they could resume their duties. Hadn't they started steaming yet? She glanced at the clock as she spoke to register both surprise and a sense of urgency. But the obnoxious man had not finished.

"I could check on Google" he was offering. Time to end this she resolved and pulled herself up to her full height, all five feet four inches of it in vertiginous heels and sucked in her stomach for increased presence.

"No. Thank you. Alex. I know what is and isn't valuable. When you have as much experience in retail as me, you know these things."

"No harm in checking" Shelley suggested. Davinia turned to face her, crushing another defenceless furry animal under her heels.

"Nerinda discussed not challenging authority with you, Shelley and will be disappointed to hear that you have not yet taken that on board." She snatched the T shirt from Alex and held it up in front of her for a closer examination. "Good God. It's from 1979. Far too old and dated to sell. Put it for recycling and then finish the sorting before you start steaming and brushing. You'll have to get your skates on to make up for lost time. Just because it's a Saturday doesn't mean you can slack you know. Your weekend hasn't started yet."

"Davinia!" A cry of anguish from the shop floor. "It's a Gift Aid!" Colin's nightmare had taken human form and appeared to him on the other side of the counter. The anguish continued, assuming a falsetto scale: "Do we take fur?" Davinia heard, perked up, handed the T shirt back to Alex, licked her lips, wheeled around and clacked out of the room in a shower of Shalimar and gall, speaking eagerly as she pranced away,

"Fur? What sort of fur"? This was more like it.

"A festival." Alex said.

"Come again?" Shelley had no idea what he was talking about.

"Knebworth." Alex laughed and explained that it was a rock music festival, really famous. His brothers had gone but he was too young. Two hirsute rockers with pungent Afghan coats and burning what they said were joss sticks, playing air guitars to over-loud pointless music had been as much as his parents could bear so they had taken him away to stay with his grandparents out of harm's way. He was rummaging in his coat pocket as he told her and pulling out his mobile.

"What're you doing? We're not supposed to use phones on duty. Davinia'll go mental." Shelley was happily shocked; Alex was not supposed to break the rules. That was her role. He was Googling Led Zeppelin memorabilia.

Davinia was expecting to find a smartly dressed woman of a certain age on the shop floor, probably recently bereaved and clearing out her mother's effects. She started to prepare her 'I am so sorry for your loss' face as she speculated about what it might be worth. Fur coats did come in occasionally and were much prized, by Davinia, if not all her customers some of whom inexplicably refused to have anything to do with them. She would control her expectations until she had seen the garment, probably a stole from the days when people dressed up for the theatre or a night out and had class. It mystified her that so many people were anti-fur. The animal was dead so why not? What else would you do with it? Double standards! So annoying. She knew of at least one so called vegetarian who wore leather shoes - boots in the winter and sandals in the summer – but still banged on about the inhumanity of eating meat. Even Head Office seemed perplexed by the issue and had left the final decision to individual managers as to whether they would accept and sell fur. Well, this individual manager would and did, with a clear conscience. It was her task to raise funds for veterans and the sale of a luxurious fur would make a healthy boost to her sales figures.

She was surprised to find a young man waiting by the counter, casually dressed but not scruffy; hair expensively cut and carefully tousled, wearing a suitably scuffed Barbour. His shoes, she noticed, were Timberland. Not high end but respectable enough and then she noticed his wrist. He was wearing a Rolex. She beamed but then frowned, empathetically; he might be grieving.

He was not. He had brought in a coat he had bought for his girlfriend but she had changed her mind about fur and refused to even have it in the house. So, he thought if he gave it to charity, she might feel better about it. Apparently, she had been to a GOOP Health wellness summit, taken up yoga, given up meat, sugar and all processed food, lost weight and gained a conscience. Although she had never tried it, she had been very taken with the idea of vaginal steaming. He wasn't quite sure what it was but she seemed very keen, had said 'Oh my God. I'm so about it' and was determined to give it a go. If it was good enough for Gwyneth, it was good enough for her. There was an offer on it in a place downtown so she and her BFF were heading there, as soon as, to get their vags steamed together. She was not sure what the benefits were but it was supposed to be very relaxing and essential for her well-being as a woman who embraced her body and womanhood. Had Davinia ever tried it? Oh well, never mind. But the girlfriend did still drink alcohol he said, more brightly, so all was not lost. Colin was shocked. The young man had talked about a young lady's – he could not bring himself even to think the word – private area without the least embarrassment, as if it was a normal conversation. Davinia clucked sympathetically and resisted the temptation to tear open the bespoke zipped bag in which the coat was concealed.

"What type of fur is it?" she tried to sound nonchalant.

"Sable, I think. I don't know. Fur's not my thing. She saw it and I bought it and now she doesn't want it. Is it of any use to you? I offered it to another charity shop but they said fur was against their company policy, so I've brought it here. I could try and sell it on the internet but to be honest, I can't be arsed. Just want rid."

"The shop about four doors down?"

He nodded. She nodded too, two nodding dogs contemplating the folly of the world. She knew exactly which shop he meant and their loss was definitely her gain. More fool them.

"We'd be delighted to take it" she gleamed, reaching for the zip to unveil the treasure. "Thank you so much for such a generous donation."

"It's a Gift Aid." Colin had found a voice. He had been wondering if Barb wore fur and what she would look like, but the remembrance that His Job came first punctured the vision. Davinia might need reminding.

She did not, but saccharine smiled and thanked him. Perhaps she should do the transaction and he could take a break? Go for a coffee? Yes, it was a little early but it was a Saturday and he was a volunteer so they had to keep him happy, didn't they? She gave a little tinkly laugh Colin had not heard before which was enchanting and he thought again what a marvellous woman she was. The young man seemed to feel the same and was chatting to her in such a friendly way, you would have thought they had known each other forever. Or were related, mother and son perhaps. And the young man was agreeing that yes, he would bring anything else he wanted to give to a good cause straight to their shop and of course, Davinia would be delighted to know if he was intending to visit and would arrange to be there to see him. No, no trouble at all. It would be her absolute pleasure. They valued their very generous patrons and their customers, equally. All part of the service – serving others.

"It's a fur coat!" Colin said to Candy who was in the corridor piling up DVDs ready for inspection. A quiet corner, aligned chakras and a cup of herb tea would help her as she worked her way through them, which would take all morning and then she could go for lunch.

"No way! She wouldn't? She couldn't?" Candy stood up, tossed her head, seized her hair like a rope and strode off to do eco-combat, Brunhilda in hiking boots. Colin was perplexed. Had he said something wrong?

Outraged Animal Rights Activist arrived at the counter as the young man was disappearing through the door and confronted her manageress with as much violence as subdued hisses and whispers could muster.

"It's disgusting. Immoral. Senseless killing for commercial gain to satisfy the vanity of the superficial rich and attention-seeking famous. We must not sell it, on principle."

"Candy. It's a fur coat. It's a valuable item which'll make a lot of money for VHS. It's for charity."

"Does that make it moral, Davinia? Does that excuse the slaughter of innocent creatures to satisfy the mindless whims of others? I don't think so." Candy's hisses and whispers were increasing in volume which bothered her boss more than her argument. So unprofessional! She took decisive action.

"We are on the shop floor, Candy. Keep your voice down. I have decided that we will stock and sell fur and that is an end of it. Of course, I respect your views" she spat out the words, "but the decision has been made in the interests of the charity we both serve. I don't expect you to handle anything made of fur, that is your choice, but I don't require your approval for a senior managerial decision."

End of subject. Outraged Animal Activist crushed, defeated, trounced and sent packing, tail between woolly tights, back to her DVDs and herb tea, chakras all over the place and badly in need of realignment.

Although he would not thank you for saying it, Corpy was sharing the same satisfaction as Davinia about a deal well closed. The PDSA had not believed him at first, it was too improbable. People just did not do that sort of thing. They knew, they spent endless hours and a fortune in cash on advertising to persuade people to donate for sick animals and it was a so often a losing battle. However, when he produced his cardboard sign, rather crushed from being wrapped around his sleeping bag and offered to show them the stocks of canine comestibles, they began to listen. If they would guarantee medical and health care for Troop, he would donate everything given to him, to the PDSA, less what he needed to feed Troop. No, nothing for himself. This was about the dog, not him. But they would need to send a van to collect the stuff which was safely stowed for the moment but needed to be lifted off the street. Suppose they had a regular collection day? Whatever was good for them; his time was flexible and he would fit in his collecting to suit. Obviously, he would not be collecting every day; he called it taking the piss but the senior vet who had been summoned by the reception staff when Corpy had put forward his proposal, referred to it as charity fatigue. He did not want a new laminated sign, thank you; that would be too commercial. If he could have a board marker there was plenty of cardboard available. Yes, blue would be ideal. When he and Troop ambled out of the surgery the vet was shaking his head in wonderment and almost skittered back to his waiting patients.

Davinia just had to try on the fur coat. Candy had disappeared with a pile of DVDs and herb tea into the ether; no one knew how she did it in such a small shop but gone she was, again, and the coast was clear. Colin had returned from coffee and a slice of carrot cake, just like

Barb's, and was proving to be the ideal audience.

"You look just like a film star!" he cooed. "Diana Dors." He sighed with approval.

Davinia was not amused. "More Elizabeth Taylor or Audrey Hepburn I think" she said to Colin who heard not a word. He was imaging Barb in a full-length fur with a collar that could be pulled up about the ears and fastened not with buttons but tiny little hidden clasps. So elegant, so glamorous. Marvellous. He wondered what price tag Davinia was going to put on it.

Having exhausted Colin's applause Davinia decided to try her luck with Alex. Shelley, of course would disapprove; people like that always did. It was a class issue. Shelley did indeed disapprove, volubly.

"Rank" was all she said, shuddered and muttered something unintelligible to herself about Hamlet's mother, whoever she was. Alex was more responsive but not as appreciative as Davinia had hoped. She had thought a surgeon who was used to cutting, slicing and stitching would be more open minded and impressed by the quality of such a sumptuous garment. She also had an axe to grind.

"Now this is worth money, Alex. Real money. It's sable you know."

"Looks like musk rat to me."

He was just being petty. The gentleman had said it was sable and he bought it so he would know. "We'll get it out on the shop floor as soon as we can. On the Glam rail, I think. This'll walk out of the shop; you wait and see."

"Not without legs it won't" Shelley said darkly. Davinia felt she had to respond but, as always, as the consummate professional, all tolerance and understanding. Role modelling.

"Now Shelley, it may not be to your taste but someone will be very happy to pay a lot of money for this." From the shop floor Colin wondered if it would be him.

"You could put it on the mannequin" Alex suggested. Davinia was surprised and impressed.

"Excellent idea, Alex. Thank you." She pushed her luck. "Oh, it's so soft and so gorgeous to wear; the satin lining is so silky. Fabulous." She did a twirl and ground her heels against the floor tiles which squealed in pain. "So Hollywood. The era of the silver screen."

"Vampire."

Davinia decided to return to the shop floor, where there was a full-length mirror.

It was Alex's turn to make dinner. As he pottered about the kitchen, Lisa was on her iPad. He had been telling her about his day and they were enjoying a glass of wine while he chopped vegetables and did his best to avoid Dave who had attached himself to Alex's leg in the hope of getting something to eat. Alex was doing most of the talking, Lisa was engrossed but occasionally muttered so he assumed she was listening. Just as Alex reached the crescendo of his account of the fur coat as it had appeared in the steaming room stretched around Davinia's ample buttocks over stumpy legs squeezed into pointy shoes, Lisa interrupted.

"What d'you think of this?" He stopped, mid-flow, suspended, mildly panicked. What was it? What had happened? "Look!" she said and gestured to him the screen in front of her. Slamming his wine glass down on the kitchen top he sprinted to her side, Dave with him, knights to the rescue.

It was a dress.

"What d'you think? Do you like it?" Lisa was serious. Alex was taken aback. Dave wondered if it was edible. "It's a bargain. On eBay" Lisa explained, under the misapprehension that Alex's concern was economic. Since the debacle at the hospital they had been on an economy drive and new clothes, especially extravagant ones, were so far down their list of priorities as to be out of sight. "It's Monsoon" she offered, as if he would know what she was talking about, "and very reasonable. There are four people watching it but no bids as yet. They all come at the end" she explained because his silence was disconcerting. "I wouldn't pay more than £20…not even £15" she added as an afterthought. Still he said nothing. "Or not bid at all if you prefer? I was just thinking of Tiger-Lily and Fern's wedding next year but it doesn't matter…Alex? What is it?"

"I've seen that dress before. In the shop."

"The Vet's Help? Well, that's alright. Maybe someone's bought it and is selling it on. People do, all the time."

"No, it wasn't for sale. It was in the steaming room. I cleaned it myself."

"Are you sure?"

"Positive. It was on a hanger, airing, ready to be priced and put out. I remember doing it because I noticed the label and thought what a ridiculous name it was. Who'd want to buy clothes named after a violent tropical storm?"

"Lots of people actually. It's a good name. Very popular, and quite expensive. But how did it get onto eBay?"

"I don't know, Lisa. … Does it say who's selling it?" Lisa squinted at the screen then swiped it a couple of times.

"Someone called Queen Dee. People don't usually use their real names but invent a username. I've never sold anything but if I did, I always thought I'd call myself Dave's Slave." Normally Alex would have laughed but now he was troubled and he tugged at one of his ear lobes, the only physical sign of stress he ever displayed, especially in the operating theatre.

"Queen Dee? ... Oh, bloody hell."

Chapter Seven
Monday

Alex could not wait to get to the shop on Monday morning, which was both unexpected and unwanted. He wanted to talk to Shelley about the eBay discovery. And yet, should he? Was he being subjective, his suspicion based on dislike, his judgement flawed by personal issues? It was a question he was almost afraid to ask after his stupidity at the hospital but one that could not be avoided. Was Queen Dee really Davinia? He had no choice but to discuss it with Shelley who would probably tell him he had a nasty suspicious mind and that although Davinia was a cow, she would never do anything so underhand. She was such a saddo that the shop was her whole life and she would never jeopardise her career or the Veteran's Help Society. Besides, it would be against Company Policy.

He arrived much too early. Lisa had dropped him off at the top of the street to save car parking charges – really, they were extortionate. No wonder Candy hiked to work and Colin caught the bus. He had no idea what Shelley did for transport or even where she came from; he must find out. The shop was closed and dark; Corpy and Troop were packing themselves up on the doorstep, the cardboard neatly folded ready for stowing behind the bins and Troop watching helpfully as Corpy strangled his sleeping bag into a rigid roll. Alex waved as he approached and Troop wagged his tail in greeting as Corpy heaved and squeezed his bedding. Apart from themselves and a stranger walking towards them from the other end of the high street, it was deserted, quiet, semi-light and cold. Winter, on the edge of the hidden world of the homeless preparing to make way for the daylight life of the domiciled. Walking down the street felt to Alex like being in a dim no man's land between a parallel world about which he had been told, but the reality of which was a complete mystery. He arrived at the doorstep at the same time as the approaching stranger who was carrying a battered sports holdall.

"This the Vet's Society?" the man asked.

"Yes." It was Alex who answered; Corpy was busy with the recalcitrant sleeping bag which had staged a comeback and refused to be rolled. Troop eyed the stranger ominously, narrow eyed, assessing the situation. He sniffed at the bag with interest, gave a low growl, raised his hackles then backed away. Corpy heard and turned around to see Alex being handed the holdall which was so heavy it made him stagger.

"I'll leave this with you then" the man said and immediately trotted away, not quite at a run but jogging, purposefully, with intent and rapidly increasing distance. He was soon out of sight.

"Morning, Corpy" Alex announced cheerfully, as if the man needed to be told what time of day it was. "How are you? Can I help?"

"Looks like you've got enough to carry. What is it?"

"A donation. I'll take it round the back and wait for the manageress to arrive. Hello Troop. How are you?" Troop was fine, thank you, happy to see Alex even without Dave and would love to have his ears stroked. Mmmm. Very nice. He kept away from the holdall however and seemed relieved when the trio moved off towards the alley, the bins and the back entrance of the shop. There Alex helped stow the cardboard mattress and watched as veteran and dog ambled away into the outskirts of town. When he had asked where they went and what they did, Corpy had merely shrugged and said the same as every other day, give or take. Did he want something to eat, Alex had asked? A coffee? No, he was fine, thank you. Would get something later but thanks for the offer. Much appreciated. Alex had had to content himself with handing over his address and phone number, written in advance on a piece of A4, "just in case…you never know". It had been Lisa's idea. And then they were gone.

Perfect timing. Almost immediately Davinia rolled up in her car, parked slowly and carefully in her allocated space and turned off the engine. If she had noticed Alex, she gave no sign of it but spent a couple of minutes in the parked car inspecting her make up in the rear-view mirror and applying copious amounts of lipstick. After inspecting her teeth, bared at the mirror and found to be lipstick free, she closed her mouth, rolled her tongue around her teeth one final time and prepared to exit. This also took time: driver door to unlock (she always drove with locked doors: an attractive lone woman had to be careful) Radley bag to check, close, open, check again and then lift from the front passenger seat, open the door, an elegant swivel of the legs to the ground outside followed by an equally elegant ladylike exit, then shut the door and lock. Check lock, turn the little Radley dog to face outwards, ready to go. Then 'see' Alex.

"Good morning, Alex. I didn't expect you to be here so early. Have you been waiting long?"

No, he had just arrived. She was looking at the holdall at his feet and mentally speculating. What did it mean? Had he left home? Well, he couldn't stay in the shop. His personal life was nothing to do with her but she wouldn't be surprised if he'd been thrown out; how much could a wife be expected to endure? His arrogance was unbearable; she would not have given him the time of day let alone married him.

"It's a donation. Left this morning" Alex explained; he had noticed her interest in the bag.

"Oh." Initial disappointment in her voice then forced enthusiasm. "Excellent. We'll add it to today's jobs. No Gift Aid I suppose?"

Alex explained that it was more or less dumped on the doorstep but made no mention of the night-time incumbents that had just left. He followed Davinia into the shop and went with the holdall into the steam room as she headed to the shop floor, surreptitiously fingering the key on the chain around her neck. Better to get the till ready before Colin arrived or he would start chatting and he really was so tedious. On Saturday he had begun to tell her about some woman he had met at Aquarium World, of all places, and she really could not bear it; he was so boring and she had so much to do. Couldn't he see that? She felt irritated, and it was only Monday morning. When she found that the till drawer was stuck and she had to prise it open with a pair of scissors her irritation was instantly promoted to annoyance. She blamed Candy; Colin would not know how.

Alex deposited the holdall in a corner of the steam room, alongside the mountain range of donations lined up morosely waiting for processing, like patients in A&E on a busy Saturday night. He began to open the bag but the zip was damaged and its teeth misaligned so it jammed and he left it where it was. Besides, Shelley had arrived and he had news. As she was unwrapping herself from copious cold weather outer garments into barely-there beach wear in preparation for the onslaught of humid tropical heat, he launched into a rather garbled account of Lisa's discovery on eBay.

"So, do you think I'm over reacting?" he asked after all the details had tumbled out, tripping over one another as dominos falling in lines. "Jumping to conclusions? I don't want to be unfair."

"Why not? She is." Shelley seemed unperturbed and unsurprised by Alex's revelation. "Queen Dee is exactly the kind of name she'd use. Yeah, it probably is her. Silly cow." Not very Shakespearian, but heartfelt and then, Shelley was thoughtful. "We need to find out for sure. Prove it. Let me have a think – this is more my line than yours. You get Lisa to buy the dress and keep looking on eBay to see if Queen Dee's selling anything else and I'll work out a plan of campaign. All very *Hamlet.* I love it. To Dee or not to Dee eh, Al?"

Alex had no idea what she was talking about but had no doubt that she would indeed work out a scheme. However, he had more to report.

"That T shirt we found, you know, the Led Zeppelin one?"

Yes, Shelley did. She had googled the band and checked them out on You Tube. "You didn't tell me they did *Stairway to Heaven*. That's an awesome song" she remonstrated. I thought they were just some hairy rockers you were banging on about. So, this T shirt, is it worth something?"

Yes, it was. A lot. Alex was excited and garbled on, "It's only about the rarest Led Zep memorabilia on the market. One just like it sold in 2011 for $10,000…." Dramatic pause. "…which is about £7,800 at today's rates."

Shelley's jaw dropped and she resisted a violent urge to swear. Instead she stared at Alex, rubbed her a hand speculatively up and down one of her tattoo sleeves and gaped.

"I knew it! I just knew it!" he crowed. "And it's in excellent condition!" His jubilation was genuine; it would be great to make a large sum of money for homeless veterans, people like Corpy, but even better was knowing that he had been right and Davinia had been wrong.

"What'll you do with it?"

"Maybe eBay. Might be better to go onto the internet though and see if there are any collectors, that sort of thing. I suggest we don't say anything to Davinia? Not yet, anyway."

"Too right. She'll think it's gone for recycling like she told us to do. Silly cow" Shelley added again, with satisfaction. Work would be almost bearable this morning she promised herself as the ancient steamer wheezed and creaked into action.

Colin was on the shop floor, as usual, excited to be at the start of another week, working with Davinia and clutching his glee about his forthcoming date like a child with an extra piece of cake. He had resolved to leave his hallowed place behind the counter when there were no customers to inspect the men's clothing section to see if there was anything suitable for him to wear, something that would impress Barb. Nothing flashy or too modern but smart, quiet good quality as his Mother would say, a 'take you anywhere and every occasion' sort of outfit. Not a suit, that was too formal but maybe a jacket? He could wear it with his polyester tie - or even buy another one - and a pair of non-crease slacks. He liked the ones with the permanent crease on the front of the legs; they always looked pressed and neat and did not need ironing, you just hung them on a hanger after washing and they dried in the right shape and everything. Marvellous. Barb herself was so elegant and stylish. She wore sparkly earrings which dangled and lots of bracelets which tinkled and jangled like bells as well as rings on nearly every finger. So pretty, and valuable. Clearly, she was a lady who liked the finer things in life and that worried him. Was he good enough? He was not rich but had a savings account as well as his pensions and the house he lived in was all his own, and Mother's of course, but she was in a home now and one day it would be his entirely.

The arrival of a customer at the counter wanting to pay for a fluorescent Benidorm fridge magnet with a thermometer masquerading as a hotel startled him to the point of abject apology. Goodness. He had to do better than this. Much as he loved Barb, he had His Job to do and should not be mixing business with pleasure. Whatever would Davinia say? He resolved to fully concentrate on Work, tucking away the prospect of Barb for quiet moments away from the shop and when he was with his fish. He had to give her the attention she deserved. Nothing but the best. There had also been a nasty moment with the till drawer which had forced him to focus on the present. It had refused to open. He had pressed all the right buttons, he knew he had, had checked and checked, but it would not budge. The customer had not noticed - was too busy inspecting the jewellery on the shelves behind glass under the counter. Colin hoped she would not ask to see anything while he was struggling with the till; how could he do both? Just as he was about to shout for help the drawer suddenly shot open with such energy that it launched itself into his stomach. He huffed and grunted with shock. The lady looking at the jewellery asked if he was alright and of course he said he was, but nevertheless stood well back when he closed it. After the lady had gone, he practised working the till while standing sideways to offset potential injury. He also placed a waste paper basket under the point where the drawer projected in case it fell out completely and he could not catch it.

Then he wondered, sweating profusely, how he would tell Davinia that he had broken it. Hot stress engulfed him; he removed his jumper and placed it carefully on the floor behind the counter where no one could see it. Wouldn't want someone to think it was for sale and buy it. More heat suffused his face and inflamed his ears as he thought of the unfortunate episode that summer when Davinia had left her sunglasses - the ones with diamonds along the top - on the counter, just for a second, while she fetched her handbag, and he had sold them. It had been a terrible mistake. He did not know they were hers. What was worse, he had assumed they were out of the 'Bargain 50p box'. Davinia was awfully cross. Said they were designer, exclusive and terribly expensive. Candy had said that he could find a replacement pair just the same from Primark but he knew that could not be right. Davinia hated Primark. Only ever went in there to look, in the interests of retail research she had told him oh, so many times. Checking out the opposition she called it.

In the back of the shop the steaming-slaves were also sweating profusely, feeding the insatiable appetite of the dragon ruthlessly wheezing and panting its way to cleansing paradise. Alex had insisted that Shelley step back and sort some of the donations in an effort to keep her cool and for once she had not argued, but done as she was told.

"Hey, Al!" She had to shout to compete with the rasp and roar of the blowing beast, "what's supposed to be in the holdall?"

"Dunno. Zip broke." Alex was doing steamy battle and talking was difficult. "Heavy though. Could hardly lift it."

"It's empty." Shelley stood up from bending over the bag which she had managed to open and held it upside down, flaccid and hollow, to demonstrate her point over the noise. Alex shook his head with absolute disinterest and returned to work; Shelley flung the bag onto the heap for recycling.

It had been a relatively quiet morning for which Colin was thankful. Less chance of injury from the till drawer which seemed to be able to detect his presence wherever he was placed behind the counter. The further he stood away the more vehement its exit from the till; even if he stood sideways it seemed capable of angled aggression and always aimed at the centre of his stomach. A complicated manoeuvre of slamming down the Sale button then instantly leaping backwards out of the line of fire had proved to be the only effective method of avoiding ongoing injury, but was exhausting. When Davinia told him he could go for lunch he was hugely relieved, not least because he had admitted his crime to her and she had been remarkably understanding. In fact, had not blamed him at all but had put it all down to Candy.

"I have no idea what she's done or how she's done it but rest assured, Colin, I do not hold you responsible. I'm just sorry you are being so inconvenienced and in the event of serious damage I will have no hesitation in laying the blame firmly at Candy's door." Colin had no idea how a door could have caused the malfunction but Davinia was the boss and she promised that she would get it repaired. In the meantime, perhaps if he stood well back…or he could put something protective down his shirt, or under his jumper? That was his jumper on the floor, wasn't it? Oh yes, Mother had knitted it. Yes, she thought as much. Well, could he pick it up please; such untidiness gave entirely the wrong impression to customers and staff alike. She would take over the till in his absence; Candy was a liability and, where was she by the way? Colin did not know and, stepping well away from the till, bent down to pick up his jumper.

Goodness, how heavy it was. He did not remember it being that heavy. Mother had used double knit wool he knew; they had discussed it at the time of creation and both had felt that anything chunkier although warm would be too bulky for comfort and smartness. What if he wanted to wear a jacket over it instead of his anorak? He flexed his knees and bent to lift the jumper with both hands, failed to move it and fell over, landing in its woolly softness … which gave way and became silky, solid and dry. Not unpleasant, but unexpected and when it moved, very alarming. True, it moved only slowly but it was a hand knitted sweater and should not be moving at all. Colin lay in its coiled comfort for less than a moment before he screamed.

Davinia was startled, turned, her elbow caught the till and slammed the Sale button. The drawer flung itself into orbit, rejoiced in the absence of any obstacle to flight and flew the entire length of the counter before crashing to earth on Colin's jumper which was languidly stretching itself out on the floor. Colin was upright, standing, appalled at the sight of the sleeves of his sweater extending themselves outwards towards Davinia on one side and the stock room on the other. Long after their knitted length had run out, they continued to extend, the body of the jumper writhing silently in uneven humps between them. Now Davinia screamed, a sound so high pitched and abnormal that the air around them seemed to fracture and shatter. The jumper continued to slither across the floor, an intriguing combination of traditional Fair Isle and brown blotches.

Alex and Shelley hurtled onto the scene, closely followed by Candy. Shelley arrived first, lighter on her feet than Alex and nearer the door for a fast exit while he was doing battle with the steamer. No time to ask what was wrong, she arrived just in time to see the sweater head off across the floor towards menswear, the till drawer toppling off it onto the tiles, musically scattering coins which jangled and rolled joyously into every crevice and hidden corner. Pinned in their drawer compartments by metal springs the notes could only stare at their compatriots' escape with envy and longing.

"It's a snake!" Shelley shouted. Davinia and Colin screamed again, in harmony with Candy the screeching backing group and accompanying heavy metal footfall. Alex and Shelley pincered themselves gladiatorially on either side of the rather beautiful if confused brown and cream pulsating pipe in a hand knitted jumper sliding smoothly across the tiled floor in search of safety.

"Catch it before it gets away!" Alex shouted.

"Both ends!" Shelley replied. "I'll do the top you do the bottom. It won't hurt you! Just grab hold of it and don't let go or it'll squeeze you to death."

Davinia collapsed against the drawerless till, clutching the dark roots of her blonde hair and trying to maintain balance in her shoes. Colin had spread eagled himself Christlike against the bookshelves, ready to sacrifice his all for the sake of the others, desperately hoping that it would be Alex who would affect a rescue and thanking God that Barb was not there. Oh, what would he tell mother when he could no longer wear the sweater? Candy was immobile, in the doorway, ready to flee but practising mindfulness and deep breathing as well as exuding karma and peace. Once she saw that Alex and Shelley were on the case, she closed her eyes and assumed a benign expression, inhaling and exhaling with measured regularity, visualising her Bach flower remedy and the sight of a snake behind bars.

Shelley was fielding the head of the terrified snake as if waiting for a drop catch on a cricket pitch except that she was bent towards the ground rather than reaching for the sky. Snake and woman, eyeing each other, biblical, apocryphal, timeless; woman in charge, flung herself on serpent, seized it just below the bulge of the head and held it tight, hard: unforgiving, indomitable.

"Catch the end Al! Now! Just like me!" A quick glance at her handhold and Alex had pitched himself on the flailing end of the snake which he gripped like death, white knuckled, then lifted up in triumph as an Olympic medal.

"Got it!"

"Don't let go!"

Easier said than done but small woman and large man maintained their grip and the snake swung like an overweight skipping rope between them, desperately trying to twist and knot itself free.

"Candy! Call the police!" Davinia had found her voice but not her mobile phone.

"No! The RSPCA" Shelley shouted and for once Davinia did as she was told.

"Yes! The RSPCA! Now. Tell them it's an emergency… Candy! Now!"

"Yes!" Colin added, arms lowered but still pinned against the shelves. "Now! Please?"

Candy exhaled and lowered her mindful shoulders, invoked a spiritually calming atmosphere with fluttering hands and scuttled towards the office, leaving Alex and Shelley sweating with the exertion of holding a half-grown Burmese python in as straight a line as humanly possible and having a somewhat breathless conversation, punctuated by gasps and tightened grips as the reptile writhed between them, still wearing the Fair Isle sweater which wafted to and fro like a flag in a light breeze.

There was a thud and a crash, a fleshy bounce followed by the crack of bone meeting ceramic and then, silence. Candy lay motionless on the floor in the doorway, her long hair gently matting in the blood from her head on the tiled floor.

Davinia and Colin screamed again, less harmoniously.

"Is she dead?" Davinia screeched.

"She's dead!" Colin howled.

"She's fallen over her bloody bootlaces" Shelley shouted from the snake's jaws which were opening and closing with outrage.

"It's going to bite!" Colin screamed again, watching the snake in Shelley's grip. "We're all going to die."

"No, we're going to call the emergency services" Alex, trying to be calm. "Colin. Go into the office and call 999."

Colin stared at him in disbelief. Me? Move? From the bookshelves? He turned to Davinia. She would know what to do.

"Yes, Colin. Go and ring for help. 999. Use the phone in the office."

Colin stared. But it never occurred to him to disobey so he

disentangled himself from his paralysis and edged away from the books towards the doorway and Candy's inert body. Tiptoeing so as not to disturb her or attract the snake which was coiling like a rope at slack anchor he slithered across the bloody floor and disappeared into the office, where he slammed the door with such force that even the python stopped to listen.

In the emergency call centre the operator was struggling. Hoax calls were sadly all too common but this one was at least original and had ambition.

"So, you have a dead body, an escaped snake and people imprisoned in a shop? …. Which emergency service do you require? … I beg your pardon? … What are the choices? Is this a joke?"

Colin was flustered. He did not make jokes. He tried to explain again. "I don't make jokes. Mother doesn't like them. There was a snake in my jumper and then Candy fell over and hit her head and is dead and Davinia can't get out from behind the counter because of the snake which is tied up with the others."

"There's more than one snake?"

"No, Alex and Shelley. They're community service…"

"Are they ex-offenders?"

"Yes. No. Not really. More like volunteers."

"And you are…?"

"Colin."

"Right, Colin. Well, where are you?"

"In the shop."

"And which shop is that?"

"Davinia's shop. In the High Street."

"I'm looking on my information screen and not seeing a Davinia's Shop. What is the exact address please Colin?"

Colin explained that it was not actually Davinia's shop but that she just managed it, marvellously, and that it was the Veteran's Help Society shop in the High Street. Then he was asked about the snake. He thought for a second before answering.

"It's too big for my jumper – comes out of both sleeves. It's Fair Isle and mother knitted it large so that I could wear a thick shirt underneath. I don't know what type of snake it is except that it's trying to bite everyone and is brown with splodges on and it reaches from the till nearly to menswear."

By now the supervisor was listening in on the call.

"No choice but to take it seriously" she sighed. "If it's not a joke it's a catastrophe. Ambulance, police and fire – combined operation. God only knows what we'll find. Just hope we don't have to scramble the chopper. Better get onto the RSPCA too – dangerous animals. I hate Mondays."

"How'd you know what to do?" Alex wheezed to Shelley as they heaved the recalcitrant python towards the centre of the room

"Boyfriend. Had one as a pet. Bloody nightmare."

"I can imagine."

"Not the snake, the boyfriend."

"Oh."

"They're quite good natured, pythons. For snakes. Popular. Grow very big though. Right, Al. We need to keep it still. You sit on its tail and I'll sit on its neck. Then we need to put it in something – that holdall it came in would do… Colin!" Shelley was shouting, "Colin!" There was no reply.

"Hell. We'll have to wait until he gets back unless…Davinia, can you get something to put this thing in? There's a holdall in recycling. … Wait, before you go, don't you think you should close the shop? What's the Company Policy on reptiles?"

Chapter Eight
Aftermath

Tuesday was always going to be an anti-climax but nevertheless, there was a frisson, a veiled excitement in the air. Who knew what might happen? The events of Monday had gripped the town and everyone seemed to know about it. What was more they wanted to talk about it, visit the scene of the crime, soak in the atmosphere of the drama and be able to tell their friends that yes, they did know the shop and had been in oh, just seconds after it had happened. A minute earlier and they would have been one of those involved, lucky to escape with their life and of course they would have been terrified but could have handled the snake – seen it done on telly by David Attenborough.

Candy had been wheeled off in the ambulance and the good news was that she was not dead, but only badly concussed. A nasty cut on her head. Head wounds bleed like buggery the paramedic had announced chirpily as he pushed one end of the gurney out of the front door through the swelling crowd. There was quite a flutter of mobile phones recording the image for posterity – a body – not moving - blood everywhere and such lovely hair but oh, what a mess. Would they have to cut it all off? What a shame. If Candy heard she did not react; she was certainly conscious on arrival in A&E and able to argue about the use of synthetic drugs and anything that had been tested on animals. She would not have any such poison thank you very much, but did allow them to shave part of her head and seal the wound. The result was extraordinary and really quite *avant garde* in a Frieda Kahlo sort of way, especially when she piled the rest of hair up over the bald patch like a badly built straw beehive.

It was the snake that caused the biggest stir. Davinia had made her way to the steam room, nimbly stepping over Candy in the doorway, but had been unable to find the holdall amidst all the vapour and heat. Alex had abandoned the antique steamer which, suddenly free from human interference had developed a determined independence and was puffing and blowing with all the energy of a once glorious youth. The room now had all the characteristics of a Turkish bath and Davinia could neither see nor feel her way even to the recycling area, never mind find a bag. Her shoes skidded and slid on the wet tiled floor, the walls rained, the ceiling had disappeared, the exit had melted into the vortex somewhere behind her. Perhaps now she'd appreciate their working conditions Alex grimly ruminated as he hung onto the snake's rear end. She emerged, moist and mascara-smeared just as the fire service burst in. The police had been close behind the ambulance and sealed off the area with blue and white tape – the crowd was thrilled. When five, fit, helmeted fire fighters emerged carrying a length of python wearing a Fair Isle sweater between them there was spontaneous applause. The snake was now remarkably quiet; it had been a hell of a day and he just wanted to rest. Besides, it was cold outside. Frankly it was a relief to be able to coil up in a box in the back of the van of the RSPCA man, who had said that he was a magnificent specimen as he closed the lid, shut the doors, closing out the light and the noise.

"But where did it come from? How did it get here?" Davinia wanted to know.

"Happens all the time" the RSPCA answered cheerfully. "People buy 'em as babies but don't realise how big they'll grow, or how fast. Can't cope. Get rid of 'em. You're the Vet's Help Society, aren't you? Well, there you are." Davinia looked blank. He elaborated, increasing the volume of his voice in case she was a bit mutt and Jeff. "Vet's. Homeless. … vets…. animal doctors?" Yes, thank you, she knew what a vet was but this was ridiculous. How could people not know the difference? They were the Veteran's Help Society not the PDSA. "Might have to change your name love" the man said, shutting the driver door. He liked Burmese pythons. Better than alligators or terrapins any day – they were always so aggressive.

Colin had other, more serious concerns. How would he get his sweater back?

The following day was not much better. Not only had Davinia been traumatised by the events of the previous morning in Her Shop but she was humiliated and mortified – had had to deal with emergency service personnel while mascara-streaked and shiny nosed. What was worse, the RSPCA man had praised Shelley's professionalism in dealing with a 'potentially serious situation'. The lady detective sent to the scene, a large woman with a variegated complexion that Alex had afterwards diagnosed as vitiligo, had agreed and said that Shelley was a remarkable young woman. Had even admired her tattoos. Now, Davinia was a deputy manageress down, Colin was in a state of shock-induced obsession about redeeming his ghastly sweater and incapable of even the most simple transactions on the till, Alex was – well, Alex and Shelley was in the ascendant. It really could not get much worse.

Then coffee/caffeine-breath Reg appeared in the doorway, meditatively rubbing his groin and surveying the shop floor full of nosy customers loudly discussing the events of yesterday while fingering the merchandise and replacing all the hangers on the rails the wrong way around.

"Reg. This is a surprise. Such a pleasure" Davinia lied brightly.

"Busy I see. Good. What happened yesterday?"

So, Head Office had heard. Not surprising really, the local radio station had been full of it and even regional TV had covered the story. Some of those same nosy customers even now examining the stock must have made small fortunes from their camera coverage. Despite her ravaged make up Davinia had made a point of appearing on the street outside the shop and had spoken at length to the earnest TV reporter of the terrible experience she – they – had undergone. You only had to look at her. Clearly the reporter, a spruce pencil-thin twenty-something had agreed because it was a shock to find that none of the interview made it to the screen. Davinia watched all evening and much of the night just to be certain. Candy had looked suspiciously composed and well-groomed on that gurney and had been much photographed. Davinia doubted if she was unconscious at all but had merely been acting – anything for attention. The python however, was undoubtably the star of the show, sharing the limelight with Colin's jumper. In fact, a number of customers had enquired where they could buy one just like it. The TV news programme had even run a short feature on the history of the Fair Isle sweater and had wanted to interview Colin who, thankfully, had refused but said only that his mother had knitted it before her arthritis became too bad. Then he had been asked for the name of the nursing home where his mother lived so Davinia really feared the worst.

"It's all publicity for us," Reg pronounced after his briefing in the office, "which is good. Puts us on the media map." He rubbed his groin for a moment. "Head Office want us to capitalise on this – maximise the potential. Promotional opportunities. Boost sales. Bit of media tartery if you get me." His hand was poised, motionless, over his crotch as he peered at her through his greasy fringe. "Public awareness, Davinia. Get the Community Service people out of the back onto the shop floor sometimes and make them visible…This Colin chap. More to him than meets the eye. How did he persuade all the emergency services to turn up like that? Brilliant. I'd like to meet him, have a chat."

And as if the Gods were lined up in ranks against her, Colin appeared precisely at that moment to be greeted by Reg like some sort of C list celebrity. He had knocked on the door and stuck his head round uttering the immortal words "It's a Gift Aid" at which point Reg had abandoned his groin, jumped to his feet and clasped Colin's hand in both of his own.

"Colin! Delighted to see you! Come in, come in. Great job you did yesterday. The Vet's Help is very proud of you, isn't it, Davinia?"

Davinia managed a smile but could not quite run to words so nodded her head slightly while forming some notion of, as yet, unidentified revenge. Then was ashamed. It was only Colin. She was just summoning the power of speech when the air shrieked and shook.

"Col! Col! Well! If it isn't my Colin!"

It was Barb. In the doorway, all of it, perched on heels higher even than Davinia's and bracelets bouncing.

Colin was stunned and thrilled. His knees wanted to buckle. Barb! His Barb! In His Shop! Davinia was aghast. Who was this woman? Where had she come from? Didn't she know that this was a private area, staff only, strictly out of bounds to customers? Her Office? The woman seemed completely oblivious to her breach of protocol and was beaming at them all like an overripe banana, soft and squidgy. Colin appeared to be in a state of barely suppressed delirium but it was difficult to be sure: sometimes he looked at the till the same way. Davinia looked at him for some sort of explanation and avoided Reg who, clearly, had no idea what was going on and was smiling politely, always the professional. Colin by now had found a slightly falsetto voice.

"This is, er, Barb. We met at Aquarium World."

"Indeed we did" she took over, chatting amiably as if she had known everyone all her life. "Colin told me all about his fish, didn't you dear?" Colin nodded vigorously as she sailed on. "We had a lovely chat and a nice bit of cake and such a nice time we decided to do it again, didn't we dear?" Colin nodded again so enthusiastically that Davinia feared for his neck. "Well, there I was, watching the television last night, and what did I see? That's Colin's shop I said to myself, the one he told me all about and sure enough, it was, and so much going on! The dead body and the police and then that snake! I couldn't believe my eyes. I looked at it and thought to myself that's Colin's jumper it's wearing – the one he was wearing at Aquarium World. It was wasn't it, Col? So exciting! You must have been terrified. But so brave! However did you manage to catch it in your jumper? Ever so clever. So then I thought, well, I really must go and see for myself and so here I am! It's ever such a nice shop floor. Aren't you going to show me round, Col? Give me a guided tour? You don't mind, do you dear?" She was addressing Davinia who was trying to emulate her regional manager's bland reaction, but without the groin rubbing.

"Of course not" she managed to articulate, then forced a smile. "Colin'll show you round; I'll get Alex to go on the till. Don't be too long, though, Colin. The customers need you!" That tinkly laugh again. Colin blushed, rosy pink, glad that Barb could see for herself just how marvellous Davinia was. He felt like a prince as he followed the braceleted bulk out of the doorway and escorted it to the nether regions of the shop. He would show Barb everything, even the steam machine and the cellar.

Davinia watched them disappear out of the door, Colin trotting behind the brassy piece as if chained to one of her cheap bangles. She turned back to Reg who was wearing a bemused expression and returned to business. What was she to do on Thursday, her day off? Candy was *hors de combat* for a week at least – resting at home, apparently, doctor's orders so no redress there. Davinia sniffed and continued. The shop could not be left to the likes of Colin and the Community Service pair and although she would try to find a stand in it was so difficult to find people at short notice; they always seemed to have better things to do. She sniffed again. Reg used his rubbing hand to pull out a crumpled handkerchief from his pocket which she declined, graciously.

"It has been a most challenging week, Reg. Traumatic. Ordinarily of course I would not hesitate to come in on my day off but these are exceptional circumstances and I really must have some 'me' time. Besides, I have already made plans which really cannot be changed." She assumed her plaintive martyr face and was careful not to sniff. Or to reveal what those plans were. A woman was entitled to privacy, even a VHS manageress and she would defend her right to confidentiality to the death if necessary. Reg observed her pulling herself up to her full short height and the look of martyr giving way to right fighter. He had no idea what she had arranged and cared even less.

"No problem, Davinia. You've had a terrible week. Terrible. I'll stand in for you on Thursday. Might need to rearrange a few things but consider it done. Take your day off, recharge your batteries. Do something nice! Pamper yourself. The welfare of our staff, especially people of your skill and expertise, is our top priority – Company Policy."

He wondered if she would ever find her pencilled eyebrows as they shot up into her hairline and seemed to disappear into the dark roots.

In the stock room Alex and Shelley were at work, business as usual. Most of the steaming had been done and now they were hanging, sorting and ironing where necessary. The room had the look of a damp abattoir lined with rows of multi-coloured disembowelled carcases ready for shipment. Alex had to duck his head to avoid them when he moved. They had been discussing the events of yesterday and laughing even more loudly than the agonised wheezings of the steamer which appeared to have pulled at least one muscle with its exertions the day before and was in considerable discomfort.

"At least now Lady Macbeth knows what it's like in here. D'you think she'll do anything about it?" There was a hopelessness in Shelley's voice that had already answered the question but, well, no harm in trying.

"Maybe." Alex was trying to be encouraging. "I think the regional manager's here. She might say something." They both knew she wouldn't.

Just as Colin appeared in the doorway with a short, jangling rather squeezed looking lady in high heels the unmistakable tones of Davinia permeated the air and Alex was summoned to the shop floor,

"To do the till. Now. Please!" He rolled his eyes at Shelley and left her to entertain the unexpected guests. No one ever came into the steam room unless they had absolutely no choice except, it seemed, Colin. With a visitor. And what a visitor. Even the steamer was rendered impotent, immobilised and silenced by her incessant chatter. When Colin finally found the space to introduce her, Shelley immediately understood.

"Oh, Barb! Lovely to meet you. Colin's told me so much about you." Colin blushed, pink verging on puce.

"Oh Colin!" the lady squealed, digging him in the ribs. He blushed, turned carmine and wiped sweat from his brow. "It is rather warm in here" she continued, unabated, a little shiny herself, "Let's move on. What's next?"

When they had gone Shelley narrowed her eyes with concentration and began slowly walking around the room, examining the limp bodies floating morosely about her. She knew what she was looking for; a few hours spent on eBay had given her a very clear idea of what she wanted.

Barb was most impressed by everything she saw but mostly, it seemed to an amazed Colin, by him.

"So brave!" she kept saying. "The hero of the hour." He began to believe it himself. "Wonderful how you got everyone there to help – even the RSPCA. How did you do it?"

"I just dialled 999" he said.

"You're too modest, Col, you know that? So sweet. I like that in a man."

He didn't know, but was very happy to oblige.

In the cellar Barb shivered and hung onto his arm; "Frightened of the dark, dear" she said but gripped him even when the lights were switched on. "Ooh it's big isn't it?" she cooed. "So much space. "What's in the bags?"

"Summer clothes. Davinia keeps them here over the winter then we have changeover and she puts them out on the shop floor. I help her. It's a big job."

"How would she manage without you?" He had never thought about it, and said so. She gripped his arm even tighter which was opportune as his knees appeared to have vaporised. "Well now, Col. Let's go and have a nice cup of coffee and a piece of cake" – she squeezed him in a most friendly way – "and a nice little chat. I'm sure Davinia can spare you for a few minutes, especially after all you did for her yesterday. Is this the back door?"

When he returned Reg had just left and Davinia was helping Alex on the shop floor, which was packed. The till had never seen anything like it and was flinging its drawer open with such vigour that it was all Alex could do to keep up with its persistent escape attempts. He had developed a technique of hitting 'Sale' while holding one hand defensively against the drawer to reduce the velocity of its exit. Colin was deeply impressed. Was there nothing the man could not do? Davinia seemed really pleased to see him. She said nothing about his extended coffee break but smiled wide enough to show her teeth and said that she was so pleased he had finally found time to join them, especially when they were so very busy. They were so short staffed but, of course, Colin had to have his own space and be able to entertain a lady friend, especially in shop hours. He was glad she was so understanding.

Alex headed back to Shelley and calmer, if steamier, waters. He found her holding a scarf.

"It's silk. Vintage Liberty. God knows why anyone would want to get rid of it but it's perfect."

"Very nice. Not quite your style though."

"Al! Don't be so thick!"

He was perplexed. Now what had he said? She explained.

"It's not for me, numpty. It's to put on eBay."

"You're going to sell it?"

"Not me. Queen Dee. The play's the thing wherein to catch the king. We're going to play her at her own game."

In the car Reg and Barb were discussing their visit. He was driving, one handed, meditatively rubbing his groin with the other between gear changes which, fortunately, were few as they were on the motorway.

"The cellar's perfect. Electricity, space, everything we need. But I don't understand why you needed me to check it out. You're the regional manager, why couldn't you do it? Colin is so boring."

"You know why, Barb. We've talked about this. I can't be seen to be involved in any way; it'd arouse suspicion. Did you get him to agree?"

"Asked him if I could put some tropical fish equipment in there. He couldn't say no. Even told me where the key is kept, under the cactus in the office. Davinia's idea of security." They sniggered.

"Good girl."

"But how're we going to get into the shop?"

"I'm the regional manager, aren't I? Master keys for entrances to all shops in my area. In case of emergencies." Here he removed the rubbing hand to a bulky trouser pocket which he fondled like a much-loved pet. "What're you doing Thursday, Mrs Sutton?"

Chapter Nine
Subterfuge

Wednesday. Only the middle of the week but it felt like a day of rest. The shop was still busy but already the hysteria about the events of Monday was starting to ease off although Reg had been right, the publicity had really put them on the map and they had become quite the local gossip of choice. Sales had soared and, it seemed to Davinia, people would buy anything. Even the pottery replacing the missing DVDs, which had still not been checked, had sold to a middle-aged gentleman who ought to have known better. The subsequent gap had been filled with some lovely ornate photo frames featuring kittens and babies. Some were even made of that silver that never needed cleaning and had sweet little motifs on them like 'Baby's First Birthday', Home Sweet Home' and 'Our Wedding Day'. Davinia thought they were charming and was certain they would sell quickly. She had marked them up accordingly.

What was more disconcerting however, was the number of dubious looking characters who seemed to be taking an inordinate interest in the shop. They loitered outside, peering through the plate glass window at the display and beyond, into the interior. It was the same ones, time after time, but they never came in which was a relief because they were so shabby, so 'street' but it gave her the creeps the way they cupped their hands at the side of their faces to cut out the light so that they could get a better view. There was one, quite a tall chap, skinny but more shaven than the others with short cropped hair and a dog, who always seemed to be in the vicinity. He was obviously down and out and most probably lived on the street, judging by the amount of stuff he was carrying. She wondered how he had the temerity to keep a dog – so unfair on the poor creature – how did he feed it? No doubt he used it as a begging tool to tug on the heartstrings of the sentimental and weak minded: disgraceful. Just let him try and camp on her doorstep: she'd give him what for. Bring it on. By the time she had gone into the stockroom that evening to find something for eBay she had already formulated what she would say to any hobo impertinent enough to sully the hallowed portals of Her Shop. There had been an occasion once before when she had had to move someone on, in no uncertain terms, and they had never returned, thank God. She smiled at the recollection. Then she spotted a brightly coloured headscarf, square, silk … Liberty! Winking at her. In mint condition. She put it in her bag.

Thursday arrived with adventure in its heart. Unshackled from the routine according to Davinia even for one day was cause for rejoicing and it meant to make the most of whatever excitement the day might bring. Reg was standing in for Candy who was always so dull and spiritual when what Thursday really wanted was a bit of fun; something different, and maybe today would be the day. Monday had had it all his own way for too long and the bragging was insufferable. Poor Sunday though. Nothing ever happened then.

Reg arrived betimes to open up promptly, familiarise himself with the intimate layout of the shop as well as to make the acquaintance of the till, about which he had heard much and was prepared to be brutal if required. Fortunately, Alex had tipped Corpy off about the change of management so he and Troop had eschewed a leisurely start to their day and removed themselves in time to see the arrival of Reg's top of the range Ford Focus slide into Davinia's hallowed parking spot and come to a silent stop. In the passenger seat was a lady Corpy did not recognise who heaved her jangling frame out of the car onto impossibly slender high heels which seemed to brace themselves for the experience and stumped off towards the Costa in the high street. Reg let himself in through the back door and disappeared.

When his troops arrived, Reg was ready and waiting with well-rehearsed instructions which he delivered at the motivational staff briefing he conducted, on the shop floor, moments before he ceremonially opened the doors to commence trading.

"Colin behind the counter please. Alex, with him to assist. Shelley. No steaming today and minimal sorting. You and Alex have done an excellent job and are ahead of schedule so I'm going to make some changes today - mix it up a bit." He rubbed his groin enthusiastically and they all watched, mesmerised. "Start off by checking those DVDs please, Shelley – long overdue – then we'll get them out on the shop floor. Perhaps try you out on a display – bit of creative flair. No, you don't need to cover your tattoos. We're multi-cultural. In touch. Company Policy." Touching did indeed seem to be part of Reg's qualifications and his trousers bore the marks to prove it so they did not argue but eagerly took up their positions ready for action. He then opened the shop doors with a flourish and let in the queueing fresh air for a second before slamming the cold out and dramatically twizzling the Open – Keeping Warm sign to prominence behind the double glazing. After which he disappeared into the office and shut the always-open door.

Shelley was delighted. Checking DVDs for pornographic intruders was a steam-free, warm doddle and then she could check out the books, find something for Al's friend, maybe herself. Nothing she liked better than cruising book shelves and this was legal! Awesome. She had tried several times to find an opportunity to peruse the shelves on Corpy's behalf but Davinia was ever-present, an unbroken Shalimar-scented ozone layer and Shelley was forever confined to the steam room. Not today though; Reg rocked. Shelley had thought about what books to look for and had decided on the meaty modern – *Cloud Atlas*, that sort of thing. The chances were too, that he had not read them. It would depend on what was available but she would put together a selection and Al would deliver them. Al had the more trying task of the day in that he was with Colin, boredom incarnate, but harmless and Al was used to listening to people. He would be doing all the till work so that would keep him busy and he had his mobile phone, not that he was supposed to use it while on duty but he was doing some deal with a collector of Led Zep stuff on the internet so he would be okay. Al could look after himself. Quite a cool guy, in fact, even if he was antediluvian and knew nothing about Shakespeare. Now, where should she place herself for Operation DVD Porn? she wondered. Where would Candy go?

Davinia was also up betimes; she had a busy day ahead. Her hair appointment was at 9.30 and from there she would go on to the nail bar and after that, the dentist. It seemed odd to be going to a tooth expert for Botox injections but the lady came highly recommended and so much cheaper than the so-called beauticians who were probably not half as well qualified. It had been humiliating not to have been on the TV but perhaps, in retrospect, it was a good thing. She had looked awful – ghastly – everything she despised in women who did not make the best of themselves. It had been a wake-up call and she was not the type to shirk her responsibilities. Today was all about 'me' time and sod the expense. Plenty in the PayPal account and more to come. The Monsoon dress had proved to be a winner, the bidding was intense and she would make a killing on it. Then there was the Liberty scarf which she would list when she returned home; that was certain to make money. Her only problem was deciding what starting price to put on it: too low and people were suspicious, too high and it put them off.

Colin and Alex had the shop floor covered. Teamwork, Alex said and Colin basked in warm glory. What was even better was that Colin, somehow, seemed to be in charge, calling the shots, chatting to the customers while Alex worked the recalcitrant till, subduing it into submission, miraculously producing the correct change and relevant receipt which Colin could then hand to the customer with a smile, as if he had done it all by himself. When the door opened and Barb entered, well wrapped up against the cold so more of a muffled jangle than usual, she was precariously perched on high heels which belonged not to shoes but shiny pincer-toed knee-high boots, Colin's breath caught in his throat.

"You alright, Colin?" Alex asked as his colleague gasped and sucked. Then Alex too caught sight of Barb as she sashayed across the tiled floor towards the counter and he caught his own breath, but for different reasons. Her progress was perilous – how did she balance? If she fell, she would break a limb for sure. Alex stood, ready to leap into action if required but Barb had done this before. She was woman to be reckoned with, who could negotiate cobbled streets without injury; a ceramic floor was no match for her.

"Col!" she screeched. The sound reverberated around the room, bouncing off the walls, assaulting the hanging garments which abruptly stood to attention with astonishment before slumping back into limp depression.

"Barb!" Colin cooed and inhaled noisily, remembering to breathe once more. "How lovely! ... You are" he added, coyly, blushing profusely at his audacity and wondering if he gone too far. Apparently not.

"Oooh, Col!" she simpered then got straight to the point. "Coffee? Cake? Now."

Alex did not know Colin could move so fast. Telling Shelley about it later he began to wonder whether Colin had actually vaulted over the counter but knew that was ridiculous; Colin's high waisted trousers would never allow it although when the Perma Prest Lothario returned to his post the same trousers were looking exhausted and not a little soiled. Colin, too, was moist with sweat and panting. His neat box cut fringe was plastered close to his forehead like a flat tasselled pelmet and there were smudges on his cheeks. His hands were filthy.

"Good God!" Alex could not help himself. "What have you been up to, Colin?" His mind was working dangerously fast in a most disturbing direction. Barb was nowhere to be seen and he feared the worst; Colin looked as if he had been devoured and regurgitated. Had he? Surely, he and Barb hadn't been ... at it? And if so, where? Was Coffee and Cake some kind of sexually charged code? Alex shuddered and desperately tried to erase the concept by slamming the till drawer so violently back into place that the whole counter shook.

"Helping...Barb..." Colin stammered, broken-breathed. "Fish... cellar." He paused and looked at his grubby fingers which he then wiped over his dewy face, etching the existing furrowed filth into a charcoal self-portrait. "Lots of it... Boxes ... Heavy." Then he sat down and put his head between his crease-free polyester knees. He had no idea love could be such hard work.

That evening, Alex had much to discuss with Lisa but it was she who initiated the shop conversation as soon as he walked in through the front door. Dave had been, as ever, awaiting his return home and flung himself bodily at his carer (Dave did not do owners or masters – carers or enablers yes, human domination no chance.) Alex was pinned against the hall wall face to face with hot dog-breath and food encrusted hair so that Lisa had to shout to make herself heard.

"It's up! The scarf! You were right!"

"How much?" Alex bellowed past Dave's nose.

"Forty-five, starting bid."

"No way!"

"It's went up today – this afternoon. Lots of views already!"

"Queen Dee?"

"Yes."

"It's Davinia isn't it?"

"Looks like it. … By the way, I bought that dress."

"Of course you did." Alex grinned at Dave who slobbered in agreement. "Shall we tell her what the T shirt's worth or make her wait?"

Chapter Ten
Friday

Colin needed his day off. He was exhausted. Having seen Barb the day before they had decided – well, she had – not to meet up at Aquarium World as arranged but to 'take some space' as she described it. Such a sensible woman, so considerate, so wise. So sophisticated in the ways of love; he felt quite overwhelmed.

"Mustn't rush things, dear" she had said, squeezing his arm in the friendliest way that made his toes tingle inside his trainers which was unfortunate because it set off the pain in his ingrowing toe nail. He would have to wear sandals despite the cold, but a pair of the thick socks mother had knitted which never wore out would keep his feet warm and probably dry as well. Marvellous.

The shop would be a man down as Candy was still recovering at home so a crisis loomed, large and bitter like an encroaching blizzard: Davinia had had to be informed. Disturbed! At home! On her day off. Colin felt terrible about it but he simply had to have a break. He had barely spoken to his fish, was completely out of cheese and Mother needed a Christmas present. So did Barb and this troubled him greatly, supplanting even the till and Gift Aid in his nightmares. What Christmas present to buy for A Woman? He had never done such a thing before; obviously Mother was female, but she was not A Woman. Besides, he always bought Mother a scarf at Christmas: it was tradition. She liked a type called Liberty which he found in the local department store. Expensive if you bought silk which he had done in the past but these days he always looked for polyester which was more affordable and so much more practical. It did not matter; you could hardly tell the difference and she never wore them as she never went outside, but he could not disappoint her. She expected it. Perhaps he would consult Alex who seemed to be a man of the world. All ideas of ponds and Koi carp had been shelved, forgotten in the throes of passion but Colin could never neglect his tropical fish. Barb would understand that. She was marvellous.

So was Davinia who had surprised them all by being quite sanguine about finding someone to stand in at short notice. And as luck would have it, one of their regular 'floaters' had had her day cancelled because her friend had just been admitted to hospital with a broken hip – fell off the kerb – never saw it – sure the council had put it a new one, higher than normal.

"Zo yah", Anna would be able to come in and help – happy to oblige – liked to keep busy – northern European work ethic. Colin was relieved that he could take a guilt-free day off and also avoid Anna who was as overbearing as she was overwhelming: her bust carried everything before her, she sailed into rooms like an old-fashioned destroyer, a Wagnerian heroine in an English soap opera. She carried her bosom just above her waist like a low-slung shelf, a hazard to shipping and was exhausting. Her enthusiasm was endless, her voice soared into the heavens. She had a German accent so strong that it was impossible to hear her and not find yourself speaking with the same staccato edge, however hard you tried not to. Colin was not the only one who worried that she would think she was being copied and mocked, but she never seemed to notice. Of course, her English was marvellous; she had lived here forever having married an Englishman who had "svept her orf her feet" she said, which seemed improbable considering his size compared to hers, but they did do a lot of ballroom dancing together so maybe it was possible. Getting caught behind the counter with Anna was terrifying; she had a way of boxing you in by the till and talking at you until you lost the will to live and certainly could no longer speak unaccented English. Colin was too polite to interrupt and too frightened to squeeze past her – supposed they touched? No, he would stay at home this Friday as usual and spend quality time with his fish, recharge his batteries, contemplate the glories of love and go to the supermarket.

Anna was always delighted to go into the Veteran's Hop as she called it.

"Zo full of old thingz and people" she told Dennis her husband, whom she banished to the shed to play in her absence. She saw him safely bundled up in layers of warm clothes then shuffle down the garden path to the diminutive summer house she had had erected many years ago to remind her of her Bavarian roots. More Heidi than Bergdorf but wooden, with a chalet type roof and tiny windows with boxes in which she grew red geraniums in warmer months. Unlike anything truly Bavarian, it was freezing in winter but Dennis was well insulated and would come to no harm if he kept moving. She herself did not feel the cold; height and rigid posture carried her big-bones and generous proportions, always brilliantly clad in capacious dresses that reached from neck to calf in a riot of colour and texture topped off with bold clip-on earrings of which she had an enormous collection dating from her youth in the 1950s. Statement dressing someone had once said, which she had liked and clung to with tenacity.

Davinia was not sure if she liked Anna but was definitely in awe of her size, if nothing else. She was organised in a Teutonic sort of way – not that one stereotyped of course, but stereotypes did not invent themselves – and it was so important for Davinia to know that she had someone reasonably competent behind the counter. More importantly, with the till in its present mood, Anna's sheer bulk would solve the problem of the airborne drawer which would never get past The Bosom, no matter how hard it tried. As long as there were no difficult customers Anna would be fine. Davinia would provide a box of tissues though, just in case.

As she unlocked the back door and let herself in to the shop Davinia felt a thrill of excitement. Yesterday had been so productive. She had decided not to say anything but to let everyone notice for themselves; infinitely more refined and meaningful; an elegant modesty was always so becoming. However, she had dressed with particular care, to set the picture off as it were, like a tasteful frame. The dress was a little tight around the body and upper arms so reaching up above her shoulders was out of the question, but no matter. There was always Alex to reach for her and he had to do as he was told. Which reminded her – Community Service report day for Nerinda. Always something to look forward to. On the shop floor she could not resist stroking her hands sensuously all the way down the front of her body then running a finger over her lips. She had thought they might be tender but could feel nothing which was amazing really when you thought how much plumper they were. Then she ran both index fingers above her nose and over her eyebrows. So smooth. Like her whole face. It felt a little tight but the dentist had said that would ease at which point to come back and see her again. As she fished the key on the chain out of her cleavage up into the light, she caught sight of her new hair colour in the reflection from the window and tried to smile.

Shelley and Alex had arrived, on time, Davinia noticed with disappointment as she glanced at her watch but never mind, plenty of other things to tell Nerinda. And, as instructed, they had confined themselves to the back so that the shop floor was left unsullied. A loud hammering on the front door announced the arrival of the redoubtable Anna, wearing a heavy-weave box-like coat over substantial fur-lined flat suede boots. On her head she had a beret and over her shoulder an enormous leather handbag in which she kept essentials, mostly lunch and snacks. It was a good thing that Davinia knew who was on the doorstep or she might have thought they were about to be invaded by an expensively dressed bear: Paddington's Herculean Russian cousin on a visit from Siberia perhaps. No need to suck in her stomach though as she went to open the door, Davinia thought with relief. She was dwarfed by Anna which made her felt gloriously svelte and slender – a reason in itself to like the woman.

Anna soared into the room in a cloud of cold air which hastened back outside as fast as it could, already exhausted by the zealotry of the woman. She stamped her boots on the floor, depositing slushy moisture on the tiles and stormed over to the till, unwrapping herself as she went, revealing the glorious pink of her dress beneath, luminous and glowing in the emerging morning light. The fresh air, now safely outside the closed door heaved a sigh of relief and shut its eyes against the onslaught of colour. Davinia was momentarily blinded, then mesmerised by the sheer amount of pink before her, topped off with huge gold earrings stretching down Anna's ear lobes as if trying to pin them to the floor. Surely, they must hurt? How could she bear such weight? With absolute equanimity apparently as she appeared not to notice and immediately launched into a hearty dialogue about the weather, her injured friend, the state of kerbs and irresponsibility of the local council, what she had for breakfast and how she was looking forward to being in the shop but hoped there would be no snakes or dead bodies. At no point however did she notice Davinia or comment on her appearance which galled. But then Anna had not been in for a while and had not witnessed Davinia's ravaged appearance on Monday – perhaps the shelved television interview was a good thing after all – so how could she know to comment on such a dramatic improvement? Davinia forgave her and attempted, again, to smile but found she could not so she bared her teeth under filled, fixed lips and oozed goodwill.

"Are you vell?" Anna enquired, looking concerned. "You have toothache maybe? That is not good. You should see a dentist. Your mouth is svollen."

Davinia closed her mouth and reassured her erstwhile colleague that she was fine – more than fine in fact, but had so much to do. She swivelled viciously on her pencil heels so that another tile shrieked silently with pain and headed off to the office. Via the steam room, she thought en route. Better check on Alex and Shelley and let them see for themselves.

They did. Stunned. Neither said a word but stared. Even the ancient steamer halted its bronchitic breathing for a brief moment to look. Davinia was pleased. So, they had noticed and she had obviously made an impression. Satisfied, she bared her teeth good naturedly at them and went to her computer to settle down over the Community Service reports.

"What's she done?" Shelley spoke first, to Alex's relief: he had no idea what to say. He mused for a moment, hesitated, then offered,

"New hair, I think."

"That's the least of her problems!" Shelley had found her voice now, and plenty of it. "She's had her roots done but gone platinum pink. Unbelievable! She looks like candy floss. But it's her face, Al. You're a doctor. What the hell's she done?"

"Botox probably. Not my field, but looks very much like it."

"She can't move! Her eyes are all starey and her eyebrows are halfway up her forehead. They look as if they've got lost and can't find their way home. But it's her mouth, Al. Her lips! They're enormous. Maybe she's been stung by something or had an allergic reaction?"

They both started laughing. The ancient steamer, momentarily silenced, wheezed back into action and huffed merrily along with them. Shock sometimes has that effect.

"D'you think she knows what she looks like?" Al asked, eventually. He was flabbergasted. Women wore make up, he knew, and as a medical man he was well aware of the advances in cosmetic surgery but had always understood them to be designed to improve, enhance and repair. To choose – and what was more to pay – to look like that was beyond his comprehension. Shelley could not, as yet, speak. Finally, she caught her breath and sobered herself sufficiently to reply, occasionally hiccupping and sniggering but managing to produce identifiable sentences.

"It's a proper trout pout! They've been blown up by a bicycle pump! Pneumatic! Inflatable lips! She'll never drown but she might get stuck to a window."

"How will she eat?" Alex asked, vaguely concerned.

"With great difficulty!" Shelley screamed. "Maybe it's her new diet!" Alex wanted to disapprove but found he was laughing too much.

"Hey, Al. D'you think she's had buttock implants?"

"Not yesterday or she'd be walking like she just got off a horse."

"You mean her bum is one she prepared earlier?" Shelley gasped for breath then rallied herself to continue. "And you know what's worst? She loves it. Thinks she looks amazing! Oh God, Al. It's too sad!" It was, but it was also too hilarious and they were loving every tragic second.

On the shop floor Anna had settled herself in behind the counter. It was a tight squeeze but cosy and the till, having nowhere to go, was firmly under control. Davinia had mentioned that the drawer had a tendency to shoot out unexpectedly but really, Anna could not understand what the fuss was about. She had no problem with it; if anything, there was not enough room for it to fully open and she had to rummage around at the back to find higher denomination notes. Sales had been steady rather than busy; Davinia emerged from the office occasionally to bare her teeth and check that all was well but Anna was very comfortable, thank you, and enjoying herself. No, no problems. Everything was "vell under control". Would it be alright then if Davinia popped out to the bank? Official shop business of course (and the launch of her new look on an admiring public but she did not mention that.)

"Yah. No problem." Anna would take care of everything. Davinia promptly left the building, graciously holding the door open on her way out to admit a smartly dressed, obviously professional couple, on their way in. The woman headed straight for the fur coat, still adorning the mannequin that felt uncomfortable about being stark naked underneath.

"Wow! It is real! We thought it was, didn't we?" she said to the tall man who smiled indulgently at her and spoke perfectly on cue.

"Why don't you try it on?"

The mannequin inwardly shuddered and hoped no one was looking but thankfully it was only the coat that they were interested in. The woman looked at Anna,

"May I?"

"Of course! Just take it off the model – that's it. Vee have a mirror in the changing room. Full length. Over here." The vision in pink illuminated their path to the corner of the shop floor where it glowed and cast soft light over the cubby hole of a changing room as she swept back the curtain with an expansive flourish. The lady carefully skirted around The Bosom into the cubicle and Anna flung the curtain across behind her with such gusto that her chest became quite buoyant and bounced up and down a couple of times, as if testing a spring mattress. Meanwhile the man was wandering around the shop floor. After studying the top shelves upon which were jigsaws and board games, precariously balanced on their sides, alluringly posed picture side out, Anna had high hopes for a large sale; he was now taking great interest in the overpriced picture frames and examining them minutely.

"They are silver" she announced helpfully. "Very lovely." He said nothing but looked politely interested – more than enough for her to continue. "Vee have many lovely things at very reasonable prices. You are looking for Christmas gifts I imagine? Vell, you vill find all you vant here and…" she was interrupted by the appearance of the woman from behind the changing room curtain wearing the fur coat and looking, it had to be said, a million dollars. So that was exactly what Anna said, in addition to much else.

… "You look like a film star. Very rich and famous. Vonderful" she finally concluded when she had to draw breath and someone else had a chance to speak.

"Yes" the man agreed, "It really suits you, sweetheart." Then to Anna, "What kind of fur is it?"

Anna had no idea.

"Mink" she answered with certainty. "Very expensive. Very valuable. And vee are only charging £55. It is an absolute bargain. Your lucky day!"

Man and woman exchanged glances and it was clear that the decision had been made.

"Well, you do look amazing. Yes. We'll take it. Do you take cards?"

Oh yes, they did, with alacrity. Anna was heading back towards the counter when there was an almighty crash followed by a series of loud clatters and then a whole storm of softer thuds and whispered bumps and slithers. She turned as fast as her bulk would allow to find the man standing shamefaced amidst several boxes of jigsaws that had fallen from the shelf and split themselves open with abandon. Cardboard pieces of a thousand different shapes and colours were carpeted across the tiles like a huge, carefree confetti rug. Some of the pieces were still sliding across the floor, skimming the shiny ceramic surface like seasoned ice skaters. The man himself was picking jigsaw pieces out of his hair and off his body which had impeded the fall of at least one box, probably two, maybe even three. Impossible to tell.

"Scheisse" screeched Anna who tended to relapse into her native vernacular at moments of stress.

"Sorry" said the man. "Just trying to get one down."

"Vot have you done? They are all mixed up. Vee vill never be able to sort them out now."

"Sorry" said the man again and backed towards the door. Anna by now had bent herself – no mean achievement with her centre of balance – over the nascent Alpine range settling on the tiles and was attempting to pick up some of the pieces. This proved difficult as they were rather small and she was unable to see most of them over her chest. She was very upset.

"Alles verschiessed" she muttered into her bosom, panting heavily and splaying her legs wide to prevent falling over.

"What happened?"

"Can we help?"

It was Alex and then, a moment later, Shelley, more concerned even than they were sweaty and moist.

"It vos that man vith that voman, the one buying the fur coat. He tried to get a jigsaw down and they all fell. Look at the mess. Vot vill Davinia say?"

"What man?" Shelley asked. "There's no one here."

Anna inhaled deeply, steadied her legs, prepared her feet and heaved herself upright. The Bosom swayed a little, hesitated, then settled and her balance was restored. She looked about the shop floor, then screamed.

"Scheisse" she screeched again. "Vee have been robbed."

The mannequin was standing, naked in the shop window. The fur coat, the woman wearing it, and her companion had vanished, considerately shutting the door on their way out to keep in the heat.

When Davinia arrived back all was not "vell" and everything was indisputably out of control. Her inability to move most of her facial muscles however, worked to her advantage.

"I thought she'd go ballistic" Shelley afterwards, "but she seemed to take it very well."

"That's the Botox" Alex told her. "I bet she was seething inside; she just couldn't show it."

"She did have an Angry Bird look. It's the eyebrows" Shelley added. "How long'll it last?"

"Long enough for us to do our time and get out of here I hope."

Davinia was indeed seething internally – a masked maelstrom of fire and rage. Fifty-five quid had simply been allowed to walk out of Her Shop and Anna was to blame. Entirely. Honestly, you'd think someone of that size would have more sense: there was certainly room for it. The female thief's coat was found abandoned in the changing room and turned out to be not the smart garment that had impressed Davinia but a cheap knock off, with torn lining, fit only for recycling. The couple were however, undeniably professional.

"It was planned, from start to finish. Get your attention then create a diversion. Distract you. That's why the man pulled the jigsaws off the shelf." Davinia was as scathing as her face would allow and exuded venom at Anna, who did not notice.

"But they fell off the shelf. He vas trying to get one but vas not tall enough and they all tumbled down, because they ver not vell balanced" she said severely. "If there had been an earthquake, they all vould have come down." Anna was not going down without a fight. It had to have been Davinia's fault.

"No, Anna. He deliberately dislodged them off to make a disturbance and occupy you so that his accomplice could leave the shop unnoticed … with the coat" she added bitterly. "The snake."

There was a silence. It was an unfortunate comment and the memories of Monday were still fresh in their minds. Even the mannequin looked a little shocked, but perhaps that was the effect of cold air on exposed flesh.

"We'd better put something on the model. Can't leave her like that. What will passersby think of us?" Davinia sighed, loudly, despite her half-closed mouth and went into damage limitation mode. But the damage was done. Anna was a wreck. Traumatised. Blamed! Ven it vas not her fault. How vas she to know that they ver robbers and thiefs? She had been victimised. Abused. Taken advantage of. And all she was doing vas her job, the best she could, at short notice, to help Davinia out because she vas a good person and her friend vas in hospital vith a broken hip and she was vorried about her vhich did not help and Davinia was blaming her for something that vas not, absolutely not, her fault. And she could not bear it. Pass the tissues if you please.

Much weeping and nose blowing ensued, the latter in vast quantities at high volume to the fascination of the customers who had come into the shop, attracted by the noise and the nudity in the window. A circle of interested strangers had gathered around the slumped pink bulk, a colossal, warm blancmange beginning to drip over the sides of an inadequate chair, heaving and sniffing and crying with no sign of respite. Really, the Vet's Help was proving to be a most exciting venue: always something going on. Quite the centre of local action.

"I think I vill faint" Anna moaned softly, wobbling with emotion.

"Put your head between your knees" ordered Alex automatically then realised the enormity of what he had asked. She had not seen her knees for years and would never be able to find them. Fortunately, Anna had other ideas.

"My blood sugar is very low. It is dangerous. I need something to eat. In my bag you vill find a snack." Shelley raced to the counter and immediately returned, bowed under the weight of the shoulder bag. Too weak to do it herself, Anna listlessly indicated to Shelley to rummage in the hallowed portals and find her something restorative and life giving. They all watched spellbound – Alex, Davinia, the mannequin, the spectators gathered in a circle around the drama – as Shelley began to unpack the bag. Only Anna was oblivious, sniffing and weeping copiously, running through the box of tissues so thoughtfully provided by Davinia at the start of the day. Sausage rolls, a Cornish pasty, low calorie muesli bars (Davinia vowed never to eat another), high energy drinks in cans and sachets with straws attached, several boxes of sugar-free sweets including humbugs and butterscotch, low salt crisps, coleslaw, a packet of coronation chicken sandwiches and finally, an unopened box of Bakewell tarts.

"A Bakevell tart please" Anna whispered, fighting to stay conscious, "something sveet. I am on a diet so I have given up the sugar except in emergencies."

"Wow!" Someone said.

"She won't starve" said another.

"My doctor has told me to lose veight so I eat only savoury and healthy food" Anna responded with considerably more strength now that she had the prospect of cake. She ate one of the tarts in two bites while her audience gazed in awe as she barely seemed to chew before she had swallowed and reached for another.

"Perhaps a glass of water?" Alex offered.

"Sveet tea vill be better. Three sugars. Thank you." No one moved so Davinia snorted with disdain and headed off to her office where the kettle was kept, ostensibly for staff use but in reality, access was restricted to managerial personnel.

By now Anna's crying had ceased and she had regained some composure; The Bosom was heaving less and was relatively steady, serving as a most useful repository for the few crumbs of tart that did not make it to the mouth above. A few deep breaths, a loud sniff and all seemed calm again. Then it happened.

The door swung open, the cold air rushed in and with it came Dave. Lisa had been walking him past the shop, he had seen Alex through the window and decided to make a run for him. Taken by surprise - he was normally so well behaved on the lead - Lisa had lost control and Dave had hurled himself against the door which had surrendered without a struggle in the face of such determined opposition. It swung open, Dave swung in and Alex swung himself forward to catch him. He missed. Dave's velocity was so great that he was propelled straight into the pink colossus that was Anna.

Now if there was one thing Anna hated - feared more even than starvation, - it was a dog. Any dog. All dogs. Especially high-speed, hairy ones with open mouths, moving limbs and intent in their eyes. She screamed, a sound so high pitched, so heart rending, so unexpected that time seemed to stop, to be suspended, frozen in the moment: a foretaste of Eternity. Davinia torpedoed onto the shop floor, armed with the kettle to investigate and she too screamed, equally high pitched but more in fury and outrage than in fear.

"A dog! In My Shop! Get it out! Now! No-one brings animals into My Shop. It's totally against Company Policy!" She glared at Lisa and shouted at her. "You're not even blind! If it was a blind dog, I wouldn't mind but you can see! You're not even disabled."

This was clearly true and Lisa put up no opposition. Alex, who in the interests of diplomacy and his forthcoming Community Service report had not acknowledged his wife, now found Dave harder to ignore. Having escaped from Her and found Him the dog was not to be deterred. Besides, there were so many interesting smells awaiting exploration and, joy of joys, a banquet spread out on the floor before him. Decisive action was required - he who hesitates goes hungry - so he launched himself on the Cornish pasty. Not so much out of taste preference but it was closest, sizeable and insecurely wrapped. Easy pickings. Then he would go for the tart things in the open box - pity about the foil things in which they sat: shiny but tasteless - although it was simple enough to lift them out and swallow whole with one manoeuvre of the tongue. He had done it before. Now Anna was faced with a double Nemesis: dog-induced starvation. She wailed, her eyes closed and she collapsed, sliding off the relieved chair like ice cream out of a cone on a hot day. She then melted across the floor, large, liquid, never-ending, all in pink.

For the second time that week the emergency services were called. Initially it was just an ambulance but then fire fighters were summoned with heavy lifting gear to help lift the patient onto a reinforced gurney that was rushed from the hospital in a second ambulance that trundled her and her shoulder bag off to safety.

"What'll I do with the tea?" Davinia hissed. "No one else takes sugar."

"I do" one of the customers offered gallantly but was ignored, and later told everyone at her lunch club that the manageress in the VHS shop was a mean cow. Davinia had other concerns.

"Look at the mess! And we're short staffed." She assumed battle formation and went into retaliatory action. "No one gets lunch or goes home until this is sorted out. Recycle the jigsaws - all of them" she said viciously without moving her lips. "And someone put something on that mannequin; it's disgusting."

That evening Lisa, Alex and Dave, who now sported a harness to which his lead was secured rather than just a collar visited the scene of the crime when they went for their evening stroll. It was cold and windy. They were worried about Corpy and Troop.

"At least Shelley's managed to get some books for him" Alex tried to reassure himself, switching the heavy carrier bag from one had to the other. "I hope they don't get wet."

"Does Davinia know?"

"No. Shelley'd found some already but in the chaos today it was easy to help herself to a few more. … I put the money in the till" he added. Lisa snorted.

"Shouldn't have had to. He's a veteran. And homeless. Least they could do." They walked on in silence towards the VHS doorstep. Lisa too was carrying a heavy bag containing a thermos of hot coffee and a huge foil wrapped parcel of cheese sandwiches, "in case he's vegetarian." Alex had just looked at her. He lives on the street he wanted to say. I don't suppose he can afford to choose, but then felt ashamed. Just because Corpy was homeless did not mean he had no principles and really, they knew nothing about him.

When they arrived, Troop got up to greet them and chat to Dave who wanted to vent about the indignity of his harness and describe the excitement of the day. Maybe there was food left? They could investigate, together, lads out on the town?

Their owners had other ideas. Corpy was delighted with the books and impressed by the choice although he could not take them all at once; nowhere to keep them; perhaps Alex could store them and change them as required, like a lending library? He would take two to start – *Cloud Atlas* about which he had heard much but never read and *English Passengers*. He liked the look of that – a bit of black humour and a dig at the colonial past. He'd been to Australia with the army, briefly, years ago and liked it very much although he'd found the Australians a little too uninhibited for his liking. They were excellent military allies on the ground though as he'd discovered in Afghanistan. That very same lack of inhibition made them brave and daring to the point of recklessness and they were always cheerful. Great blokes. He'd like to go back to Oz one day, check out the Barrier Reef and Uluru.

No one spoke after he said this. It was too sad. Even the dogs were quiet, watching the two-legged ones with knowing eyes.

"Yes, of course he could keep the thermos" Lisa said as they were leaving. "Anything to help."

Davinia was recovering at home, in a hot bath with a glass of extremely cold Prosecco sweating on the side. She had her eyes closed and was concentrating on relaxing. Another glass would help later but at the moment she was shattered. She would finish the Community Service reports tomorrow; Nerinda had been informed that they would be delayed because of yet another incident in the shop but would not even open the email until next week so it made no difference. Unfortunately, Reg and Head Office had had to be told; anything involving the emergency services was a notifiable event: Company Policy. Added to which the police had had to be told about the theft and statements would have to be taken, reports filed, in-house investigations conducted and insurance companies notified. It was all such a bloody nuisance and all because of that stupid, pink, oversized German hausfrau. Who would never darken Davinia's doors again, not if she had anything to do with it.

She took careful another sip over the edge of the glass (gulps were not possible until her lips softened a little) and felt comforted. Her eBay sales were flying. She also knew that when she emerged from her watery cocoon and peered in the steamed-up mirror, she would be smooth-faced, plump-mouthed, strawberry blonde verging on platinum and gorgeous. Marvellous. That made her think of Colin. It would be almost a relief to have him back in the shop the next day and after finishing the bottle of Prosecco, she might even look forward to it.

Chapter Eleven
Saturday

The good news was that Candy was feeling much better and would be back in the shop next week. Possibly Monday, depending on her chakras but she had been using healing stones which had helped enormously and she felt oh, so much better. Quite realigned and reinvigorated. Her energies were strong and vibrantly coloured; her hair would soon grow back, although she was rather taken with her new piled-on-top look and several people had commented on it. Wearing her knitted hat was out of the question but if she put on her ear muffs from the back instead of over the top of her head, then she could keep her ears toastie warm and not disturb her hair. Her aura was strong and glowing – everyone said so – and the positive side of the whole dreadful experience had revealed itself in a moment of pure enlightenment when she was concussed. She knew now that she had to become not just vegetarian, or even vegan, but fruitarian. It was the fur coat that had done it. The Spirit of the Sable had spoken to her and ordered her to atone for the sins committed against their kind in the name of vanity. Eating only fruit with some nuts and seeds was the way forward and she embraced it. With joy. Since leaving hospital she had begun a strict regime of raw veganism and the effect was sensational. She was liberated, energised and made whole. Everyone should do the same. It was if she had been reborn and she wanted nothing but to spread the word among others and bring them to the same salvation of body and soul.

Davinia relayed the above to her staff in somewhat less jubilant tones and an air of general dejection descended. Colin did not understand how someone could not eat cheese, and what about bread? Would she never eat another sandwich? Alex and Shelley could only anticipate with longing the completion of their sentence, but first, there was Christmas to get through.

"We're doing the Christmas window display on Monday" Davinia announced as loudly as her lips permitted. They all strained to hear. "So, use the weekend to think of ideas, although I do have a rather wonderful surprise for you. All will be revealed on Monday!" She would have liked to beam but had to carry on talking instead, "We're also putting together the Christmas raffle so lots of donations please. Anything festive and attractive would be fine – the sort of thing you would like to win is always a good guideline for giving I like to think. Be as generous," here she eyed Alex, "as you can. It's all in aid of the veterans and I would like us to raise more than any of the other shops. We came second last year so let's make this one a winner. Right; back to work everyone. Customers to serve, money to raise, veterans to save." She disappeared towards her office but just as they thought she had gone she reappeared, with further instructions, this time aimed at Colin.

"We'll need the Christmas decorations from the cellar, Colin. Get Alex to help you. Before lunch if you can. Thanks." And then she really was gone: they watched and listened for the door to close, just to be sure.

"Marvellous" Colin pronounced in wonder. Shelley and Alex thought he was joking and wanted to laugh, but then remembered it was Colin.

Sunday

Corpy was enjoying *Cloud Atlas,* or at least he would be when he worked out what was happening. He loved the challenge to his perceptions and to some extent identified with the displacement but had to concentrate on the text which was sometimes difficult in the wind. It was determined to turn the pages before he was ready although it seemed to understand the book better than him in that it was constantly shifting between what had happened and what was to come. In the end he propped the book up against Troop, lying at his feet and pinned down both sides of it with gloved hands so that he could focus. Hard as it might try, the wind could not then return to the past or skip to the future and Corpy could finally settle down with the present. Troop was an excellent reading companion: quiet, still, the perfect book rest. No interruptions or inane conversation, just solid, fleshy warmth close to Corpy's crossed legs as he sat in his doorway corner, bent over his book, oblivious to reality. Which was being amiable today – no rain, virtually no traffic or footfall until 10.00 am at least when some of the shops opened (but that was further down in the more salubrious part of the High Street). Here it was more private with a real Day of Rest feeling. He even had a thermos of coffee to look forward to. The Sally Army chap had filled it for him late last night so chances were, it would still be hot enough to enjoy; that Lisa was thoughtful. She had given him a top of the range all-singing-all-dancing-keeps-everything-hotter-for-longer thermos which was obviously brand new and really did the job, but was not too heavy or cumbersome to carry around. Nice lady.

He returned to his book and was lost to this world.

Sometime later - he was never able to say exactly when as he did not wear a watch and was too absorbed in his book to notice - it was Troop that ended the idyll. Without notice he growled, his hackles rose as his body lifted and *Cloud Atlas* tumbled page down to the dirty ground where it was spread eagled in the dirt, a supplicant begging for mercy.

"Troop!" Corpy was annoyed, then disturbed. "What is it?" The dog ignored him and emitted a low warning rumble as if to say,

"Listen".

So, he did. And heard. Not loud noises but more sustained: sporadic bumps and scrapes and what sounded like high heels on cobbles, hisses, whispers and swearing which became more frequent. The sounds were coming from around the corner, the rear of the shop. Nothing seemed to be happening inside it - they both peered in through the front door and plate glass windows. Corpy noticed that the mannequin was wearing a sequinned mini dress rather than her usual fur coat and looked extremely cold, but apart from that there was nothing to see, nothing out of the ordinary. However, as they watched, a light went on at the far back of the shop - they could just see it slyly winking at them from behind an almost closed door.

Man and dog looked at each other and considered. Corpy wanted to say no but Troop but was more curious, more insistent so, reluctantly, man followed dog who led the way to the alley, the bins and the back door. Where they found only a parked car that they did not recognise in Davinia's designated spot, innocent and unoccupied apart from the fact that it was trespassing, but it was a Sunday, the shop was closed and Davinia would never know. Dog looked at man and they considered again. To do or not to do? Could be quite legit. Obviously, no break in; no damage to the door; must have had a key so must be okay? Mustn't it? Yeah. No worries. They both shrugged, trotted back to their doorstep, solitude and *Cloud Atlas.*

Monday

Colin was excited. Davinia had a big surprise for them all and he could hardly wait. Plus, they would be dressing the shop window for Christmas and he always loved that. He had been down to the cellar as required (anything for Davinia) to collect the boxes of decorations – old friends now, well acquainted, resurrected year after year, all a little older, a little shabbier, a little more creased but still game for the festivities of the season. Alex had offered to help but no, this was Colin's pleasure and he did not want anyone else to see Barb's tropical fish equipment. There appeared to be so much; she must be going for it in a big way which was thrilling. So much to share together, so much to look forward to. The boxes were unlabelled and he was terribly tempted to open them and have a look but she had told him, "strictly no peeking, Col" so he absolutely would not, however strong the temptation. Perhaps she was even considering keeping Koi carp? His heart raced and he had had to sit down for a moment to recover his senses.

Alex and Shelley were less enthusiastic as they were assembled on the shop floor before the doors were opened for the onslaught of custom. Davinia was glowing, smooth and dewy beside a substantial rectangular something covered with a tablecloth borrowed from the linen section. As she perched on her high heels and braced herself for the great reveal, smiling tightly at her retail warriors, Colin inhaled and held his breath. The other two mentally girded themselves and prepared to be as astounded as unrehearsed expressions permitted. With as much flourish as precarious balance and painted nails could muster, the tablecloth was swept aside to reveal an enormous open, plastic-wooden stable, peopled with the holy family, angels, podgy cherubs, kings, shepherds, assorted farm animals, a camel, one palm tree and a great deal of plastic straw. The infant Jesus lay smirking divinely in a large manger, definitely oversized for a new born and profoundly chubby. Behind the entire scene, watching over it as a fairy godmother who had lost her way and ended up in the wrong story was an enormous star, points outstretched and threateningly angular.

"Like a bloody hypodermic" Shelley muttered and Alex nudged her. Davinia however, had not heard; the surprise was not over.

"Watch!" she said, clicked a switch and stood by for them to be amazed. The Nativity scene had set itself alight with the wonder of electricity and was a thing to behold. A halo beamed out over the baby in the manger casting his face into horribly malevolent shadow. Standing over him in adoration were his parents, similarly illuminated. Mary had the appearance of a prematurely aged dwarf, bent double in a blue veil while Joseph held a staff like a shabby garden gnome angling a fishing rod over a non-existent pond; at any moment he might catch the baby Jesus and reel him in. The surrounding guests stared at the glowing baby with chipped pink-cheeked joy as the animals resolutely chewed the cud or nosed in the straw vainly searching for something to eat. From below the fixed fronds of the palm tree a bilious green light radiated, infecting the tableau with *mal de mer*. And above it all, gleaming and flashing with infernal gusto, the star winked and leered by turns as it flickered on and off with alarming regularity and even more disconcerting strength: the Samson of the star world without fear of any Delilah to curb its power.

They were, to a person, speechless and Davinia was duly gratified.

"Isn't it magnificent?" she cooed.

Clearly it was, their reactions said it all. "We'll have this as our centrepiece and arrange the other decorations, the tree, tinsel and cards around it. No one will have a window like it."

That was undeniably true. Now all that remained to do was to arrange the window to Davinia's satisfaction and that would take time. Shelley was banished to the stockroom unless particularly small hands were needed for fiddly fitting, while Alex and Colin were commandeered to lift, shove, lift again, move it over a little, a bit more, no the other way and then finally unpack the tired annual Xmas regulars from their comfortable boxes for another seasonal airing. The electrical glory of the Nativity scene had an unfortunate effect on these stalwarts which rendered them even more tired and morose than ever. The tree, last of an ancient lineage was undeniably balding and even when clothed in the creased and flattened tinsel seemed to be suffering from a severe arboreal mange. It bent its despondent branches ever lower as the same old baubles were suspended from them, all trying to fling themselves to earth to end their suffering and beat the angel from the top of the tree to self-destruction. She leant dangerously forward, wings unfurled, halo askew, hands clasped in desperate prayer silently invoking the Gods of mercy to grant her an end to her prickly torment.

"We'll display the cards on their cardboard racks artistically around the whole thing, filling the window" Davinia dictated when the Nativity and tree were in place. "Lots of tinsel on the shelves throughout the shop for colour and then we're done."

"Marvellous" said Colin.

"What d'you think, Alex?"

Davinia had cornered him. He tried not to flinch and said he agreed with Colin who nodded heroically. The pain continued.

"So, let's find out what you've brought for the raffle. … Shelley!"

Shelley, summoned, duly appeared. The inquest began.

Alex was up first. A bottle of whisky and some Duchy of Cornwall shortbread in a suitably regal box adorned with the Prince of Wales' feathers and an image of Highgrove; Davinia was gratified and quite impressed. Unable to smile properly she nodded approvingly. Then it was Shelley's turn. This was not so successful.

"But what will people do with a tattoo template? Even if it is Christmassy?" Davinia was aghast. "I don't care if they will get a discount from the tattooist you recommend. It's really not the sort of thing one expects to find in a Christmas raffle." She turned to Colin; surely it could not get much worse? She was wrong.

"Fish food?"

Even Alex stared.

"But you said what would we want to win" Colin protested,

perplexed. How could anyone not want fish food? "It's the best there is" he added. "My Guppies love it."
Davinia rolled her eyes towards her unreachably arched eyebrows.

Later, as she sat in the office with a skinny latte and Danish pastry to soothe her unfurrowed brow, she found additional comfort in writing Alex and Shelley's overdue Community Service reports. Alex was still arrogant but becoming more of a team player; he had proved himself useful in an emergency and maintained a cool and steady head under stress. Good news for a surgeon. Shelley, although making some progress in terms of reliability and punctuality was, regrettably, resistant to constructive criticism and lacked insight: she continued to flaunt the tattoos she insisted on calling body art and demonstrated a spirit of independence and defiance, verging on entitlement. She had responded well to the incident with the snake it was true; apparently, she had experience with reptiles that had proved invaluable in the circumstances, but this was not in itself enough to exonerate her wilfulness and an unfortunate tendency to mutter under her breath. Davinia had not stooped to find out what she actually said, the mere muttering was surely unacceptable enough. However, the VHS would continue its programme of support and positive reinforcement for them both, but especially Shelley, whose attitude was exemplified by her contribution to the shop's Christmas raffle prizes. What a pity she could not include Colin in her report Davinia lamented, but even Nerinda would not be able to do anything about him. And the fish food would have to stay. Perhaps it would be seen as a seasonal jest, a bit of Christmas jollity and good humour? She could only hope.
The mouse had just clicked on the send button and the report was winging its way to Nerinda's inbox when there was a tap at the door. Davinia wiped the crumbs off the desk and called "Come in" as she changed the screen. Just in time as it was Alex who appeared in the doorway.
"Alex. What can I do for you?" She exuded a smile as she was learning to do now that her mouth would not move. Her lips shivered slightly with the effort but remained plump and pert, settling back into solidity almost at once.
"It's about that T shirt – the Led Zeppelin one – remember?"

"Of course… Does this mean you didn't send it for recycling?" Davinia, on guard, prepared for battle.

"Yes, I'm afraid so." Alex charged straight on, confident that he had the firepower to avert a skirmish. "But when I tell you what it's worth, I hope you won't mind."

Silence. Action suspended. Alex misread the eyebrows and answered what he thought was a questioning glance. Davinia was momentarily blind-sided; Alex pushed on.

"There's a collector on the internet, in Germany, who's prepared to pay £5,000 for it." He ploughed on, pressing home his advantage. "Obviously that's not as much as we could get if we sold it ourselves but this guy's got the contacts and there has to be something in it for him. It seems a very fair offer to me but, obviously, it must be your decision."

"£5,000?"

"I could try and negotiate more but I think he's just about reached his limit."

"You've already negotiated?"

"Yes. Sorry. I thought it was better to have something concrete for you rather than just an idea that might not come to anything."

"£5000?" Davinia was incredulous. "For a T shirt?"

"A very rare one. In good condition."

Another silence. Even the air held its breath as tension circulated the room like a predator. Everything was still, afraid to move. Davinia's eyebrows seemed to have gone into orbit, a pink hairy ozone layer above while her pout remained chained to earth, fixed and immobile. Then the lips trembled, the corners of her mouth stretched, the end of her nose drew marginally closer to her upper lip and Alex realised she was smiling. Crisis averted. He realised that he too had forgotten to breathe; transplant surgery was less stressful than this.

"Super! What a pity I've just finished your weekly report for Nerinda. Never mind, the money will make a material difference to our veterans. Head Office will be delighted." They looked at each other, he thinking 'if you tell them it was me', she thinking 'they'll never know it was you.'

When Corpy and Troop came home for the night after a busy day on the street they were tired. Christmas was coming, the goose was getting fat and people were generous; the collection for the PDSA was generous and weighed a ton: as heavy as full kit, weapons and extra ammo on a long yomp when you have not eaten and have been on the move for over 24 hours. Troop was most unhelpful when it came to lifting which Corpy understood, but rather resented as he stood sweaty and panting in the cold air. Rain was inevitable; it always was after a couple of dry days, which had just passed, and he hoped it would not be snow. Only those with shelter, heating and money enough to use it advocated a white Christmas. Man and dog were ready for rest; a quiet night in their secluded doorway, tucked away from the pavement, just the two of them.

"Christ!"

Yes, it was, in his manger, surrounded by his acolytes, garish, illuminated, back-lit by *mal de mer* green and overseen by a pulsating disco dancing star. The silent scene was loud with light, fully electrified, throbbing with energy in the darkened window with the impenetrable darkness of the shop behind.

"For effect" Davinia had decreed, and had not been wrong. Effective it certainly was; no one could miss it.

"How'll we sleep?" Troop did not answer; he had no idea. For himself he did not mind, could sleep anywhere. Had learned to, especially when the small human had arrived in his before life and the crying kept everyone awake. Then they had all shouted at him and were cross and he spent most of the time in the tiny garden, even at night. He was better off with Corpy because then at least both of them were outside and even if he was cold, he was not lonely. And he never went hungry, not even when Corpy did.

They settled down as usual, bagged and crumpled in the left side of doorway, back to the wind. Corpy was in the foetal position, completely immersed in his sleeping bag on his cardboard mattress with Troop curled up to him, body to body, umbilical, but neither slept. Corpy was in torment; Troop went with him. Into the past, Afghanistan, blood and dust, the sound and the fury. The IED under the chassis, the explosion, the torn flesh and body parts and then silence, which became a ringing in his ears and the sound of death. The heat. The smell: liquid iron, sulphur, metallic and wet, overflowing. But no pain, not at first. That came later and made him scream until it gave way to the sense of loss, which had never ended. As he shook inside his non-sleeping bag and clenched his hands, the flashing star in the shop window became a white flare and the IED went off all over again. Corpy screamed, reached for his gun even though he knew it was too late and prepared to die once more, except that this time, Troop was there to save him.

Only when the sobbing and the shaking had ceased, overcome with exhaustion, did Troop finally close his eyes, but even then, he did not rest. Not fully.

Chapter Twelve
Jingle Bells

Christmas was coming in fast, inexorable, speeding up as the deadline approached only to grind to an equally inexorable halt when the schools broke up and small people had to be contained until the arrival of the morning itself. The Veteran's Help Society was making the most of it and even Davinia was surprised by the tat that people would buy to give to others, most of which would be back on the shelves by mid-January. But before the arrival of St Nicholas, the shop had the return of Candy to look forward to.

She blew in on the Tuesday morning in walking boots with Nordic poles, King Wenceslas running ahead of time wearing not a hood but a buoyant top knot, precariously pinned and enthusiastically releasing itself from all restraint like an evolving octopus. Messianic. This was the season of goodwill and she was going to share her message. No sooner was she on the shop floor, bundled and layered against the cold when she began, but not quite as they anticipated.

"It has to go!"

Davinia was thrown off track. Her over-cheery carefully rehearsed spontaneous greeting of welcome never made it out of the birth canal. So instead of solicitous managerial enquiries about the health and well-being of her erstwhile colleague, she found herself rather inelegantly asking

"What has?"

"That. In the window." Candy was brandishing one pointy pole at the illuminated Nativity behind her, still leering and winking remorselessly out into the street. "It's not appropriate."

Davinia was stunned; Colin was perplexed. Both were silent, shepherds on the hillside blinded by the word of Candy, heavenly-hostless and without wings but nevertheless filling their world.

"We're meant to be multi-cultural. What about other religions?"

Head shepherd Davinia found small voice.

"But Candy, it's Christmas."

"Not if you're Muslim. Or Buddhist. Or Hindu, or Jewish, or Jehovah's Witness."

"Or Roman Catholic?" Colin was interested. That was not English was it?

Candy ignored him and fixed Davinia with a gimlet look, piercing; John the Evangelist confronting an ignorant unbeliever about to get it in the neck.

"It has to reflect all faiths or else it's discrimination. We could be sued. It has to go."

"Sued?" Davinia was on heightened alert. The one word no manageress ever wants to hear on her shop floor. Candy was clearly barking mad but even the remotest possibility of any type of legal entanglement had to be avoided. Action would have to be taken but if they removed the Nativity, at Christmas, what would the Christians say? Then inspiration struck, divine, manna from heaven.

"We can adjust it! To include other religions, reflect other faiths. We'll just add them to the scene so that no one feels left out."

Candy was caught off guard, archangel without an agenda or an immediate reply but always ready to find the middle way and already her brain was turning over the possibilities.

"Yes" she proclaimed and the choirs sang.

"Perhaps you'd like to do that then? A special project?" Throw it back to her, let her take the responsibility so that if anyone sues it's not my fault, Davinia was thinking as she eased her mouth into a friendly grimace and Candy glowed with pleasure. Then, inevitably, it came.

"This is what comes of giving up everything except raw fruit and vegetables, Davinia. … Colin." She had noticed that he existed.

"Creative awareness, intense sensitivity and understanding. My whole life has been transformed. My Body and Soul are working together, united in perfect harmony, cleansed and purified. I am at one with the organic universe which speaks with me and through me; my body is its temple, my life is now part of its infinite cycle of growth, renewal and regeneration and I am here to spread its message. I know that now. It's as if I've been reborn, a seed in the fruit of the world ready to grow and bloom until I ripen into wisdom and perfection. I have so much energy! It's wonderful."

That was not quite the word Davinia would have chosen but she nodded and let it go. And avoided Colin who was clearly struggling hard with the concept before him and wondering how it would feel to be an apple.

Thus it was that the VHS Christmas Nativity display changed the life of window dressing in the High Street forever. Even the local paper got onto it and took pictures which were emblazoned on the front of the pre-Christmas issue to general rejoicing in Head Office. Reg was a little more ambivalent about the publicity, which Davinia took as a sign of jealousy and pique; her branch of the VHS really was outperforming all the others and Reg had the unenviable task of trying to raise them all to her high standard. The addition of a chubby Buddha sitting next to the Virgin Mary, beaming at the baby Jesus, was rather endearing and less startling than the vision of Durga waving all her arms at anyone and everyone: the donkey was quite bedazzled but not as confused as the lamb, which tried to hide in the straw. A cow, open mouthed and mooing for all eternity had also been included among the animals in deference to Hinduism while a large Star of David was placed on level pegging with the Star of Bethlehem. Together they shared the responsibility of overseeing proceedings and twinkled amicably together, though not quite as greenly as the palm tree. Candy was not quite sure how to represent Jehovah's Witnesses then decided that nothing was best as they did not recognise Christmas and anyway, the gifts from the Wise Men, one of whose faces she painted black and the other she adorned with a rainbow ribbon turban, were redolent of a Witness Present Day. That would have to do. As for Islam, she settled for a shepherd in a burqa, which also dealt nicely with the transgender issue and demonstrated equal employment opportunities in the agricultural sector. All in all, she was very satisfied with herself and even when Alex asked about Rastafarianism, she had an answer in the form of a tiny, crocheted red, yellow and green hat over yarn dreadlocks which was placed on the head of the black King. Her suggestion that a medley of multi-faith music should be broadcast to accompany the display was turned down so she inserted a Jedi knight with an LED light sabre under the palm tree, beside the camel, as an act of both defiance and a nod to the spiritual force of science. Who knew what lay out there and beyond? Shelley was less than helpful, asking only which of the figures represented the ancient and sacred art of body painting. Candy drew the line at inking any of them and concentrated on scattering judicially chosen healing stones amidst the plastic straw to create ambience and positive energy. The end result was a cacophony of colour, a Nativity tableau somewhere between a disco and a shrine to political correctness. Colin had proved himself indispensable and glowed as brightly as one of the illuminated figures themselves. By virtue of his expertise with fish tanks, he had saved the VHS in a fortune in electrician's fees by rewiring the plug for the electricity supply to the window and Candy was delighted, Davinia amazed. Colin was ecstatic, dazzled with his success and the glare from the festive scene; the local newspaper reporter could honestly say that had never seen anything like it. Nor had the High Street and Corpy had such broken sleep and recurrent bouts of PTSD that he seriously considered relocating to another doorway.

The window display certainly had the desired effect of creating a diversion and attracting attention. The shop was exceptionally busy and Candy made a point now of being seen on the shop floor instead of her more customary invisible who knew where? Her Kahloesque appearance was an additional source of curiosity for customers lured into the shop by the psychedelic Nativity which pleased Candy so much that she stopped plucking her eyebrows altogether and very soon sported a sturdy line of hair that loomed over her eyes like an overhanging valley. A significant growth of hair on her upper lip was not required however, and she continued to pluck, wax and thread it with assiduous regularity.

It was about 4.00 pm on Saturday, the end of another busy week was in sight and they were weary. Colin had been doing battle with the till all day and was, frankly, exhausted. The racks of Christmas cards for sale strategically arranged around the Nativity scene were also exhausted. Every time the door was opened, they collapsed, their flimsy cardboard racks blown over by the incoming draught so that they repeatedly tumbled and fluttered to the ground. Battered, windblown, crumpled and creased they were returned to their positions only to be assaulted again and laid so low that they longed to be left to die, alone. Perhaps Colin understood because eventually he gave up replacing them and only did so every third or fourth time they hit the decks. Colin still had not decided what to get Barb for Christmas; time was running out; his stomach ached from the sustained assaults on it by the till drawer and, as he rearranged the hapless cards yet again, he longed for his fish and a cheese sandwich. Davinia had said that no one was available to repair the till drawer until after the New Year so they would just have to persevere until then - but the shop would be shut over the Christmas holiday period so it would be fine, wouldn't it? Colin certainly hoped so, and trusted that the bruising would have healed by the time they reopened.

Raffle tickets had been selling well and, strangely, although there was no great enthusiasm for the fish food, the template and discount voucher for the tattoo had proved extremely popular. Lots of scantily black-clad, heavily-mascaraed men and women had seen the window display and come in to find out more. There had been a run on everything retro, especially belts, chains, boots, short skirts, leather, vinyl and cassettes. One chap had asked what they had in the way of rubber. Davinia had been summoned and seemed quite disconcerted by the request. She had ever so politely asked him to vacate the premises but not before he had bought a raffle ticket, sales of which were increasingly lively. Initially there had had been a slight problem until Colin had been made aware that he was supposed to retain the ticket stubs rather than asking people to fill in their details and then returning the whole sheet back to the purchaser. But it had not been so many that the raffle was compromised, Davinia said, and it was all in a good cause so she was sure they would not mind, which was a relief. Colin bought a whole book of tickets to try and make up for his mistake.

Outside it was dark; the Nativity scene beaconed forth its message with unrelenting vigour and strength. The wet pavement was streaky with fractured coloured light and the faces of those who peered in through the window were like antique stained glass, rhythmically disparate and angular in the light of the flashing stars. It was a little distracting, especially when adding up, as Colin did, when there was more than one transaction to complete at the till for a single customer. It was so much easier to write down the amounts, add them up on a piece of paper then enter the total into the till than negotiate the minefield of technology and give change that way. It was slow, admittedly, but Colin preferred it like that: slow and steady wins the race Mother always said and he knew she was right.

"…And 3 then carry over 1 to make it 4 which makes it £22 and 35 pence. Then 5p for the carrier bag but that can go in the charity box. So, it's £22.35!" Caesar Augustus decreeing that all the world should be taxed could not have matched the jubilation of Colin's declaration. The customer, however, was unconvinced.

"Seems a lot to me. Are you sure you've got it right?"

Colin was crushed. Then the panic set in.

"Alex! Alex!" A cry in the wilderness, lost in the void, but saved by the appearance of the Man from the Steam-room. "Can you check my adding up?"

Alex resolved to buy a calculator as a secret Santa and deposit it by the till, his gift to the world, but until then yes, of course he would check the sums. He set to. Then stopped. Sniffed.

"What's that smell?"

The customer, bored with waiting had perked up considerably at the arrival of another member of staff and sniffed enthusiastically.

"Burning" he said.

Colin sniffed but could smell nothing. Alex sniffed again, slow and loud, head raised to the ceiling, nostrils in the ascendant.

"Burning" he agreed with the customer.

There was a bang and a flash and the lights went out. All of them. The shop floor, the stars - both of them, Jesus in his manger, the stable, the steam room and even Davinia's office were plunged into darkness. Now there was nothing to distinguish between the outside world and the shop interior; they were as one in black night, melting out onto the pavement, leaking away into the vortex. Heaven and hell.

Someone screamed, high pitched, female. Unseen. Polar night. And it was then that the miracle happened. An iota of light, an edge, a suggestion that began to grow, became a flicker and then took form. The window display was on fire.

The fire fighters greeted Davinia like a long-lost friend.

"Hello darlin'." A hearty wink from their leader while his team smirked a greeting. "No need to ask what's happened this time. Don't worry. We'll soon put you out. My appliances are always at the ready for you".

He grinned and Davinia's eyebrows achieved the impossible and rose a little higher. Unfortunately, he interpreted this as encouragement. He stood very close to her as his team rushed about fetching equipment and stamping their boots on the bewildered floor tiles, reeling from the onslaught of heavy tread and bulky bodies.

"Always happy to get my hose out for you, eh, darlin?" He nudged her as he spoke and Davinia nearly fell off her shoes - but no matter, he would have rescued her in a moment. Thankfully for her complexion it was dark. The eyebrows tried to return to base but got lost, gave up the attempt and resigned themselves to a new elevation.

They set to work and in a twinkling the window was full of foam, drowning the Holy Family and their entourage until only the two stars remained, damp and dark but defiantly angular. Once the flames were extinguished - fortunately before they had had time to blossom and flourish - the ever-practical fire fighters rigged up an enormous flash light in the shop floor to enable their investigators to identify the cause of the blaze. The light also enabled Davinia to attempt to restore some semblance of order in her staff who had, she noticed with ill-disguised disapproval, taken the opportunity to stop working. Colin alone, while shocked by events, was secretly relieved. Without electricity the till was incapacitated, powerless and its drawer confined to barracks. The customer at the counter who had witnessed the incendiary excitement was more than happy now to simply hand over the correct cash - had not had such fun in years, had enjoyed every minute, glad to have been of help and would be back very soon. The shop was closed over Christmas? What a pity; Christmas went on forever and the kids needed some form of entertainment once they tired of their gifts.

What with the snake - he'd heard all about it - and now a combustible window display, they were the most exciting retail premises for miles. Davinia did not even attempt a smile but thanked him for his contribution with trout-lipped iciness and wished him the compliments of the season.

It did not take long to discover what had ignited the infant Jesus in his humble abode.

"Faulty wiring, love. Some cowboy sparky's overloaded yer system and it's all gone up in smoke. Yer wanna use a reputable electrician - I've gotta list of recommended tradesmen if yer like."

No one said a word and Colin was grateful for the Stygian darkness behind the counter, away from the glare of the artificial light.

"But it's Christmas. What about my sales?" Davinia was desperate.

"Oh, no problem. This'll soon be cleared up. Just a bit of foam and dirty footprints. Nothin' to worry about. Yer system's fused but that's soon fixed.... Yer overloadin' yer system. Usin' too much power, darlin', know what I mean?" He winked; she shuddered. "Might have to change yer window though."

They all stared at the blackened stable sitting in the coagulated plastic straw which had melded into a dense yellow cloud, mustard gas in a trench suffocating the recumbent animal population. The lamb had become ostrich-like, head buried in the sand while the Virgin Mary, still recognisably blue under the drying foam, looked as if she had dug herself a shallow hole in a sandy beach and was trying to lay an egg. All the figures in the scene appeared to have newly emerged from a blizzard of shaving foam that had dribbled and dried upon their persons; the black faced king was grey and streaky, Durga's arms were festooned with drops of liquid snow, snotty and sticky, while the Buddha's generous torso was swathed in so many bands of white that he looked like a morbidly overweight Egyptian mummy in the process of being unwrapped. It was a scene of desolation and damp sorrow, framed by the singed outline of a wooden stable in need of major repair and refurbishment. The palm tree drooped, the camel had lost leg and with that, its balance. It lunged forward towards the holy babe in the manger, miraculously unburnt although a little grimy. The gurgling infant was still smiling and had his hands outstretched, as if to catch the camel before it collapsed, while Joseph's fishing rod had snapped in two, one half of which was to be seen impaled in the straw perilously close to the bedazzled donkey.

Candy wanted to cry but did not. Later, she put her resilience down to her new found fruitarian strength and the healing stones now forever sealed within the carpet of melted straw. Davinia was as distraught as her face would allow and considerably more distressed.

"What will people say? What will they think? How would she explain it to Head Office?"

Alex and Shelley, to her surprise, found they were concerned and tried to console her. They failed, so began a campaign of action. Alex un-tripped the boxed fuses at the back of the shop and then there was light, which was good, but also bad because it revealed the exact extent of the damage and Colin, who could no longer remain concealed behind the counter. However, Davinia was magnificent and said not a word, partly because she did not have the vocabulary and partly because her mouth would not stretch wide enough to accommodate that amount of wormwood and gall. That evening they went home subdued and demoralised. Not so Corpy and Troop however, who had the best night's sleep they had had in ages.

Apart from the dejection of the charred Christmas window, the damage was not great - a little smoke damage and a very dirty floor, mostly from firefighters' footwear, so the shop could be up and running within forty-eight hours. Davinia insisted on opening on the Monday morning promptly at 9.00 am, even as the clear up operation was underway. Instead of sweating and steaming in the back Alex and Shelley had been given permission to do the same on the shop floor and were to be seen mopping, wiping, sweating and steaming in full view of the fascinated public who had turned up in droves to witness the latest VHS drama. Indeed, many of the so-called customers were simply there in anticipation for whatever might happen next. Colin was disconcerted at the numerous requests for advance information about the next 'event' and no, at Davinia's insistence, he would not take telephone numbers 'in case something happened and they did not want to miss it'.

Reg arrived to inspect the premises and assess the situation for Head Office who were rather of the same opinion of the interested customers and eagerly awaited the next instalment from Davinia's outpost of their empire. They loved the publicity; no one had been hurt and it came at no real cost. A small insurance claim with minimal paperwork and then it was business as usual and everyone was happy. Yes, plenty to celebrate this Christmas.

Sales of raffle tickets soared and the draw was soon upon them. Originally the idea had been to make it an event, to ask a local notable to choose the winning tickets and publicise the results with festive flourish, but in the light of the fire and forlorn Christmas tableau still smoky and streaky in the window Davinia decided on a less ostentatious approach and opted for a quiet ceremony. Consequently, she asked Candy to select winning ticket number one and then each member of staff would choose the others. Shelley had suggested, straight-faced to the amazement of Alex, that they ask the lead fire fighter to do the honours but Davinia had adamantly refused; she was still trying to find her eyebrows and the bad dreams about men with hoses winking at her were causing sleep deprivation.

It was deemed appropriate that Shelley should dip into the box of folded ticket stubs and find the lucky recipient of her tattoo template and discount visit to the tattooist, whom she personally recommended. Not the one who had done her ill-fated most recent addition that her landed her in hospital but another guy, she said, clean and really fastidious.

"OCD. Obsessed with detail. Takes hours" she announced. "Gifted when it comes to artwork but only does the designs he likes. He's doing this for me as a special favour so whoever gets this prize is dead lucky." Alex looked enthusiastic but fervently hoped it would not be him; the others watched, impassive. It was only a tattoo.

Shelley stuck one small hand into the box and rummaged about, taking her time, waiting for inspiration. Then she triumphantly pulled out one yellow ticket stub and waved it in the air.

"Here we go!" she said and opened it. Her mouth gaped, fishlike, shut again and she stared goggle eyed at the ticket.

"What is it?" Davinia spoke for them all.

No reply. Instead Shelley looked up and silently handed the piece of paper to her manageress. Davinia was aghast. Not me? her face said. No, Shelley's face replied, not you. Read it.

It was for Colin.

He was overwhelmed. Him! Colin! With a tattoo!

"But are you sure you want one?" Alex asked. "I'm sure you could have a different prize if you wanted, couldn't he, Davinia?"

Yes, even she had to agree to that one.

"Oh, but it's marvellous! I've never had one before. And…"

Breathless silence. They waited, absolutely at a loss to know what was to come.

"I can get one for Barb! For Christmas! We'll have matching tattoos!"

At least the bidding was brisk on the Liberty scarf, Davinia consoled herself at home that evening. In fact, it was unprecedented. Dave's Slave, whoever he or she was, seemed determined to have the scarf at any price and was assiduously bidding and outbidding to maintain a steady lead in the scarf stakes. The finishing post was coming up fast, Dave's Slave's finger was resolutely poised and pressing, victory was in their grasp. When the red numbers reached zero and those lovely noughts flashed to signal the end of the auction, Dave's Slave was the proud owner of a silk vintage Liberty scarf and Davinia was quids in. Literally. Now all she had to do was send it off it before the last post before Christmas jollifications and hope it arrived before the holiday. She shoved it in a brown envelope, printed out the paperwork and attached the address label which she glanced at, in passing. Local! Thank God for that, then it would almost certainly arrive in time.

Alex broke out in a sweat at the price Lisa had had to pay but accepted that it was necessary for the stratagem Shelley had devised, although he wished it had cost a great deal less.

"But what are we going to do with it?" he moaned.

"I shall wear it." Lisa's reply was that of a primary school teacher at the end of a long winter term dealing with a class of five-year olds. "Unless you want to?" Alex ignored her and focused on another problem.

"What happens if Davinia recognises the name and address?"

"She won't. I've registered on eBay in my maiden name and she'll have no idea who Ms L. Birtley is. The fact that she lives locally is mere coincidence. Chance. Could happen to anyone." She grinned. Alex was appalled. This was a side to Lisa he had never seen before and he began to understand why MI5 recruited housewives.

"What happens now?" he asked.

"Wait till after Christmas. Shelley'll deal with it in the new year." And it was left at that; Alex dared not ask more. Instead, he and Dave focused on the thorny issue of what to get Lisa for Christmas and Alex wondered how Barb would greet the news that she was to receive a tattoo.

So did Colin, but with a great deal more excited energy than Alex. The dilemma that replaced the spectre of the till at night was multi-faceted. What design? To consult with her or surprise? Should he get his down now, or would they visit the parlour together? If they did that, would they get a discount? Perhaps he should lead by example - the first principle of successful management according to Davinia. That would show his commitment but what image should he have inked on his person? And where? Oh dear, and what if it was very painful? Or got infected? That night he dreamt of snakes and fish and Barb, gloriously plump in their midst and in the morning, it was decided. That was what he would get. A 'B' lovingly entwined with a fish – no particular species – and a curling (friendly) snake, but not in a Fair Isle sweater. On his left arm, above the elbow, next to his heart. And Barb would have the same but with a 'C' and it would be marvellous. Now his biggest concern was how soon he could get his done and show Barb. Strangely, he had not seen her for a while, nor heard from her but of course it was Christmas and her nephew would be too busy to bring her into town. But she had said she would see him before the holiday began and he knew he would.

"Chrissie pressies to buy, dear" she had said in such a way that his heart fluttered and his ingrowing toenail throbbed. "I do love Crimble, don't you?" He had agreed with his whole being although unsure exactly what Crimble was. Later he had worked out what she meant and laughed at himself for thinking it was some type of pudding.

Davinia had plans for Christmas which did not involve the shop, charity or anyone else except the attentive staff at the exclusive spa into which she had booked for two days, effectively cancelling out Christmas for another year and giving herself the opportunity to lose a few pounds instead of gaining them like everyone else. That alone made it worthwhile. It also provided a chance for her Botox to ease a little and become a little less rigid without losing any of its tightness.

Her eyebrows would descend and she would be sensational. Fortunately though, in the interim, the Kate Middleton effect had resulted in a vogue for heavy eyebrows so she had been able to colour in the underside of her own to give the impression that they were closer to her eyes so no harm had been done. And her forehead was so smooth. Who needed feeling there anyway?

Lisa and Alex would spend Christmas with Dave and Shelley would be at home with her mother. At least she had plenty to read. Smile, nod, agree with all things and hope that the anger would only simmer. She had lived with her Mother's fury for so long it had almost become a sibling: she could not remember life without it. Not that she really minded even though it was exhausting, especially for her mum who was wizening and shrinking before her as her resentment about her unfulfilled life destroyed what was left of it. She was also afraid - frightened that Shelley would go the same way - intelligent but thwarted, abandoned, wasted in menial jobs, prematurely aged by the degradation of her life when it should have been so different, so much better. Her daughter knew and understood, but had nothing to say. So, she kept on getting tattoos as a way of expressing her pain and hopes, a kind of constructive cutting resulting in illustrations rather than scars.

Candy's Christmas plans revolved entirely around fruit and vegetables to her joy and their dismay. She had again been invited to join the protest in the frozen turkey aisle at the local supermarket but had decided against it this year, conserving her energies for her forthcoming campaign promoting Fruitarianism. Meat of all kinds was so last year. Even veganism was becoming a bit of a cliché. What was the point of vegan bacon? No, better to eschew the entire concept of flesh and convert to fruit, an organic world, the path forward, the future of healthy personkind and the salvation of the planet. Truly, this Christmas was a joyous rebirth. She had never felt so good.

As for Corpy and Troop, well, it was just another Christmas wasn't it? Their first together of course, which made it more meaningful, but just another day when the High Street was quiet and inside the shops the lights went out. It used to be two or three days of inactivity but now the obsession with spending money meant that Boxing Day was busier than Christmas Eve so their p&q was limited. Not that it really mattered as they would not be in their doorstep anyway. Christmas was the time when those on the streets made the news. These days there were always cameras in the Crisis at Christmas venue, mostly focused on the celebrities who left their dining tables to hand out festive fare to their local hobos, newly washed and laundered for the event, clad in warm clothes, shaven and fragrant. It was always a shame that most of the really bad weather they would have to endure occurred well after the Christmas bun fight was over, but at least they had access to dentists and doctors in preparation and could stock up on new-old clothes in readiness. Corpy had wondered if dogs would be welcome but need not have worried; they were as much a part of street life as he was and Troop was something of a celebrity in his own small way. The PDSA had a vet at the ready in the hall and he had told everyone about Troop who was greeted with acclaim. 'The dog that donates' the local rag had headlined him and all the celebrities wanted to be photographed as close to him as possible. Corpy could have sworn that Troop was laughing at the camera but that was absurd. Corpy had plenty to read, company if he wanted it and a warm place to sit. The lending library arrangement with Alex was working well and he was looking forward to tucking into *Brave New World*, an old favourite. Not a bad kind of Christmas all things considered.

Barb had 'just popped in, dear' to see Colin as the shop was about to close for the holiday and had much to say about the visit when Reg picked her up at the end of the street afterwards, most of it in a less than festive spirit.

"This is your bloody fault, Reg. If you think I'm getting a tattoo on your behalf you can think again I'm not getting a tattoo for you or anyone else never mind a snake eating some kind of horrible fish around a C if I'd known what I was getting into I'd never have agreed to go along with it Colin is a nightmare he's so boring and he wears hand knitted sweaters." She paused for much needed breath and Reg leapt in to soothe and cajole.

"I know, I know. And you're doing a marvellous…" he hesitated as she glared at him "…job. You know I couldn't do this without you and it'll be worth it in the end. We're going to make a fortune."

"Yes, well. We'd better. That's all I can say." If only, he thought. "But I'm not getting a tattoo, Reg. No way. And when it's all over I sincerely hope you'll make it worth my while."

"I will, darling, I will. You know I will."

"Hmm." She was mollified, seeing platinum and diamonds and an exotic holiday somewhere hot and expensive. Reg grinned as he looked out of the side window of the car where she could not see his face. Women! So predictable. But she was useful and he couldn't do this without her.

"Did you buy Colin a Christmas present?"

"What? Colin? Of course not."

Reg rubbed his groin thoughtfully and frowned into the rear-view mirror.

"Should I have done?" Barb suddenly felt abashed. Colin had looked so eager when she had called in and so crestfallen when she left, at speed, even as his sleeve was rolled up his arm revealing the cling-film-covered, inky, red blotch he said was some kind of reptile and in which her own initial was just about visible.

"We need to keep him onside."

"It's too late now."

"Not necessarily. I know where he lives. We'll swing by Aquarium World now and drop something off on our way home. Don't worry, you won't have to see him. Just ring the bell and leave it on the doorstep. He'll love it."

He did. It had been a great disappointment when Barb had exited the shop as fast as heavy legs in pointy shoes on slippery floor tiles could go. Even just a card would have been nice and he had covered his tattoo, which really hurt, with his sleeve before anyone could see it. Then it occurred to him that she had been overwhelmed by his devotion and he felt ashamed. How could he be so insensitive? She was such a lady, proper in 'the right kind of way' as Mother would say, that any such demonstration of emotion was bound to be embarrassing and she had done what any real lady would do and fled the scene. He felt such a … cad. Yes, that was the word. He had read it in one of Mother's women's magazines. Oh, how could he have been so stupid? He had spoiled everything, was a brute, did not deserve such an angel and Christmas was ruined. When the doorbell rang, he had gone to answer it with heavy heart, aching arm and pulsating ingrowing toenail after a day standing on an unforgiving shop floor. The end of the world felt nigh until he opened the door and found the parcel, in - oh joy - an Aquarium World carrier bag. Could it be? Yes, it had to be; could only be. With trembling hands, he parted the closed lips of the plastic bag to reveal … a mermaid. A real live plastic mermaid! Sitting on a plastic rock, open mouthed, calling to him. She had long luxuriant blonde hair, a bit like the colour of Barb's, tumbling down her back and huge blue eyes matching the elegant oversized scallop shells demurely adorning her, um, chest. Colin blushed and switched his attention to her tail, bright teal, shiny, coiled beneath her like a cushion with two little fins peeping coyly out at him from the side of the rock. And what was amazing, even more amazing than her beauty, was the fact that she was a fish tank oxygenator and would blow bubbles at him forever and Barb had bought him a present after all, but had been too shy to give it to him in the shop but had left it on his doorstep like a real live Santa Claus because he did not have a chimney, only an electric fire, and there was a card with the present which simply said Happy Christmas Colin with a B and a great big X. And Christmas was not ruined but wonderful, his arm no longer hurt, the toenail was subdued and Colin was in heaven.

So, the magic of Christmas night came and went, and the shop was closed. And no-one witnessed the visitations via the back door throughout the whole of the two-week holiday or noticed the smell and the occasional glow leaking through the back of the shop.

Embers sing; empty echoing. Calm darkness crying.

Chapter Thirteen
The New Year

Apart from Corpy and Troop, who would miss the warmth of the Christmas shelter, most of the incumbents of the Veteran's Help Society shop were looking forward to returning to work, but for very different reasons.

Love had rendered Colin restless. Until now, his fish and to a lesser extent, Mother, had been all he needed but now he felt dissatisfied. Even Swiss Railway Journeys on the telly seemed to be lacking somehow: predictable, even a little dull. He had begun to want more than a cheese sandwich as it were, had developed a yearning for excitement - pickle or something more exotic than mature Cheddar to spice up his life and satisfy a new appetite. Barb had brought him alive and awoken in him strange longings and urges. He seemed to see her everywhere: on the street, around corners, on the television, even staring out at him from his pink back-lit fish tanks which was weird and he knew was impossible. The little mermaid bubbled at him day and night and he swore he heard her singing or calling him 'dear'. It was exhilarating but disturbing and he knew he needed to get back to His Job to restore order to his mind and his turbulent emotions. Of course, he had not seen Barb in the flesh (he gasped at the thought and suffused crimson all over) throughout the festive period so could hardly wait to get back to normality and the possibility that she would waltz onto the shop floor and into his dreams at any moment. Maybe, into his arms, the prospect of which made him go hot and very sweaty, so that he had to roll up the sleeves of his jumper and then he saw the glory of his tattoo once more (he looked at it constantly throughout the day and much of the night) and that made him hot and sweaty all over again. It was all very exhausting and costing a small fortune in deodorant. Then there was the challenge of Barb's tattoo to organise and he had begun to wonder if a mermaid shouldn't be incorporated in the design somehow. Goodness, Love was such hard work. He had had no idea but did not regret any of it. No, not a thing. It was all marvellous.

Davinia was eager to display her slim-mer torso to the world, swathed in a cerise bodycon like an overtight sausage skin. The colour was designed to complement her hair but was rather overwhelming in that she appeared to glow, not unlike one of Colin's fish tanks. She also needed new stock to sell on eBay. Candy was also keen to show off her reformed body and mind, both of which had reduced in size and vigour since she had cut out everything except raw fruit and vegetables. She was pale to the point of being not just interesting but utterly fascinating and had lost so much weight that her woolly tights sagged around her ankles and dripped over the top of her walking boots. She still had her Nordic poles which she leant on with relief as she strode out, but the best news was that her hair was growing back and she no longer featured a bald patch. So taken had she been with the Frieda Kahlo effect however, that she had retained the coiled-up hair and the monobrow, which looked more and more like an overhanging valley under which her eyes, nose and mouth fought for light.

Alex did not want to get back to the shop so much as to get the ordeal and his Community Service over, so the sooner he went back, the sooner he could leave. Shelley shared his desultory vision but had the added frisson of exposing Davinia to look forward to, not to mention the relief of avoiding her mother. It had been a typical Christmas and she had done a great deal of reading in her room, out of anger's way. She had also been doing a great deal of thinking and had started to devise a plan for the future but still had some way to go before she would share it with anyone, except perhaps Alex. She would mark the occasion of a new year and evolving ambition with another tattoo, but just what and when had yet to be decided. However, it would have to feature a serpent.

There was something sad about the shop after Christmas. The battle-torn Nativity scene had been removed from the window and unceremoniously consigned to the 'not sure what to do with this so I'll leave it for the time being' heap in the stockroom. Davinia knew it was destined for the bins but could not quite bring herself to sign its death warrant, thereby condemning it to rot. There seemed something sacrilegious about chucking the Holy Family and their guests in a bin, even the blue one for recycling. On the other hand, it would be a kind of rebirth for them, a resurrection she reasoned, but Candy had put the kybosh on that by reminding her that reincarnation was a Hindu belief, not Christian, and what if they came back as something unholy, like a pedal bin or a child's potty? It looked as if the Son of God would be left in his forgotten corner for some considerable time.

The unsold Christmas cards, bearing the scars of their annual display longed to be discarded or, hope against hope, recycled but knew that they would be packed away for another eleven months and resurrected the following year to undergo the same humiliation. All they could hope for was more secure display units upon which to rest in December. There was another equally sorry pile of exhausted Christmas decorations, bedraggled and a little smoke damaged but "good for another year or two" so they too lay in dejection awaiting newspaper and cardboard boxes before resuming their sojourn in the cellar. If only they could be included in the Sale; they stared with longing at their compatriots being awarded bright red dots on their price labels. The mark of freedom.

The Sale. Colin dreaded it. The challenge of new numbers over old. He lay awake dreaming of 50% until he worked out that he could add up everything as normal then divide it by 2. Then he slept undisturbed. Davinia loved Sale time - decisions, deadlines - all down to her. It was a time for her entrepreneurial skills to shine and she felt energised and powerful and very svelte. Head Office left Sales very much to the discretion of individual shop managers, dictating only the time and duration of when they should be held. Davinia always went for an 'everything half price approach' and the punters rolled in. They bought anything. People did when it was cheap enough; the dross she cleared in Sale time was legion. All the dodgy garments and bric a brac that had been festering in the 'not good enough for full price but too good to be thrown away' piles were brought out, dusted down, promoted to hangers and shelves and given the red dot treatment. Not only were they fresh stock on the shop floor to the joy of regular customers, but they were half price! They practically wrapped themselves in carrier bags and walked off the premises. It was also an excellent time for Davinia to select and secrete items for eBay; in the midst of all the activity and alteration no one ever noticed the absence of the more expensive donations and designer labels which found their way into her capacious tote bag. The Radley and its little dog had been kennelled in Davinia's wardrobe for a well-earned rest for the duration of the Sale and replaced by a more commodious receptacle better suited to her needs.

Except that this year, Shelley was watching, and had noticed. But said not a word. Not yet. Alex silently watched the drama unfolding before him with trepidation. It occurred to him that there was much to learn from quietly observing. He had known that once but wondered when it was that he had forgotten; perhaps when he had reached the heady heights of consultant surgeon? That disturbed him. He also realised that for someone who knew so much about the human body, he knew nothing of the workings of the female mind.

This was brought home to him on the first day back. Even though everyone was supposed to be skint after Christmas they were rifling through the racks of clothes with the care and clinical determination of pathologists. Arms were heavy with clothes slung over them as the forensic examination continued, meticulous and methodical.

"We could have done with some supermarket trolleys" Alex quipped, not entirely in jest as he stood with Davinia at the back of the shop. She was surveying her domain with hidden pleasure; smiling was still difficult.

"I don't think so" she retorted. "Health and Safety. You should know that."

"Against Company Policy?" Alex asked, sweetly, exactly as Shelley would have done.

Davinia nodded sagely. Hope for him yet, she was thinking. Alex would have liked to grin but was distracted by an outbreak of hostilities at the till. A petite woman, carrying almost her own bodyweight in Sale merchandise was giving it large to Colin over the counter. She wanted a discount for buying in bulk and yes, she knew perfectly well, thank you, that everything was already half price, but she wanted more. Deserved more.

"How about 50% of 50% for 10 or more items? That seems fair don't you think?"

Colin did not think and was beginning to panic, rolling his hand knitted sleeves further and further up his arms until they were so bunched around his armpits that he could not lower his upper limbs. It appeared that he was wearing only a vest beneath the jumper and his tattoo was soon basking in the light, the letter 'B' still a little pink-edged but the snake and the fish both looking healthy and extremely well nourished. Before Alex could act however, Davinia had arrived at the till in an adept pincer movement. The customer was trapped; cut off from the door, disadvantaged by her additional weight and rendered vulnerable by this and the element of surprise which was all her opponent's.

"Can I help?" Davinia. Polite. Impassive. Deadly.

"Marvellous" Colin muttered but neither woman heard. Their eyes were locked; positions were being taken before they began to circle like boxers in the ring. Who would strike the first blow?

The customer.

"And you are?" A tentative jab designed to test and disarm.

"Only The Manageress."

Alex flinched. Colin gaped. Davinia bided her time.

"Of a charity shop?"

Alex winced. Davinia stood firm and, oh God, inferred a smile. Alex froze.

"I wouldn't expect you to understand. Otherwise you wouldn't be asking for a discount."

Now Davinia's mouth did move - just, and only at the furthest corners but it was unmistakable - with the words came a smile. Alex and Colin exchanged glances and it was a shock to the former to realise that even Colin had sensed danger. Both men, Time and Place crossed their fingers and held their breath. Not even the air stirred while the floor tiles shivered in fear and braced themselves for action.

"Taking away from those who already have next to nothing."

They faced each other. Davinia's eyebrows had the advantage of height and body over those of the enemy, but she was the proud owner of substantial false eyelashes, reinforced with a thick coating of mascara which could give as good as they got. More or less evenly matched, Alex reckoned, in the eye department, but the customer was much slimmer than Davinia which could work either way. Although physically weaker she was undoubtably lither and more athletic, plus she was wearing flat shoes - all the better to pounce with - unless Davinia chose to use her stiletto sharp heels in which case the customer would be crippled. He hoped she would not underestimate Davinia.

"Charity begins at home." The woman smiled as she spoke, full-on, brazen, unrepentant.

Davinia's gaze never faltered, her forehead never moved but her nostrils twitched, like a fox's, smelling its quarry.

"If you have a home."

Alex was impressed. Colin awestruck. Davinia however, had not finished; she went for the jugular.

"We're here for those who don't. For those who have sacrificed so that those of us who do, can shop."

By now all the other customers in the shop were transfixed by the confrontation, avidly watching and listening. Initially, sympathy had been with the petite woman - who would not want a discount? - but then Davinia's argument had struck a chord. Also, none of them wanted to be seen to be uncaring, so allegiance rapidly lined itself up with Charity and the hapless woman knew it was all over.

She submitted. Completely; a total surrender. She put the goods down on the counter, smiled disingenuously and assumed martyrdom.

"Of course. You are quite right. I should of thought". Alex winced at her grammatical error but rejoiced at the wisdom of the capitulation and everyone relaxed except Davinia, who never backed down until the enemy had not only bowed but fled. Which she did, with alacrity and three carrier bags for which she put a whole 50p in the charity box.

Magnanimous in victory, Davinia merely swivelled silently on her vertiginous heels and headed back towards her office. Shelley was watching from the doorway and had heard every word.

The following morning Alex was nervous. He and Lisa had discussed the events of the previous day and Lisa had been unusually interested in everything said by Davinia. Alex had had to repeat the entire exchange, word for word to her more than once and he could not understand why. She was normally very dismissive of VHS dramas and crises unless they reduced her to tears of laughter. On this occasion however she said little, looked thoughtful and nodded knowingly. Even he recognised that this was ominous. He suspected it was connected to the imminent showdown between Shelley and Queen Dee and did not dare even to speculate how Lisa might be involved. Ignorance is bliss he decided, and envied Colin. Who had his own problems. There had been no sign of Barb since the shop had reopened and he was becoming concerned. Was she ill? Had something happened to her? Perhaps she had had an accident -fallen - been run over - mugged - kidnapped - sold into white slavery. Such things did happen, he knew, to beautiful women; he had read about it in Mother's magazines. What should he do? He decided to consult Alex.

It was very cold and the rain was threatening to turn into snow. As ever there was no sign of Corpy and Troop when Alex arrived at the shop and he wondered where they had gone; would they be able to keep warm and dry? At least it was comfortable in the shop and for once the prospect of the steamer looked relatively attractive. The smell in the nether regions of the shop was getting worse: ingrained dirt, dust, mould and something else that could have been anything dead or decaying, it was hard to say what. He had mentioned it to Davinia who had told him it was normal after the shop had been closed for a while and told him to increase the use of air freshener; he could use as much as he thought necessary. She would tell Reg about it when he next called but, and she meant this in the nicest possible way, perhaps Alex was being a little too pernickety? This was his Community Service, after all, not a holiday camp. Alex did not like to remind her of the noxious aromas he regularly encountered as a surgeon; she had obviously never had to do a laparotomy for faecal peritonitis or incised and drained a sebaceous cyst or a perineal abscess. She should try working alongside wet gangrene or rotting limbs on a vascular ward.

He and Shelley now dressed for undressing. Davinia did not comment just as long as they were wearing their lanyards and remained concealed, mostly by the clouds of steam that billowed around the room desperately seeking escape and then weeping copiously against the walls when denied freedom. Sometimes they could not even see each other and Alex would occasionally call out, a sort of audio-flare system, to try and locate Shelley and make sure she was still alive.

It was the arrival of Candy that threw the day into confusion however. She appeared at the front door, all hair and boots, pinched and bony, scantily clad. Her legs were bare, her thin cotton skirt had absorbed slush and rainwater as a sponge and was clinging to her calves with the determination of an Olympic athlete; she was coatless, gloveless and hatless. Her ear muffs alone protected her from the elements.

"Candy! What's happened?" Alex had stepped out for a moment from the onset of steaming to check on Colin when he saw her and ran to open the door, while Colin stood sentry by the till and looked his concern.

"You're frozen!" By now Alex had shut the door behind her and was ushering in the emaciated figure, mottled and blue, leaning on her Nordic poles and gasping for breath. As she warmed up, she became pinker and her skirt began to steam, gently at first but with more vigour as the heat of the shop increased the evaporation of its watery load. Drops of water began to descend onto the tiles and Colin watched with alarm, uncertain whether or not to fetch cardboard to place under her to absorb the mess.

"Where's your coat?" Alex asked but before Candy could reply, snatched an XXL jumper from the menswear section and wrapped it around her. The reaction was astonishing.

Candy shrieked, lost all her newly regained colour and fell to the floor. She skidded in the puddle at her feet, lost her grip on the poles which torpedoed off in opposite directions as she came to rest on the hard tiles where she lay, sobbing, cradled in the sweater.

"She's dead!" Colin screeched.

"It's wool!" Candy screamed and began clawing at the sweater.

"She's alive!" Colin screeched again and clung onto the till for support.

"Get it off me! I can't have wool! It's abuse."

At which point Davinia appeared.

"Whatever is going on? I could hear the noise from my office … Oh my God! She's dead again!"

"No, she's not!" Colin shouted from the safety of the till.

Candy was indeed very much alive, kicking and scrabbling wildly to escape from the confines of the substantial jumper which seemed intent on remaining as close to her as possible, to warm, to comfort and to soothe as all good sweaters should. Unfortunately, the harder it clung, the more frantic she became.

"Candy! What's the matter?" Now Shelley had joined the fray, drawn from the torrid depths of the steam room by the commotion.

"It's wool! I can't touch wool!"

"Why not?" Alex, the voice of utterly baffled reason. He and Shelley were now raising Candy from the dead, as it were, by lifting her upright into a sitting position while Davinia did her best to extract the resistant garment from Candy's body, which seemed to have shrivelled inside it. Alex was shocked to feel how thin she was: birdlike, brittle. She felt as if she would snap and was clammy with cold. "What's wrong with wool?"

"It's abuse. Like fur. Sheep shouldn't be sheared."

Even Colin's eyebrows sought refuge from surprise in the upper reaches of his forehead. They all stared at the bedraggled heap on the floor.

"But sheep have to be sheared. That's normal. It's good for them." As soon as had spoken, Alex sensed he would regret his words but at least they had the unforeseen benefit of re-energising the eco-warrior in Candy, who now stood up (a little shakily) to deliver her message.

"They're genetically modified sheep. They shouldn't need shearing but we've bred them like that and it's not natural and it's wrong to take their wool - it's abusive and they suffer and get cold and it's no different to killing animals for their fur."

There was a heavy silence, broken only by the soft slop of water dripping from Candy's skirt onto the moist floor. Candy inhaled, drew herself up and was about to continue when Shelley saved all their sanity and intervened.

"But who says so? The sheep don't get killed and their coats keep growing so they have to be sheared or else they wouldn't be able to walk."

Candy was severe.

"The animal activists; the people who care about animal welfare and know these things. They do investigations and find out all sorts of abuse and cruelty and the only way to stop it is to stop wearing wool." She glared defiantly at their doubtful faces. "It says so on the side of the bus."

Colin was intrigued.

"Really? Which one?"

Sensing a weakening in the ranks, Candy assumed a look of triumph and focussed her attention on Colin, still standing by the till but now leaning over the counter with undisguised interest.

"Lots of them. They're big, like adverts. You can't miss them."

"I've seen them." It was Alex. "But it's not the whole truth. You shouldn't believe everything you read on the side of a bus."

Candy was sorrowful as she answered.

"Oh Alex! Alex, Alex, Alex. And you're a doctor." And with that she gathered herself up and dripped her way to the back of the shop, ignoring her Nordic poles lying like discarded javelins in an arena and disappeared out of their sight.

"She's bonkers."

For once, Davinia had to agree with Shelley.

Later, to their mutual astonishment, Davinia sought out Alex to consult him about Candy and what they should do about her.

"Does she need psychiatric help?" Davinia asked, *sotte voce,* glancing uneasily at the closed door of her office in which the consultation was taking place.

"No. Just some protein, a hot meal, warm clothes and a filtering mechanism. At least we can deal with most of those. I don't suppose she's eaten properly since before Christmas. Did you see how thin she was?"

"Yes". Davinia nodded resentfully. "So, what do you suggest?"

"Vitamin and mineral supplements, protein in the form of nuts and pulses - we can tell her that they're fruits of a kind and she'll believe us, you know what she's like - warm clothes which don't offend her sensibilities. Bamboo socks, cotton, anything made of hemp, vegan leather…"

"Vegan leather?"

"Made from apple peel…Honestly. I looked it up on the internet."

Davinia put her hand to her mouth and held it hard; laughing was out of the question and would hurt but her muscles were out of control so she sniggered with her mouth shut while her eyes narrowed in a most unflattering way. Alex was mesmerised. Davinia - amused? He shivered.

The happiness did not last. Alex returned to his vaporous duties and Davinia had overcome her temporary lapse into levity to return to managerial responsibilities. There was a pile of post to be opened and dealt with, which always infuriated her. Hadn't the advent of email meant that letters and mail were a thing of the past? Why did they still land on her desk and have to be opened? Such a waste of precious time. Her precious time which made it infinitely worse. Sighing she picked up the first letter and ripped into it, flinging the dismembered envelope into the bin beside her. Gimlet-eyed she gave the first page of the correspondence a cursory glance then went straight to the bottom of the page, and gasped. As wide eyed as Botox would permit, she turned to the second sheet and studied its break down of figures with laser-sharp precision.

"How dare they?"

It was an electricity bill, of astronomical proportions. Not just a little higher as expected at this time of year, but huge. Enormous.

"Totally unacceptable. I'll sue them for incompetence and negligence. Clearly the meter is faulty or they've read it wrong, or both." She grimaced "This will have to be dealt with." Unaware that she was shouting to herself she had reached for the phone and was dialling Reg's mobile number.

Reg was unusually sanguine about it.

"Probably just a clerical error. Nothing to worry about."

"What shall I do?"

"Nothing. Leave it with me; it's not the first time they've done this. I'll be in as usual this week and we can talk about it then. …Oh, hang on, what day is it today?"

"Tuesday."

"Change of plan this week, I'll be in on Thursday."

"That's my day off."

"Damn. Never mind, I'll see what I can do. Might pop in on Saturday afternoon instead if that's okay? I know it's a busy day for you. Don't want to get in the way!"

That was so like Reg, Davinia thought. Considerate. Understanding. He appreciated the pressures his managers faced and always had their best interests at heart.

"You're never in the way. It'll be a pleasure to see you, as always. Oh, before you go, there's a bit of a smell in the shop, at the back. The Community Service people are complaining I'm afraid. Not that they have any right to, as we both know, but when has that ever stopped them?" Perhaps I'm a little too familiar she thought as she spoke but Reg was really so accommodating and besides, was reported to be a happily married man so would recognise that she was just being pleasant. Nothing complicated or compromising; nothing to worry about. She had never met Mrs Sutton, but imagined that she would be the ideal wife for a successful regional manager, probably a bit plain and mumsy, keeping a clean hearth and steady home-cooked meals sort of home for her hard-working husband who was so often out on the road. "Any idea what time on Saturday?"

"Not yet. Afternoon, probably. I'll let you know. Meanwhile, Davinia, no worrying about your electricity bill, d'you hear me? I'll sort it out for you. And don't worry about the smell, it's always like that after the shop's been closed for a while. Tell them to use more air freshener and they won't notice it."

A heartfelt "Thank you, Reg, that's just what I said" and she meant it. He was an excellent managerial role model and she would follow his example. Unable to smile she began practising a less mobile expression of conciliatory niceness as she opened the rest of the post. She would test it out on her staff later.

"What's the matter with her?" Shelley asked Alex after Davinia had 'just popped in' to check that her Community Service volunteers were alright. "Has someone died? Why's she being nice to us?"

"I have absolutely no idea."

What I do know is that all women are a mystery to me was Alex's next thought but he had learned enough about them to keep that to himself.

On the shop floor, Colin was entranced all over again by the vision that was Davinia asking if he was warm enough and had he had a break? His ingrowing toenail was getting worse and standing for long periods was not helping. He did not like to complain but perhaps a chair, or even just a stool to sit on behind the counter sometimes? Only when it was quiet, of course, he would always stand up to attend a customer - only polite - especially a lady. Mother would expect nothing less of him. When Davinia agreed and said she would look into it he was thrilled. Colin worried that he could smell something unpleasant and wondered whether it was his toe but he never noticed the smell when he was at home. Now he had only to see Barb walk in and his life would be perfect - as long as the toe did not get any worse. It was with a light heart and a tuneless hum that he went about his duties and even when his lanyard became caught in the till drawer, which shut for once, and attached him like a dog being brought to heel on a very short leash, he did not mind.

Chapter Fourteen
Wednesday

Davinia was as good as her word and Colin was overcome. On his arrival at the till the following morning he found a high stool for him to sit on, which was fortunate because he had been kept awake most of the night by the pain from his ingrowing toenail and that musty smell had returned. The stool was perhaps a little too high for the cash desk so that when he sat on it, he towered over the till and had to lean with tense arms at full length on the counter to avoid losing his balance. Davinia said it was an old bar stool which she had had in her kitchen for yonks and no longer used; would it do? Colin thought it was marvellous and developed a way of slumping on it with an impressively bent back so that he looked like an antiquated gnome perched on a plastic and chrome mushroom. At least he could take the weight off his feet, he thought, as they dangled in mid-air, although descending to earth in order to stand and serve was both precarious and painful. To avoid landing too heavily on his sore toe when he descended from the stool, he put the good foot down first then followed with the rest of his body, which dropped heavily to one side so that he looked like the hunchback of Notre Dame with a severely shortened right leg. This continued once he was standing as he put all his weight on his left leg and stood unevenly behind the counter, peering up at the intrigued customers like an inquisitive cat interrupted in the act of washing its privates.

As soon as the shop floor was empty of customers, Colin bellowed for Alex, who came running.

"Colin, what's happened? Are you okay? Is it the till?"

"It's my toe."

"Your toe?"

Alex surveyed the foot that had been thrust before him like a votive offering. For reasons of comfort rather than style, Colin was wearing open toed sandals of vintage origin with a pair of Mother's hand knitted socks, four-ply for warmth and durability. Always mindful of waste and thrift, Mother had constructed them with leftover wool from other, very varied projects and they were resplendent in their striped brightness while their bulk spilled out like muffin top between the straps of the sandals.

"They're wool" Colin said, guiltily, glancing uneasily at the back of the shop. "Don't tell Candy."

"What's the matter with your toe?"

By way of an answer Colin sank to the floor and immediately proceeded to divest the affected foot of its coverings.

"Should we perhaps go somewhere more private?" Alex had no idea what to expect, or, worse, what was about to be exposed.

"I can't leave The Till." Colin was shocked that Alex could even contemplate such a dereliction of duty. Anyway, he had already removed shoe and sock so would have to stay where he was.

"Look."

Alex looked and tried not to inhale because of the smell. He studied the white blob of Colin's foot before him: pulpy, soft and hairy-toed with decayed overlong yellowing nails and the *piece de resistance*, the big toe. It had swollen to almost twice its size and was red with anger, tight skinned, tender, like a chorizo sausage. One side of the toe nail had twisted into the flesh and disappeared, leaving only a sticky wound tinged with infection and inflammation. The sultry aroma of sweat from incarceration in thick wool and the fact that Colin had had the first of his twice weekly baths on Sunday and would not be bathing again until that evening, not only added to the vision but began to permeate the shop floor. It was overwhelming and Alex knew that prompt action had to be taken.

"You've got a severely in-grown toe nail, and possibly a fungal infection, Colin. It looks painful."

The wounded soldier nodded ruefully.

"Well, there's nothing we can do at this precise moment so put your sock back on … that's it, keep it covered. Have you seen your GP?

"GP?"

"Your doctor?"

"I'm seeing you."

"Right… Okay. …Well, you ought really to consult your own doctor or better still, a chiropodist. Obviously, it needs treating."

"A chir o po dist?"

"A special foot doctor."

"Oh! Yes. Mother saw one of those. After she fell off the back of the sofa."

"How did she do that?"

"Getting rid of cobwebs. She lost her balance."

There was a silence. Alex was confounded. Colin was ashen. He looked imploringly up at the surgeon-steamer.

"What's the matter, Colin? What is it that's worrying you?" Alex had seen the signs before: fear of the unknown, uncertainty, panic and the patient's acute awareness of their own mortality.

Colin gazed at him, choking back tears and said in a very small voice,

"Will they have to amputate?"

"No. I think I can safely promise you that no amputation will be necessary."

Now Colin was swallowing his tears, the light of relief in his face.

"Oh, Colin. Is that why you haven't been to see your doctor?"

It was. Alex wanted to pick him up, hug him and call him an idiot. Instead he offered to make him a cup of tea with, yes, three sugars and plenty of milk, just the way he liked it.

Colin slowly sipped the tea, a picture of misery.

"Is there something else?" Alex was troubled. He had never known Colin drink a cup of sweet milky tea without a smile and at least one "Marvellous."

"It's Barb."

"Has something happened?" Alex thought he could guess. Colin's great romance was cause for concern in the shop. None of them much liked Barb. Their dislike was based entirely on first impressions and her physical appearance, which they acknowledged was wrong, but they all mistrusted her and were afraid that Colin would get hurt, have his heart broken or at best, be scammed. Shelley had been particularly vocal on the subject.

"It's all over the internet. Scamming lonely old people, getting money off them. Cat fishing it's called."

Surprisingly, Davinia knew all about it.

"No, it's not cat fishing because he knows the person. She's real and he's met her, not just some distant voice and a photo. Anyway, Colin doesn't use the internet. He doesn't even use the phone."

This was true. However, Shelley was still suspicious.

"Yes, well, she might still be out to rob him. Get his life savings or something."

"Colin?"

"Or his fish."

At which point the conversation had lapsed as Davinia had left to be important and even Shelley had had to admit the weakness of her argument. Her suspicions had remained though, and she told Alex how she feared that Colin was being taken for a ride and would end up a broken man. Looking at him now, Alex rather shared her concern.

"I'm worried that Barb's had an accident or she's ill and no one knows. What if she's fallen and hurt herself? Or she's been abducted? I haven't seen her for ages, not since before Christmas when she left me a present on the doorstep, a mermaid with blonde hair and …"

"Yes, I know." They all knew. Colin had spoken of little else since the shop had reopened and they were all heartily sick of the endlessly bubbling Siren on the rock. "I expect she's just busy" Alex offered. "It's a busy time of year and didn't you say she lives in the Forest of Dean?"

Yes, he did.

"Well then, she probably hasn't been able to get a lift into town, and you know what the buses are like."

Yes, Colin knew all about buses, especially after 9.30 in the morning when he could use his bus pass and at which time all buses seemed to vanish off the face of the earth.

"And the weather's been bad. Terribly wet and cold." It was the last thing Alex could find to say but Colin accepted it with equanimity and began to drink his tea with more enthusiasm. He had been such a silly, hadn't he? Of course, she would be alright, she was marvellous, wasn't she? If anything dreadful had happened he would have heard, wouldn't he? When Alex said, with his fingers crossed behind his back and eyes cast upward on the lookout for the thunderbolt that would strike him down for making false promises, he was sure that Barb would be in touch and probably in the shop before you knew it, Colin was restored to his former gentle, trusting self. Alex hoped to God he was right and that Barb would put in an appearance, even if he had to go and track her down himself. He decided to change the subject.

"Perhaps you should go and see the same chiropodist as your Mother did. If you bring in the contact details tomorrow, I can help you make an appointment if you like?"

Oh yes, please. He would like, very much. But how would he telephone? He could not possibly use the VHS phone for a private call. What would Davinia say? What? He could use Alex's mobile? A mobile phone? Goodness. He had never used such a thing before! …He did not how to work it… Alex would show him how and even put the call through for him? Oh, that was marvellous. Simply marvellous. …Another cup of tea? Yes! Why not?

Under doctor Alex's orders, Colin then tried to walk as little as possible and spent most of the day perched precariously on his bar stool, propped up over the counter, an eagle in his nest atop the heads of the customers. He even found a way of working the till from his lofty elevation, employing the knee of his good leg to prevent the till drawer from escaping. Occasionally Alex would quit his steaming responsibilities and visit the shop floor to check that Colin was alright: tickety boo as Colin called it, and at lunchtime offered to get him something to eat to save him having to limp down the High Street.

"Usually I have a cheese sandwich," Colin explained, "but today I fancy a change. I feel so much better. I shall have a treat!" He thought hard. "One of those meat pies in a tin that are all ready to eat - you just heat them up in the oven. They're marvellous!"

Alex thought he knew what he meant and was about to depart on his mission when accosted by Candy, who had overheard the conversation. How did she do that? Alex wondered, not for the first time, as she asked him to get her an organic apple. The staff rarely saw

Candy; her wherewithal was generally a mystery, she was never there when wanted but would suddenly unexpectedly appear, of her own volition, like a hairier type of lurcher: thin, bony, silent and suddenly there. Then gone again. However, Alex was glad that she was eating and decided to chance his luck. Would she like to sample a vegan sausage roll? Not that she would be abandoning her fruitarian diet of course, but he had been told they tasted very good so perhaps she might like to try one, purely in the interests of research? He would value her opinion.

It worked. She hesitated for the briefest of moments then agreed to help him out. She did know about such things - no one more informed - and although she took issue with the concept of vegan sausage anything - such a contradiction in terms - she would always be happy to help out a friend. As long as he told no one. She wouldn't want anyone to think she had been unfaithful to her Fruitarian principles. Alex was out of the main entrance before she could change her mind or anyone else got wind of his shopping spree which had, by necessity to be swift. They were behind with the steaming and he did not like to leave Shelley alone. The steamer was in a particularly vaporous mood that morning, puffing and blowing with bronchitic eloquence and the enthusiasm of a chain smoker in a tobacco factory.

Candy ate the sausage roll with equal enthusiasm. She said it was unethical, artificial, tasteless and a mass-produced mockery of everything she stood for but, if that was the closest people could come to a proper diet than they could do worse. As she was tipping the crumbs into her mouth from the paper bag in which it had been transported, Alex nodded sagely as he concentrated very hard on the state of the till roll. He and Candy were on watch, guarding the till in Colin's absence as he had sandal-slap-limped off to visit the little boy's room, a meat pie in each hand. Unable to decide exactly what it was that Colin wanted, Alex had erred on the side of caution and bought two, one in a flattish sort of sealed tin and the other in an open foil container. Colin had been delighted with both and had carried them away into the back with reverent awe, suffering from a bad case of option paralysis. He had no idea which one to eat but whatever he decided, he would take the other one home so it was all simply marvellous.

They soon found out which one he had chosen. What could only be described as a spontaneous combustion of pyrotechnics exploded into life at the back of the shop. White light, golden sparks, flashes, whirrs and bangs lit up the shop floor, racing towards the ceiling, exuberantly shooting along the floor, glorious, energetic and unrestrained. An explosion of light and sound, all the more entertaining when all the lights went out and the till died. Even in the murky January daylight the firework display was bright and beautiful, although all too brief. It ended with the surge of power that fused the shop's electrics, to be replaced by screams of outrage from Davinia's office, the door of which opened with astonishing vigour as she hurled herself on her heels out onto the shop floor, screeching,

"What the hell's happened?"

"The electricity's gone off."

"What? Again? How?"

Colin had appeared in the doorway with the answer. He looked somewhat shaken and if not exactly singed, extremely hot and bothered.

"My meat pie caught fire."

Davinia stared. "How?" she asked incredulously.

"In the oven."

"We haven't got an oven."

"Yes, we have. The little one, on the shelf, beside the sink."

"I think he means the microwave" Alex offered. Then, heavy-hearted, he went further,

"Colin. Which pie did you put in there?"

"The one in the tin."

Davinia had heard and seen enough.

"I don't care what happens or what it costs, but we are absolutely not calling the fire brigade. Do you hear me?" And she stumped off towards the fuse box to inspect the damage, to slam switches, to stamp her heels on the long-suffering floor tiles and to curse Colin. On the way there she met Shelley.

"Davinia! The steamer's not working. I think it's died."

It had. Finally, after long years of dutiful service it had pressed its final garment, exhaled its last moist breath, exuded its ultimate burst of steam and closed its rheumy eyes, worn out by over work and neglect. One single protracted gasp of air and it had departed forever, never more to heave and puff and blow. It was a solemn moment: death, the great leveller, that comes to us all.

"Damn and blast. What the hell are we going to do now?" Davinia's lament.

Candy had a solution. "Is this a good time to tell you I'm changing my name?"

Thursday could not come soon enough for Davinia, who was desperate for respite. Never had a day off been so welcome she mused as she luxuriated in bed with tea and her iPad, checking on her eBay account and watching with satisfaction the ongoing activity. The bids were steady rather than spectacular; bread and butter sales rather than the glory of a vintage Liberty scarf but she had no complaints. Really, her high record of sold items against those that remained unsold was most pleasing; she glowed in the validation of her retail expertise and excellent taste.

"It's all about knowing your market" she informed her mug (such an ugly word for such an expensive, elegant bone china cup she thought).

Then she remembered.

"How could she? Candy - or Orange Pippin, as she was now to be called, had completely lost the plot.

In the shop everyone except Orange Pippin was struggling. No one had ever noticed how often the name Candy had been spoken before, but now it seemed to be required all the time and remembering that she was now not Candy, but Orange Pippin, was a challenge. She of the apple nomenclature was refusing to wear her lanyard until it was updated with her new identity but as Davinia was absent, no one cared. With the demise of the steamer Alex and Shelley were enjoying a brief renaissance: civilisation, a cool, dry climate, quietness, time to sort properly and to chat. Neither of them could understand why black bags were still being used to pack and carry clothes and Alex resolved to suggest, again, that they be replaced by hangers on mobile rails. He would have a word with Reg this time - go straight to the top.

Colin was ensconced on his high throne at the till, besocked and besandalled, full of optimism and anticipation. He was very much looking forward to using a Mobile Phone and in moments of quiet, gazed longingly at the doorway through which Alex might appear at any minute. At last the time came and there he was, phone in hand, approaching Colin, who had the number written on a piece of paper, much creased and folded after repeated viewings and being constantly checked for safety in his pocket. He had made a special trip to see Mother in The Home to get the number and could not wait to give her the sequel to the story. Then there would be the appointment itself to look forward to; his toe really was awfully sore but now that his foot was safe, he was no longer worried. There had been a sticky moment when he had arrived in the shop and bumped it against the base of the counter which had hurt, very much. He had nearly said a rude word but shouted "Ouch" very loudly instead. Shelley had appeared in the doorway and asked if his day had got off on the wrong foot? Apparently, it was a joke because she and Alex were laughing so he did too, but he would be glad when the toe was fixed.

It felt very odd talking to the air rather than into a proper telephone receiver but the lady at the other end seemed to hear everything he said. He had told her he was using Alex's mobile phone - not the proper one in the office - so that she would know what to expect. Yes, of course he could make an appointment. When would be convenient? … Tomorrow was his day off? …He was in luck. They had had a cancellation so there was just one slot available, in the late morning. How would that be?

"Marvellous. My toe is very sore."

There had been a short silence at the end of the line before the lady asked,

"Your toe?"

"The big one. I'm wearing socks and sandals to help but it's very red. It doesn't need amputating though. Alex said so, and he's a doctor."

More silence. Then,

"You do know we're a chiropractor's?"

"Oh yes, Alex told me all about it. He said surgeons don't do toes now, they leave it to you."

"Alex is a doctor, you say?"

"Yes, in the hospital."

"A real doctor?"

"Of course. He gives injections and tells people what to do and everything."

"I see. And what does Alex say is wrong with your toe, if you don't mind my asking?"

"Not at all. He says it's an ingrowing toenail and you can put it right without having to cut anything off."

"Well, we certainly wouldn't be cutting anything. A chiropractor uses hands-on spinal manipulation to enable the body to heal itself without surgery or medication."

"Gosh! That's marvellous. And that will fix my toe?"

"I'm afraid not. ...perhaps it is a chiropodist you are looking for?"

At this point Alex signalled to Colin to hand him the phone, and took over the conversation. It did not take long to clear everything up and to ring a chiropodist, whom Alex just happened to know. He agreed to see Colin the following day.

"Happy to help, Alex. Just send him along and we'll sort it out. How's Lisa? … and Dave? …Great. Let's do dinner soon. Our turn."

"Will it hurt?" Colin wanted to know. He had been very taken with the idea that having his back massaged would mend his foot.

"No more than the toe at the moment and he'll give you a local anaesthetic before he treats it, so you won't feel a thing."

Fortunately, a sudden influx of customers distracted Colin from the perplexities of a debate between alternative and traditional medical practices and he turned his attention to something much more topical and pressing - Gift Aid.

Anxious to impress Davinia and to compensate for his recent disasters, Colin had made a momentous decision. He had determined to persuade new customers to sign up for Gift Aid, no matter how difficult or terrifying he found the experience. It broke his heart to think that Davinia was disappointed in him, and he could always ask Can…Orange Pippin or Alex if he got stuck. A family had come into the shop and was enthusing over the prices of the clothes, especially the heavy weight jumpers and winter coats. Or at least that's what Colin thought they were doing; he could not understand what they were saying but they certainly seemed keen and were piling armfuls of clothes onto the two children to hold, while the parents continued looking. The smaller child, a boy of about five, had more or less vanished under his burden and some of the longer garments were starting to trail behind him as he followed the adults around the store. Had his toe permitted, Colin would have gone over and taken the purchases from him to load onto the counter. As it was, he could merely call from the till. He was ignored, so called again, louder. This time the whole family stopped what they were doing, suspended, mid-movement, frozen in fear, and turned to face him.

"Please. We wish to buy."

Colin beamed. "Of course, you do! Marvellous. You can put those things on here if you like?" He patted the surface of the counter invitingly, as if encouraging a shy lover to sit down next to a suitor. The family exchanged glances and tacit agreement landed the responsibility of dealing with the crisis on the elder child, a girl; she who had spoken.

"We are good people. Not thiefs."

Colin nodded vigorously in agreement. The atmosphere cleared with the faces of the customers. Encouraged, the girl became more expansive.

"We like this shop. Very cheap, yes?"

"Oh yes. Very. But very good quality. Davinia insists on it. Nothing but the best she always says."

An interchange between the girl and her parents ensued before she spoke again, this time holding up a pair of lady's shoes.

"We like this shoes."

"Marvellous!"

"They are small. You have the bigger size, please, for Mama?"

"Cand…Orange Pippin!" No reply. Colin tried again. "Alex! … The Till needs you."

Once the confusion had been sorted out and the customers had been made to understand that the goods in the shop were not in fact new, but second-hand, or 'pre-loved' as Alex attempted to explain but then gave up, international relations were resumed. He spoke no Spanish and 'second hand' was comparatively easy to communicate in sign language, however 'pre-loved' was entering territory into which he refused to go. It was all very jolly and Colin enjoyed the banter with the nice foreigners who had come all the way from Spain and were on holiday. They seemed perfect for Gift Aid and, undeterred by the used nature of the goods were happily amassing a substantial sale. They had, apparently, according to gesticulation and action, been caught unawares by the ferocity of the rain and cold temperatures they had encountered and were desperate for warm clothing. While Colin could not imagine why anyone would want a holiday at that time of year it was not up to him to question the wisdom of their decision and he got out the Gift Aid application forms with a feeling of excitement and adventure. He would do this! He would do this and make Davinia proud! Then he would be able to tell Barb all about it and she would be just as proud, if not more, and he began to wonder why he had not taken the plunge before. Ah, the power of love to spur a man on to great things!

There was a slight moment of doubt when the man came to pay. Using the calculator that had magically appeared on the counter after Christmas (Davinia was so thoughtful), Colin had carefully added up the total and entered it into the till. He had intercepted the drawer on its way to freedom, checked that the total in the little window was the same as the one on the calculator and felt like royalty: lord of all he surveyed. Then the man had opened a fat wallet and produced a handful of notes, none of which Colin recognised. Alex said they were Euros which was fascinating, but not legal tender and Colin knew that to accept them would be Against The Law. But it turned out that the man had made a mistake and his daughter took over the transaction, rummaging in the wallet to eventually produce English money so everyone laughed. Colin helped her work out which denominations were required and held up the £50 note with awe. So much money! Alex assumed he was checking it for authenticity but in fact he was just admiring the picture of the Queen and imagining Barb in a tiara. He managed to place the money in the safety of the back of the till drawer without the metal clip biting his fingers and meticulously counted out the change according to the little window. Handed it over. Stuffed the clothes into three carrier bags and decided to forgo the challenge of demanding the small change to pay for them: too exhausting; he would pay for them himself. Then, it was The Moment. Grasping a Gift Aid form Colin thrust it into the man's hand as he babbled out his well-rehearsed sales pitch,

"Do you do Gift Aid? If not, would you like to sign up for it? My name's Colin and I'm a volunteer - look" (here he waved his lanyard proudly at the end of its ribbon so that they could all get a good view of it) " and I like fish and it only takes a minute and we get ever so much more money from the government which makes all the difference to the veterans who need our help who served their country so now we serve them and that's the application form I've given you; you just sign at the bottom - here - and I'll do the rest, or Alex or CandyOrange Pippin will, and Davinia will be so pleased"

Triumph. He had done it!

"Government?" The girl repeated in a low tone, looked aghast and spoke to her father, who gasped,

"El Gobierno?"

He looked terrified and turned to his daughter for assistance. She stared at him, then at Colin, bypassed Alex, shook her head sorrowfully, said something in Spanish and they fled. Fast. Clutching the full carrier bags against their chests they sprinted to the front door, which the father reached first, heroically held open for his family, then slammed behind him as he followed them out and they disappeared at speed along the High Street. Never to be seen again.

Colin was devastated. "What did I do wrong?" he beseeched Alex, who was trying hard not to laugh.

"It might have been the lanyard. I think they got the wrong end of the stick…Colin, why did you ask them if they wanted to be Gift Aiders?"

"They seemed so nice. And I wanted to help Davinia." He sighed. "She's not very happy with me at the moment."

"She's not very happy with any of us. I think it goes with the job."

Colin looked blank, so Alex changed tack.

"You do remember that only UK residents making donations qualify for Gift Aid?"

"Oh no! I forgot! They were buying, weren't they? Not giving?"

"They were… I don't think they were UK residents either, were they?"

Food for thought, which Colin swallowed and digested before answering.

"No" he said slowly. "They weren't English, were they?"

This was getting complicated and Alex began to regret entering Gift Aid territory. He also began to feel some nascent sympathy for Davinia as manageress.

"It's not so much that they weren't English..." he started, then lost his nerve. "They were on holiday, from Spain, wasn't that what they said? So, they couldn't have been living in the United Kingdom - not England, Scotland and Northern Ireland... or even Wales."

Indisputably true. Colin nodded his head gently and regretfully.

"You won't tell Davinia, will you?"

"Not even Orange Pippin."

They giggled, like small boys behind the bicycle sheds eating contraband confectionary. It really was the most absurd name and irresistibly funny, even to Colin. Alex was moved.

"Why don't I put the kettle on? Davinia's out so we can use it as much as we like. Three sugars?"

"Yes please! And plenty of milk!" Colin beamed. He would get it right next time.

It was late afternoon when the door opened and Barb breezed in onto the shop floor, all bracelets and bangles and sporting a new pair of shiny, sharp, high-heeled boots that made the floor tiles wince and cringe.

"Colin! Happy New Year, dear! Did you have a nice Christmas?"

"Barb!" He could say little else, speechless with joy. She was here! Barb! His Barb! Just as beautiful as ever and looking oh, ever so smart. Made him feel quite shabby by comparison even though he was in his second-best sweater with the multi-coloured diamond shapes that had nearly made Mother go boss-eyed when she had been knitting it. But then he remembered that he was wearing a proper shirt underneath, with a collar, and cuffs that he could unbutton and roll up to display his tattoo - the manifestation of his love for now and all eternity, just like it said in Mother's magazines.

No matter, Barb could speak for both of them and many more besides.

"How did you like your present? Was she what you expected?" Here a coy glance and arched eyebrow above a slowly squeezed eye which passed for a wink, that sent Colin's heart racing. "Bet that was surprise, eh? Finding her on your doorstep!" Barb laughed heartily and her bangles shook merrily in time with the flesh around her neck, which shivered and wobbled as if it had an advanced case of palsy. Colin was entranced; her hair was even more golden than before which was amazing and made her look like an angel; her nails were shiny like her boots and almost the same shade of red, while her eyelids glimmered blue and flickered under the unforgiving shop lights. She was wearing an elegant skirt, tight and narrow and very business-like which, goodness, showed her knees, which were soft and dimpled. Colin was embarrassed and having involuntarily located them, carefully averted his chaste gaze to higher up her person but then found himself in potentially even more perilous waters. He pulled himself together and focused on the safety of her right shoulder, swathed in fur.

"You're admiring my jacket, aren't you, naughty boy?... Father Christmas brought it for me. He's got good taste, don't you think? It's not real fur of course; no one wears real fur any more but this is just as good and not so expensive but you'd never know, would you? I like the shorter length best - shows off my new skirt and boots. Aren't they lovely? Bit tight over the toes but I do like the pointy ends, don't you? Ever so fashionable and flattering."

The floor tiles had a different view but Colin was overwhelmed with admiration and showed it. Barb was delighted.

"I just knew you'd like them" she cooed. "Now, how about a nice cup of tea and a piece of cake? Naughty but nice! We've got so much to talk about and catch up on. You won't mind taking over, will you?" This was addressed to Alex, who was on the shop floor, as was Shelley, but Barb ignored her.

Since they could no longer steam and because it was Davinia's day off, both the Community Servicers had thrown caution to the winds and ventured out into the public domain. Shelley was 'sorting the books' which meant replenishing Corpy's library and reading whatever caught her fancy, while Alex wandered about, ostensibly checking for stock that had gone past its sell by date but in reality, keeping an eye on Colin least he attempted further ambitious plans to impress Davinia.

Love's aging dream departed together, in a flurry of piercing heels and bouncing bracelets, Colin majestically holding open the door for his lady love through which she sailed like an overloaded container ship, leaving only a slick of cheap scent in their wake.

"Wow!" Shelley said, as their senses were assaulted by the perfumed

Exocet. "I hope he's safe."

"Afternoon all! How's tricks? When the cat's away, eh…?"

It was Reg. He had arrived via the back entrance, unseen and unexpected, let himself in and had a wander around, he said, just to check that everything was hunky dory and was now coming to have a chat with the staff.

"Where's Candy?" he enquired, hand on groin.

"You mean Orange Pippin?" Shelley suggested.

"Who?"

"She's changed her name. From Candy to Orange Pippin."

"What kinda name is that?" Reg could not help himself and rubbed his groin animatedly as he exhaled his coffee/cigarette breath with alacrity where it clashed and fought with Barb's scent.

"It's her new identity. As a Born-Again Fruitarian."

"Bloody fruit loop if you ask me…So where is she, Orange Blossom or Apple Juice or whatever she calls herself?"

Neither Alex or Shelley had any idea and Reg knew better than to pursue the subject. "You'll have to do then" he said, offending them both. "How's it going?"

It was going fine, thank you. Takings were steady and there had been an increase in donations.

"Always happens after Christmas" Reg told them. "People sorting out their crap. After they've been stuck in the house together for two weeks, they get restless and decide to redecorate or move or get divorced. Highest divorce rate is just after Christmas. Very good for business, divorce: lots of donations, then people come in wanting to buy back all the stuff they've just given away for their new homes. Big bunce for us. Any more fires? Exotic animals?"

No, it had been very quiet and uneventful, thank you. Nor had the emergency services been required. Neither of them mentioned the microwave incident but Alex did report thc untimcly dcath of the steamer.

"Hm. That's a pity. It'll need replacing but I'm not surprised, it's been on the way out for years. Expensive though. I'll have to take it to Head Office…I'll call in again when Davinia's here. This is just a social visit. I was in the area and thought I'd drop in; wish you a Happy New Year and all that. Now that that's done, I'll be on my way…"

Before you go, can I make a suggestion?" It was Alex. Reg was astonished. He did not normally entertain the possibility of suggestions from enforced volunteers serving their time in the community but Alex seemed a sensible sort of chap and did not conform to the usual profile of a petty criminal. Reg decided to hear him out. When Alex had finished, he put his hands into his trouser pockets and ruminatively fiddled with the contents.

"Well …" he searched his memory, "…Alex. It's an interesting idea but not appropriate for our *modus operandi*, if you get my drift." He did, which forced Reg to rapidly reassess his level of condescension. "While using hangers to transport garments might work between a few closely located outlets, it's not appropriate for our wider operation. We don't have the equipment or transport available to implement such a policy nationwide and the financial outlay required to fund such a venture would exceed any logistical advantage it might provide. While you might consider our current system of bagging and unpacking cumbersome and inefficient, it's been proved to be the most cost effective and reliable means of moving our goods between shops. However, it's a most interesting idea … and I'll certainly give it more thought and pass it on to Head Office. Your contribution to the improvement of our working practices is appreciated and does you credit. I'll be sure to let Davinia know. And if you have any more suggestions, do please share them with us. Thank you. Now…" he leant over to consult the watch on the wrist of one jiggling hand, "I must be gone. I'll be in again on Saturday."

"What time?" Shelley asked, "So that we can let Davinia know."

Cheeky baggage Reg was thinking to himself as he smiled and answered. "Mid to late afternoon. About 4.00 pm. I'll see myself out." And he was gone, in a fog of coffee and nicotine, hands in pockets. They heard him head to the back door and then a thump as it thudded to a close.

Chapter Fifteen
Nemesis Wears A Scarf

Saturday arrived, as it always does, with all the expectation and elation of the first day of the weekend when time seems long and possibilities endless. Davinia was refreshed and recharged. A day of valuable me-time followed by a Colin-free one certainly rejuvenated her spirits, as well as her complexion. Stress was so aging but the Botox was working well, she had noticed with repeated satisfaction, as she made her daily final examination in the hall mirror before launching herself on the world. Best face forward. It was a nuisance about the steamer but she had emailed Head Office who had said that Reg was on the case and that a replacement was already being sourced. He would tell her more when she next saw him, which she was expecting to do that afternoon. It was essential to get something in place as soon as possible if they were to maintain their high standard of merchandise and also, she did not want Alex, and especially Shelley, at a loose end. Or on the shop floor if she could possibly help it. He was okay but not her, the ink-stained barbarian.

"Looks just what she is" Davinia snorted derisively to herself as she drove to the shop "common little tart."

Additionally, there had been a surge in donations: always exciting, not least because of her potential eBay sales. She was also looking forward to expanding her wardrobe and was even considering skirts now that she had shed a few pounds. How satisfying it was to run her hands down her body these days, contained and contorted even more by shapewear, which although pricey, was worth every penny. Yes, she was looking forward to the day and she was smiling as she let herself in the back door, even though her face was a mask.

Shelley was also looking forward to the day but for an altogether different reason. So was Lisa, but Alex knew nothing about that. He had been surprised when she had quizzed him about Reg's visit and had seemed unusually interested in the time of his expected return. But then Dave had thrown up, spectacularly, so they had both been distracted and the subject was dropped. Dave was fine. He had eaten the best part of a rotting frog on his walk which now put in an unscheduled appearance on the kitchen tiles. Once the corpse was out of his system Dave never looked back, but Alex had spent a large part of the previous evening assiduously scrubbing the floor while Lisa nursed and soothed, then prepared a nourishing, easily-digested scrambled egg for the eminently cheerful invalid.

Colin too, was in high spirits. The visit to the chiropodist had been marvellous. Armed with Alex's written directions he had found it easily enough and there had even been a bus which took him almost to the door, and he had not waited more than ten minutes before it had arrived at the bus stop. And it wasn't even raining but it wouldn't have mattered because the bus shelter had been repaired and had a roof again. He could not understand how 'youths' broke so many bus stops; they must have been waiting a very long time for buses to cause so much damage. Anyway, he had gone into the chiropodist's and the lady at the desk knew who he was and the chiropodist was a lovely man who knew Alex and said he was delighted to meet any of Alex's friends, which made him feel very comfortable so that when he had the injection for the pain in his toe, he wasn't in the least bit worried. And apart from the stinging of the anaesthetic, it was marvellous because the toe stopped hurting and when the man started cutting into it, he didn't feel a thing. Honestly! Not a thing! Then all this green stuff came out and started mixing with his red blood, turning it a very strange colour. At that point he had felt a bit sick; it hadn't felt nice when it welled up in his throat but he had managed to swallow it down again. The chiropodist said it was very infected and he had to take tablets for a whole week to make sure his toe got better. Look - a whole packet of them! Three a day for seven days and he had to be sure to take them all, every single one, or the toe might get nasty again. Anyway, when he had got rid of the green stuff, the chiropodist started to make a big hole and chop away at the edge of his toenail …At which point Davinia, Alex, Shelley and Orange Pippin all, to a body, curtailed his description of His Visit to the Chiropodist and no matter how hard he pursued the subject throughout the day, absolutely refused to let him continue. Never mind, he consoled himself. At least he had shown them his bandaged digit. He was still wearing socks and sandals and perched on his high stool, but earthly descent was getting easier and walking, although cumbersome, was a lot less painful. It was disappointing that Davinia had forbidden him to discuss his condition with customers, with no exceptions, but there would be plenty to tell Mother and of course, Barb, who would want to know every detail.

Reg's arrival was prompt and discreet. The first those on the shop floor knew of it was when Shelley presented herself furtively in the doorway and hissed

"He's in with Davinia." Neither Colin or Alex knew what she was talking about until a moment later, when the duo appeared in the doorway behind Shelley, who had not seen them. Alex tried to warn her, opened his eyes wide in a frantic 'It's behind you' kind of expression but failed to raise the signal in time. Shelley was busted: tattoos, short skirt, tights and Doc Martens, all caught red handed on display to the public. Whether it was the effect of the Botox or the presence of Reg, Davinia was magnificently restrained in her response to this most recent outrage.

"Shelley! I did not expect to see you here. Have you finished all that ironing already? Goodness! I shall have to find more for you to do at this rate! Can't have you getting bored, can we?"

There was a sudden chill in the air. Even Reg noticed. Colin was absorbed in the machinations of changing a till roll, the latest of his Herculean labours to please the lovely Davinia and remained oblivious, but Alex felt his stomach drop into his pelvis, heavy with foreboding. Nothing good would come of this.

He was right. What he had not anticipated however, was the arrival of reinforcements or, more precisely, one reinforcement, but a power to be reckoned with nevertheless. Lisa opened the door and walked into the shop. She was dressed for the weather, wrapped up against the cold and the enemy in snow boots for stability and a lightweight puffa coat for a quick getaway. No hat, and the gloves were off, but around her neck she had ostentatiously draped the vintage silk Liberty scarf she had bought on eBay. From Davinia. Who recognised it. Alex was appalled but helpless. He was not a cowardly man and knew he possessed the emotional and physical strength to conduct arduous surgical procedures back to back, but this was different. This was brutal; naked warfare. He reckoned Davinia's chances quite high on her own against Shelley, but the combined forces of Shelley and Lisa made him tremble. He ignored Colin's plea for help with the till roll and stood, immobile, transfixed behind the protective barrier of the counter. Lisa completely ignored him but smiled amicably at Colin before striding nonchalantly up to Shelley, with whom she stood, shoulder to shoulder.

Alex braced himself. Colin smelt the fear in the air and suspended his act of devotion in mid-air, to stand firm beside his friend. Reg stopped rubbing his groin, mid-motion and froze. Davinia stepped forward, a single pace. Lisa and Shelley stood firm.

Silence. Then, Lisa broke ranks.

"Dave's Slave" she said, holding out her hand by way of greeting to Davinia. "You must be…?"

"Queen Dee" Shelley answered, before Davinia could speak.

"Who?" said Reg. "Is everyone changing their name?"

"That looks like Mother's scarf!" announced Colin, pointing at Lisa's neck. "Well I never!"

Alex kept quiet but resigned himself to the inevitable; swift and painless was the best that could be hoped for.

"Davinia will explain." Shelley said, swinging the axe.

They all looked at Davinia, who said nothing, but whose gaze was fixed on Lisa's neck.

"What's going on?"

A voice from the recesses, the unknown. It was Orange Pippin, who had chosen that moment to reveal herself and wafted into the midst of the assembled company like a wandering spirit.

"Who's Queen Dee?" she asked.

"I am." Thus, spake Davinia, standing steady in the face of the artillery, impassive. "That's my eBay name."

"EBay?" Reg hissed.

"EBay." Shelley said.

"What's that?" Colin aimed his question at Alex but it was generally received and everyone waited for Davinia to reply. She took the hint.

"Online trading, Colin. I sell, and people buy, like in an auction."

"But it's what they buy and you sell that's so intriguing, isn't it, Dee?" Shelley, all gentle smiles and bonhomie; serpentine, deadly.

"It had better not be" Reg hissed again, horribly suspicious.

At this point Lisa made a tactical move designed to bring the enemy out into the open. She stepped forward, unwound the scarf from her neck and held it up, stretched out taut and straight between both arms for all the shop to see. Colin gasped.

"It is Mother's scarf! I knew it was! It's the one I brought for a donation. It's ever so old and Mother has so many, she hardly ever wears them so we had a sort out and she gave it to me for the veterans. There was a cardigan as well. Have you got that too?"

Davinia ignored Colin and continued; he might as well have been a golf sweater on a hanger for all the attention she took of him. It was his words she addressed.

"Yes, it was a donation. Which I sold and you…" a shot, at blank range, aimed at Lisa, "must have bought." Then, defiantly, "But how can you be so sure I didn't pay for it? I might have put the money in the till?"

"Did you?" Shelley fired back. "Villain, smiling damned villain" she muttered.

Davinia did not speak; she did not have to. Even Botox could not conceal heightened colour and guilt leaking from the eyes.

Dave's Slave nodded grimly - a direct hit - and Shelley charged in from her flank to follow up the advantage but was intercepted by Queen Dee, whose retaliation demonstrated exemplary military precision. Attack to defend. Pick out the weaknesses in the enemy: target the unarmed behind the lines; use sarcasm to soften, then hit them hard.

"Very clever. A set up, of course? Orchestrated by you and her…" she had half turned to Shelley, whom she stabbed with a stiletto glance …"to catch me out, I suppose? Were you in on this?" Now she had turned to face Alex, full on, and he was exposed: alone. Stranded in the cross fire across a desolate no man's land, helpless, a male caught between battling women. He knew everything depended on his answer: survival, marital harmony, companionship at work, his Community Service reports.

"Think" he told himself. "Choose your words carefully, Alex, or you're done for and there'll be no coming back from this."

Suddenly another voice was heard and Alex was saved. It was Reg, he of the bad breath and greasy hair with a hand on his groin, who had come to the rescue and Alex wanted to hug him.

"It doesn't matter who was in on it, Davinia, it's the fact that you've done it. Not for the first time, am I right?"

He was.

"You do realise how serious this is?"

Yes. Oh yes, she was only too well aware.

"Taking away from those who already have next to nothing" Shelley said, quietly, but Davinia blushed as she remembered every word of the conversation she had had with the customer who had been so keen to get a discount.

"Who exactly are you?" Davinia asked Lisa, staging a desperate comeback. Lisa smiled and said nothing. Alex looked at the floor and Colin piped up, helpful as always.

"You're the lady with the dog that frightened Anna! I knew I'd seen you before. But I still don't understand. How did you get Mother's scarf? How could you buy it from…Fleabay?" he stumbled.

"E Bay" Shelley pointed out.

"Davinia stole it from here and sold it online. Then she kept the proceeds for herself, isn't that right?" This was Orange Pippin's contribution to the battle that was now beginning to lose momentum as the Scarf claimed victory and shimmied in triumph between Lisa's outstretched hands. Then, as after every bloody encounter, the field had to be cleared. Reg took command.

"Close the shop! We've all had enough for one day. Colin and Alex, you tidy the shop floor. Candy …" Orange Pippin was about to correct him but jumped ship, "…cash up. Ladies…" he spat out the word, "…Come with me. I'm going to get to the bottom of this. The rest of you can go when you've finished. I'll lock up." Alex watched in awe as the three women followed Reg meekly to the office. You had to hand to Reg, he had crowd control.

Colin and Alex left the shop together. Both were uneasy. Alex felt he should wait for Lisa but had no idea how long the interrogation was going to last. More importantly, or was that cowardly? he asked himself, he would prefer his connection with Dave's Slave to remain undetected, certainly for the moment. He had his Community Service report to think of. Besides, Lisa and Shelley had hatched this scheme between them; he would like to have felt hurt at being excluded but was actually vastly relieved which made him decide he was a not so much coward as a lucky escapee. So, he went home, alone, to confide in Dave.

Colin was hobbling painfully in the opposite direction towards the bus station. He was confused. How could Davinia have done such a thing? He would happily have given her the scarf and lots more if she had asked; Mother would have been proud to know such a smart lady wanted her things. And what had happened to the cardigan? As he was limping along the street, he resolved not to tell anyone, especially Mother, what had happened. He admired Davinia so much. It was all probably just a horrible misunderstanding, like the time he had switched the shop's energy supplier. How had he been to know? The man came in and was ever so friendly so that when he asked if Colin would like to save £350 a year, of course he said yes; all he had to do was sign the form the man gave him and he would see the savings almost at once. His pension had not increased so he was not sure how the money would be paid to him, but he was looking forward to it and had planned to take Mother to Aquarium World by taxi. Then Davinia had found out when a chap came to fit something called a smart meter and she had been ever so cross, but did not blame him in the end and said it could have happened to anyone.

His toe was throbbing, persistent and determined to be as sore as possible, so he stopped for a moment outside the furniture shop. The bedroom scene looked very inviting, which made him blush until his face was as hot and red as his bandaged digit. To his discomfort, the bed made him think of Barb which was shocking but vaguely exciting and he felt his chest tighten. That seemed to make the toe throb even worse so he shifted his balance a little more onto the other foot and rested against the shop window, which was cold and comforting. He had had no idea that Love could be so heating. He knew that emotions rose and turned into Passions, but had not anticipated the same for body temperatures. On recovering his equanimity, he decided to shortcut to a bus stop where he might have to wait, but at least he could sit on one of those narrow seat things that folded out to lean against, so that you felt that you were sitting, but in fact, you were standing as well. So clever. He levered himself away from the shop window, turned into the alley behind the shop where the bins were kept, and saw It. A vision. Just beside the bins. Glorious, heavenly, holy, in full colour, as much like the real thing as was humanly possible: Barb. It could almost have been her! And when the vision clattered its high heeled red boots on the cracked tarmac of the uneven road exuding a delicious, familiar scent, he realised that it was her. But how? It was unbelievable. It was a miracle! Barb, the only thing his heart desired, there, in front of him, almost as if he had wished her to happen and lo and behold, there she was.

"Barb!"

The vision, strangely substantial and plump, faltered for a moment.

"Barb! It's me! Colin!"

Then it began to move, slowly at first being somewhat handicapped by a tight pencil skirt but once this was hitched up above the knees and stretched over ample thighs, the movement became more swift and the heels clacked purposefully towards the back entrance of the shop which was opened, and then the vision was gone. Disappeared! Dematerialised, vanished; it had melted through the doorway. Had he imagined it? Perhaps it was the tablets from the chiropodist, making him see things? But what if he wasn't? What if it really had been Barb? He had to know. Abandoning all thoughts of buses, pain, cheese waiting for him in the fridge at home, the bubbling mermaid on her cosy rock, he accelerated his open toed sandals in the direction of the shop and slap-limped to the back door.

It was solid enough, firmly closed, mundane and ordinary. But it was unlocked, which was odd and Colin was surprised but not deterred. What if Barb was in there but in trouble? In distress? She might have been sending him a message, an SOS (he had heard about such things and seen it on the TV) and Love had made him see it. Smell it. Hear it. Pushing the door open he did not even feel frightened, although he yelped when he caught his toe against the step and hopped onto the premises.

It was dark. All the lights had been turned off and it was difficult to see. It was also very, very quiet: almost silent. He could hear, or thought he could hear, a faint, constant hum, like a murmur, whispering spirits from another time speaking in vibrations. The discussion in the office was obviously over and there was no sign of Davinia, Shelley or the other lady, the one with the dog. Reg must be somewhere about because the door had not been locked and if Reg had said he would lock up, he most definitely would. He was the Regional Manager! Was more important even than Davinia. As Colin's eyes became more accustomed to the gloom and he moved lopsidedly further into the shop, he became aware of a greenish glow, bright but suffused, creeping furtively out from beneath the door to the cellar like an ill-concealed smirk.

Colin never hesitated; he leant on his good foot and tried the cellar door which opened at once. He was bathed in green light and the hum was now almost song, a wordless tune in his ear. He seemed to be enveloped in light and sound and smell, lured in, impossible to resist, like the call of the little mermaid on her rock.

"Barb? Barb, are you there?"

No reply. Colin tried again, louder.

"Barb!"

Only the humming answered, persistent and prolonged, never even pausing for breath while the green light beckoned. No other choice, Colin barely thought, as he went through the doorway and stood at the top of the steps leading down into the cellar. He peered into the watery translucence and remembered the long-ago story of the Wizard of Oz he had been told as a child. And now here he was, in it, standing on the threshold of the Emerald City but he was on his own. Why wasn't he frightened? Shouldn't he be terrified? But he wasn't and that could only be because he had to save Barb who was down there, somewhere. He stepped forward and turned clumsily on his good foot to push the door fully open but slipped, hit his toe on the door frame and howled with pain. The door swung back into place just as he had extracted his sore foot and he began to sweat. Suppose he had got it caught in the door? So engrossed was he with his narrow escape that he failed to notice that his lanyard, his precious lanyard, had caught itself on the door latch as it had swung shut. The door had locked itself; he was on the wrong side of it and he was also tethered to its handle, penned like an animal in an abattoir. Added to which his toe was agony. Now he began to panic. He called, he shouted with as much volume as his restricted neck would permit but nothing happened; no one heard. He shouted again, then listened. Nothing but humming, humming, humming. Then he heard what he dreaded most: the muffled sound of a door closing outside the cellar and he knew that Reg had indeed locked up and gone home.

But where was Barb? He had to find her, but how? How could he free himself from his ribbon chain? Leaning against the door as much as he could to enable himself to breathe, and to avoid strangulation, he concentrated. What would the little mermaid do? Or Alex?

Twenty minutes later, still concentrating and trying not to imagine what would happen to him if he was imprisoned for ever in the green singing cellar, he realised how uncomfortable he was, semi-perched against the door, neither standing nor sitting. His knees were hurting and the pressure on his toe was horrible so he eased himself a little further down into a crouching position, back still against the door and edged towards the floor. The lanyard was pulling on his neck, most uncomfortably, so he stood upright and lifted it off over his head. Then he could sit down unimpeded and felt, oh so much better. Only when he was sitting on the top step, leaning against the door for support as he rubbed his sore foot, did he realise that he had untied himself.

Descending into the cellar was easy but he went very carefully; he did not want to fall, or bump his toe but he was becoming accustomed to the green watery light and no longer heard the humming which seemed to have become part of his own mind. As he descended and peered ahead, he was astonished. It was very warm, which was unexpected, and the floor was covered in plants - hundreds of them, growing tall and vigorously into the light above, as if engaged in a race to be the first to touch the ceiling. The further he ventured into the room the more he found, some smaller and less well developed than their colleagues but clearly all from the same family. They were housed comfortably in pots, one apiece, packed snugly in rows the length and width of the cellar. There was no sign of the black bags of summer clothes that should have been there and it was not until he had limped his way right to the back of the long room that he found them, piled high against the back wall. Nor was there any sign of Barb's boxes of tropical fish equipment. It was like being in an underground greenhouse he thought, and was glad it was so warm. He slap-limped his way back through the foliage the way he had come, carefully watching his step; he did not want to damage the plants or bump his toe against any of the pots – there were so many of them. It was like threading a seam through a never-ending curtain, smelly, green and soft, which tickled and caressed his face.

He found his way back to the foot of the steps and sat down, easing the sore toe out in front of him at the end of a straight leg which he examined ruefully. The socks at the end of it were looking grubby and baggy; they needed washing and he wondered if he should take them off. It was also warm, very warm indeed, so he made a courageous and daring decision, and removed his sweater while leaving the socks in place, to protect his feet and because the musty smell was very strong. He folded the sweater, just like Mother had always said he should and placed it reverently at the side of the step. And that was when he saw it. A fur jacket - not real fur because no one wore real fur anymore, but the one that Father Christmas had brought Barb and which made her look like a film star. The one she had been wearing when he had seen her earlier in the week. He picked it up and buried his face into it for comfort. It smelled of Barb, of her perfume and something else he could not identify but which was sweet and soothing.

But where was Barb? She had been here; she must have been – he held the evidence in his hands. But where was she now?

Then he recalled that he was locked in. He began to cry.

Chapter Sixteen
On the Sabbath Day

Corpy and Troop had had a disturbed night. It was extremely cold, the temperature had fallen below freezing and keeping warm in a doorway in such conditions was at best, challenging and at worst, impossible. Sleep was out of the question; it was simply too cold and no matter how much cardboard you had beneath your sleeping bag, the cold permeated everywhere, got into your bones, froze your blood, made it hurt to breathe and paralysed your extremities which would not work, could not curl into warmth and began to freeze your body from the digits to the marrow. Getting up and moving around while wearing your sleeping bag was the only option: a macabre sack race where first prize was survival and the wooden spoon, death by hypothermia. Even Troop shivered and shook so that Corpy abandoned all pretence of discipline and tried to squeeze him inside the sleeping bag with him. It would have worked if Troop had backed in, but he burrowed down head-first and then attempted to turn around so that his head was up against Corpy's chest; a dog liked to have his nose in the air, even if it was freezing. After squirming like two larvae trying to shed the same cocoon, they abandoned the attempt and Corpy wrapped them both in their blanket; he was swaddled in all the clothes he possessed inside the sleeping bag, with Troop recumbent on his lap. They looked like a pieta, Native American style. Thus, they managed to doze until the early hours but then the cold became too much and they had to get up and move. Their lives depended on it.

"C'mon Troop. We'll go round the back into town. The lads'll have a brazier under the railway bridge which'll keep us warm. We'll put the gear by the bins. Might even get a cup of tea if we're lucky."

The street was deserted under the orange glow of the street lamps, silvery stone in the settling frost. As they turned into bin alley the light faded and became a glow in the past as they moved slowly along the unlit narrow lane, the bins their only companions. It should have been quiet and peaceful: dark, undisturbed, so the singing bouncing off the walls and rebounding against the road was a surprise. Not tuneful or melodic or gentle in the still night but raucous and lusty, interrupted by hysterical prolonged laughter. Someone was singing a sea shanty, *My Bonnie Lies Over the Ocean,* except that the name Bonnie had been charged to Barbie. But where was it coming from? Apart from Corpy and Troop the alley was empty, except for the bins and clearly it could not be them. Corpy toyed with the idea of inspecting their contents lest some inebriated naval rating on leave had taken up residence but that was absurd; there simply was not enough room. Had they been industrial bins … His attention was diverted by Troop who was sniffing furiously beyond the bins, making his tail-wagging-way devotedly towards the back entrance of the Veteran's Help shop. Nose to ground he was darting and twisting, following who knew what scent? but his trail was lop sided and uneven. Only when it stopped at the doorstep did Troop look up, plainly signalling that the door had to be opened and the search continued within. And all the time the singing persisted, high volume, cacophonous, a joyous, solo, unaccompanied male voice blasting to the heavens.

Well, obviously whoever it was, was not in distress, but surely, they should not be inhabiting the VHS shop over a Saturday night? The music aficionado was locked in and ought to be let out, but how? Corpy and Troop mulled over the problem for just a few minutes before a decision was reached. It was Corpy's idea and Troop whole-tail-waggedly agreed. Involving the police was not an option; Corpy lived on the street and Troop was a stray; neither wanted to take on the authorities. No, they would have to resort to plan B: Alex. There was no one else. Deep down inside his kit bag, somewhere, was the folded piece of A4 with Alex's contact details. Corpy knew it was there;

now he just had to find it and the darkness did not help. In the end he hoisted the whole bag onto his shoulder and they returned to the well-lit street at the front of the shop, where the singing could barely be heard. Yes, there it was. Right at the bottom - sod's law - but the paper, though much folded and rather grubby had the information that they needed. 'Phone number wasn't much good, but they could find the house easily enough.

"It's a bit of a walk, Troop, but it'll keep us warm. Nothing better to do, eh?"

A long trudge later, vagrant and stray stood awkwardly in the sedate tree-lined avenue where the Whiteleys lived. Lit up by the eminently respectable street lamps condescending their light upon such an unsavoury sight - thank goodness it was dark! - Corpy and Troop appeared small, scruffy and insignificant, marked more by the vapour of their warm breath against the cold air than their presence. They were standing under the shelter of a smug imposing tree, substantial, established, reeking of ownership, inspecting the houses opposite, one of which was Alex's. But which one? Squinting at the address on the piece of paper in the half-light, they crossed the Rubicon and began peering at the numbers on the gateposts. Or the names, which was confusing. Why did people give their houses a name? They still had to put the number on the address. After shaking his head in disbelief at Bobannas and sniggering about the kind of person that might inhabit Rivendell, Corpy found what he was looking for. A bay-windowed Tudorbethan statement of respectability, with its original 1930s leaded windows, much repaired, and a solid oak front door. Quite the period piece sitting self-righteously behind a sturdy wall and wide gate, firmly shut but not locked. Man and dog inhaled determinedly together, stepped forward and undid the gate which opened easily, well oiled; quite friendly really. The pea gravel drive was short but a little intimidating the way it crunched under Corpy's heavy boots and he walked as lightly as possible, willing himself into lightness and walking inelegantly on the steel tipped toes. But it did not seem to matter. The house was asleep, eyes closed, expressionless. Even the fake black beams seemed to be snoozing, leaning against the white stucco walls and ornate brickwork. They walked up to the arched porch and eyed the boot scraper at one side with suspicion. Troop would have liked to growl. Ignoring the pert little bell hanging jauntily from an iron arm just waiting to dance into action and disturb anyone that would listen, or not want to listen, Corpy looked at Troop who agreed, and softly tapped a gloved knuckle on the slumbering wood.

"Alex! Wake up. I think there's someone at the front door.!

"Dontberidiculous. It's…" he opened one eye and eventually focussed on the digital alarm clock beside the bed, "six o'clock on a Sunday morning. I'm not on call. Go back to sleep."

"But I heard something!"

"You're imagining it. Dave's not awake, is he? He'd have barked if there was someone there."

He should have done, he knew it, but Dave was not taking any chances. Six o'clock in the morning, pitch black outside, freezing cold. No dog in his right mind would bark and get out of basket for anything less than a full-scale armed robbery. A soft tap at the front door was of no interest or importance. Maybe, if it persisted, he would change his mind.

Damn. There it was again and this time Alex had heard it so Dave knew the game was up and he'd have to react. He leapt off his cushion on the floor beside the two-legged ones and hurled himself at them, still prone in their bed, barking ferociously. If he had to get up and make a noise, he was jolly well going to make them do it too. Might be a biscuit in it if he played his cards right. Lisa had huddled under the duvet but Alex was up and saying lots of those shouty words that he was always being told off about; Dave, like any self-respecting canine took no notice and barked even louder as he followed the Tall One down the stairs to the front door. The Shorter One had stayed in bed which made the Tall One even more grumpy and mutter about something called 'so much for bloody equality' but Dave had heard it all before and was curious to find out what lay on the other side of the door.

He was delighted to see Troop. What an unexpected pleasure! The two dogs sniffed each other's rear ends amiably and wagged their tails on finding each other in good health and high spirits. The two-legged ones seemed less comfortable however, although Dave's person had stopped saying shouty things and had invited Troop's person in, out of the cold, to "tell him all about it." In the kitchen, which was deliciously warm, Troop fully relaxed and stretched out on Dave's downstairs bed as if he owned it, totally ignoring Dave's warning growl. Troop only had to throw him a look to remind him of canine social etiquette: guests get the beds, all food is shared, including table scraps and two-legged ones are their dog's responsibility at all times.

By now Lisa, in dressing gown and slippers, had joined the happy throng and they were discussing the dilemma over mugs of tea.

"Who is it?" Lisa asked. "How did they get there?"

"No idea" Corpy replied, "but they can't sing."

"We'll have to let them out" Alex mused, "But how are we going to get in? We haven't got a key."

"Davinia?" Even as she said it, Lisa knew it was a bad idea.

"No!" Corpy and Alex said together.

"I've got a mate who might be able to help" Corpy suggested. "I think I know where he'll be."

"In town?"

"Yeah. Under the railway bridge, by the fire."

"Right. I'll get dressed, then we'll go and find him. We'll take the car" Alex added, remembering that it was below zero outside, that Corpy and Troop had walked for the best part of two hours to find him. Also, they had no idea what they might find at the Vet's Help shop when they got there, so they might be glad of the means of a quick getaway.

"You stay here" he told Lisa. "We'll all want a hot breakfast when we get back, won't we Corpy?" And maybe a hot bath and a change of clothes and at least one day out of the cold he thought, even if the veteran insisted on leaving later. Corpy did not look too sure but Troop liked the idea of breakfast immensely. No bath for him though, under any circumstances.

There was a moment of hesitation outside the car. Troop was reluctant to get in, not after his last ride in one of those things. He was not going through all that again. However, Corpy was with him so that made it okay and he leapt up into the back seat which was leather and odorous but not unpleasant, although his claws skated on the surface and it felt like sliding on ice. No way was he going in the back though, behind that grid thing, no matter how much the two-legged one might love his top of the range Land Rover Discovery. He was telling Corpy all about it, who seemed to be really interested, and was agreeing that the charcoal oak veneer dashboard was stylish without being over the top. Troop shook his head and flapped his ears. He would have stroked his beard in disdainful contemplation if he could.

It took barely fifteen warm, comfortable minutes to reach the centre of town where Corpy took charge of the directions and Alex followed, silently, wondering just what he was getting into. They were now driving in a part of the city that was unknown to him and almost everyone who did not live on the streets, especially at night. He was surprised how populated it was in a discreet, quiet way. Everyone on foot if they were moving, many just unidentifiable shapes and heaps in doorways, all of them cold. As they approached the station not from the main thoroughfare but a dark, narrow, slimy back street, barely wide enough for the car, Corpy told him to stop and wait.

"Troop and I'll go from here. The lads don't like strangers." Then they were gone and Alex was left sitting in the dying warmth of the opulent car with its engine cut off, in the middle of another world. He wondered if he should lock the doors, then felt ashamed and sat in silence.

It felt like an extremely cold eternity and getting worse before Corpy reappeared. With him was a shapeless figure festooned in indiscriminate layers of clothing in an attempt to stave off frostbite and a filthy deer stalker hat of dubious vintage, flaps down over the ears and brim low over his eyes, assuming that he had some. It was hard to tell.

"This is Fingers. He's come to help."

Don't ask the look said as Alex watched him get into the back seat with Troop. So, he didn't, just started up he engine and headed up the alley - there was no other way to go - to find himself emerging out onto the illuminated ring road, the known world, so close but so far.

Fingers said not one word so Corpy spoke for him.

"Fingers'll be able open the door for us. He's clever that way…I said he could come for breakfast afterwards if that's okay?"

"Of course. Delighted." Alex wondered if Lisa should be forewarned, especially as Fingers was beginning to give off a rather pungent aroma redolent of a long life on the streets in old clothes without facilities for washing, as he warmed up in the back of the car. Neither Corpy nor Troop seemed in the least bothered however, so Alex was not either, but felt ashamed - again. Besides, they were pulling up outside the back of the VHS shop so there was no time to call Lisa and all attention now was on what might happen next.

"Fingers'd prefer it if you stayed here …while he opens the door" Corpy said in a way that clearly left no room for negotiation. "He also wants to know if there's an alarm?"

"No. It's a charity shop."

With that, Alex got out of the car with the others, but loitered outside the driver door and pretended to be interested in the car's bodywork while Fingers, Corpy and Troop sauntered up to the back entrance, as relaxed as a High Court Judge walking to his chair from his chambers. If Alex had wanted to call Lisa he did not dare; what would he say that would not be overheard and cause offence? Then, while Fingers plied his trade, Corpy and Troop loitered nonchalantly behind him, masking him from the street, prying eyes, Alex and even the bins. The picture of relaxed innocence they were strangely at odds with the discordant singing which had now escalated into something between an intermittent howl and a holler, with only the word Barbie being occasionally recognisable. Whoever was in there had a magnificent set of lungs Alex thought, with medical appreciation. Enviable. Clearly never smoked. Perhaps he was a swimmer with lung capacity like that?

Fingers took barely three minutes to open the door, which slid away from its chains without damage, protest or voice. Corpy hissed to Alex to join them while Fingers stood modestly to one side while Alex gaped with awe. The man should have been a surgeon.

"Listen!" Alex had stepped forward and pushed the door open as he spoke.

"I can't hear anything" Corpy said.

"Exactly! I hope he's alright. Something might have happened. We'd better be quick."

They filed into the dark interior, Alex leading them towards the shop floor, but they did not get far. The sickly green light leaking out from behind the cellar door arrested them mid-tentative-step, still in single file. They stopped, celluloid cartoon villains suspended for a moment to confer in whispers before unanimously nominating Alex, by virtue that he was in the lead, to open the cellar door.

"It's locked!" he said with secret relief as he tried the door "It's one of those self-locking ones: automatic, when it shuts."

Fingers shrugged. "Give me a proper challenge" his shoulders seemed to say. Alex was on the case, however.

"I know where the key is. Under the cactus in the office. You stay here while I get it."

"Put the lights on!" Corpy was right. No one would notice and it was absurd the way they were sensing their way around when all they had to do was flick a switch. As soon as they were illuminated the green light from the cellar door disappeared, absorbed into the glare of the overhead strip lights and no one would know that it existed. No wonder it had never been noticed; Davinia always switched on the lights as soon as she opened the back door. Whatever was in happening in the cellar was hidden in plain sight - completely unnoticed. Except for the smell which seemed to have swallowed all the air freshener in the world over the course of one night and was really strong. Horrible. Something decaying in a cesspit. Alex wondered how long it had been like that as he retrieved the key from its secure niche under the limp cactus plant that never seemed to grow and managed to give off an air of deep depression. It looked at him reproachfully as it was half lifted up and the key removed, as if to say, I know I'm just being used, it's alright, I can live with it; I'm used to the rejection. Alex took no notice and headed back to the cellar door, trophy in hand to do the honours and unlock the door.

It swung open, outwards, over the top of the steps and settled itself comfortably against the wall where it rested and stayed, as if keen to reveal its secrets, releasing its musty perfume. Alex sniffed, was reminded of Colin's feet then carefully launched himself onto the top step and began to descend, slowly, a great deal more calmly than he felt. He held onto the wall as he went, a small child descending a staircase, clinging to the security of the one steady side, unsure what to expect. Not exactly afraid but, definitely, not happy. Half-way down he gasped. And stopped. Then laughed out loud.

"Oh my God! It's cannabis!"

Behind him Corpy had seen the same thing. "It's a bloody weed farm.

There's tons of it."

"Now I know why they call it skunk. It stinks." It did. The men recoiled: Troop sneezed.

They surveyed the cellar, all of it, swathed in rows and rows of tall, sap green cannabis plants, bathed in a perfect storm of intense white lights suspended like Christmas decorations from the ceiling. Seven fingered leaves were pointing at them from every angle, reaching out to touch them as they approached from the stairs and began to thread their way through the burgeoning forest. As they made their way towards the back of the cellar, where all the black bags of summer clothes were piled up against the wall, they found him. Colin. Dressed only in a string vest and a pair of over-washed ancient Y fronts and his socks, comatose in a bed of bin bags, clutching a faux fur jacket.

"Is he dead?" Corpy asked.

Alex was bent over the body with a wrist in his hand.

"No. Pulse is good - strong, regular and slow. He's fine, but out for the count."

Alex had lifted both eyelids to inspect Colin's pupils which were dilated and unseeing; his breathing was slow and deep, but he was absolutely unrousable. Nothing Alex did or said would wake him; he tried. Even when Troop licked his face then trod on his sore toe, Colin did not move. In the end Alex rolled him over into the recovery position while they discussed what to do.

"He can't stay here. We'll have to move him."

"What's the matter with him?"

Alex grinned. "He's high. Stoned. Off his face. It's my guess he's eaten some of the leaves; probably thought they were lettuce or spinach or something, knowing Colin. He'll be fine; just needs to sleep it off."

With difficulty they managed to carry/drag Colin, utterly comatose, up the steps out of the cellar and into Alex's car. It took all three men and a dog but eventually the reeking invalid was slumped across the back seat of the car, knees bent to fit him in, while Troop and Corpy crouched in the boot, out of sight, behind the grill. Troop had only consented to travel thus if Corpy went with him. Alex hoped against hope that they would not meet the police on the way home. The plan was to get back to his house, unload Colin, put him to bed then work out what the hell to do about the cellar. Shelley had to be consulted he decided as he drove home though the mercifully, deserted streets. Thank God for cutbacks and austerity: there was not a policeman or a patrol car in sight. Fingers had neatly sealed all doors behind them as they had vacated the VHS premises and was now seated comfortably, if pungently, beside Alex in the front of the car enjoying the ride and revelling in the warmth. He seemed perfectly at home and had even pushed the brim of his hat up so that he could get a better view out of the car window. Alex half expected him to give a gracious royal wave to the watching street lights as they eased through the suburbs towards Tudorbethan sanctuary.

If Lisa was surprised to find a dog, four men, one of whom was unconscious and another a total stranger, on her doorstep, first thing on a Sunday morning she did not show it but merely smiled and opened the door wide enough to enable Colin's inert body to be lifted into the hall and dumped on the sofa in the living room. No one had the strength or will to get him upstairs. He seemed to be getting heavier every time he had to be moved so, still clutching the fur jacket, he was laid out on the three-seater sofa and covered with a blanket. The ever-adept Fingers had retrieved the intoxicated volunteer's discarded pot-infused clothes from the cellar which were meticulously folded and strategically placed over the arm of the sofa, ready for him when he awoke.

Everyone else gathered in the kitchen where, although it felt a little odd to introduce his wife to a man known only as Fingers, Alex found to his astonishment that he was enjoying the occasion. It was very lively. Even if Fingers did not speak, he had a way of joining in the conversation which was extremely relaxed and breakfast was a jolly affair in an Enid Blyton high-tea-after-an-adventure sort of way. Lashings of hot buttered toast and tea and marmalade followed a spread of bacon, eggs, sausages, tomatoes and amazingly, hash browns. Quite how and where they had come from, Alex could not imagine but Lisa was a wonder and he vowed he would never whinge about supermarket expenditure again. What she kept in the freezer was her business. Troop and Dave were in heaven; no one seemed to be monitoring how much 'fell' from the table and, although they eschewed the tomatoes, the sausages were particularly well received.

They had even come to an understanding about Dave's cushion beside the Aga and would both avail themselves of its comfort once the food supply dried up.

Inevitably, the conversation focussed on the VHS shop and the contents of its cellar.

"What are you going to do?" Lisa asked Alex. Even the dogs stopped begging, all the better to hear his reply.

"I don't know. I don't really want to go to the police, not with my record and Community Service and all that."

Corpy and Fingers now also stopped eating and were visibly fascinated. This was news of a most unexpected kind and they were intrigued. How could this be? Both looked around the affluent kitchen bearing all the hall marks of solid, honestly earned respectability: cappuccino machine, designer dog, Emma Bridgewater pottery and their minds went into overdrive. It was irresistible.

"Really?" Fingers had spoken and they all stared, even Corpy. Fingers ignored them and addressed himself to Alex. "What was it? White collar crime?"

"It's difficult to define…there's no legal precedent so it's unknown territory and they don't know what to do with me."

"Fascinating. I would like to discuss it more, if you are amenable? Not now, obviously - other fish to fry - but perhaps on another occasion?"

They all stared even more, especially Corpy. This was not the Fingers he knew, the down and out, hirsute, unwashed demon locksmith. Where had the Received Pronunciation voice come from? And the vocabulary? He had removed his deerstalker to reveal vast quantities of straggly grey hair, eyebrows and beard and under his outer layers, which were unwrapped with the care of a nurse removing bandages from a third degree burn, a shabby but once very sharp double breasted suit jacket was revealed, circa 1985, sporting peaked lapels and two back vents. Alex concealed surprise and agreed that a conversation about the legal intricacies of his case would be opportune, but they ought now to deal with the matter in hand. Time, as lawyers always said, was of the essence.

"I'm going to call Shelley, the other Community Service volunteer and talk it over with her. We're sort of in this together and she should have her say. In fact, I'm going to go and get her if she'll come, and we can discuss it properly, here. Is that OK?" This to Lisa who was fine, yes, it'd be great to see Shelley, soon as you like. Would you like me to call her for you? Alex had forgotten that Lisa and Shelley were co-conspirators and decided to be independent. No thank you, that was kind, but he would ring her, now. He thought she knew where she lived but would need to confirm the exact address. He'd be as quick as he could and was gone.

He described the events of the morning thus far to Shelley in the car on the return journey to casa Whiteley and she howled with laughter to the point of asphyxiation.

"Oh my God! I can't wait to see Colin! Stoned? You're kidding? In his vest and pants?" And she was off again, snorting and gasping with the effort of retaining sufficient breath for life as her diaphragm convulsed and heaved, a reincarnation of the steamer that was no more. But by the time they reached the tree-lined avenue that Alex called home she was much more serious and asking all the questions that were perplexing Alex.

"Who can have done this? Not Davinia - she's a cow but this is way out of her league. Orange Pippin?"

"No. She might smoke a bit of weed - I'm sure she probably does - but this would never occur to her. Apart from anything, cannabis is not a fruit."

"How did Colin get in there? How long was he in there? And what are we going to do about it? We can't just ignore a cannabis farm on the premises of our place of service to the community, but I don't want to go to the police. No way."

"Me neither" Alex agreed and wondered about the grammatical accuracy of his endorsement. "Colin is out cold on my sofa, so he hasn't been able to tell us a thing. Maybe when he wakes up, we'll find out more, but I wouldn't count on it."

"There's something rotten in the state of Denmark" Shelley concluded as they pulled into the drive. "Nice house."

It was quiet in the kitchen when they entered. The dogs were asleep, companionably curled together on Dave's cushion, Lisa was loading the dishwasher and there was no sign of either Fingers or Corpy.

"They're freshening up. Both bathrooms" Lisa explained. "I've also said I'll do their laundry and that they can help themselves to anything of yours they might need in the meantime. I knew you wouldn't mind. Just milk isn't it, Shelley?"

Alex noted not just that his wife and Shelley seemed to be extremely well acquainted, but that the washing machine was busting a gut. No doubt it had seen the size of the second pile of clothes awaiting attention at its feet.

"And Colin's still flat out on the sofa. I checked him just a few minutes ago."

On this count however, Lisa was wrong. As if on cue, a semi-naked figure had appeared in the doorway.

"Banquo lives" Shelley announced. No one got it.

"I don't feel well" Colin moaned. He would feel a great deal worse, thought Alex, when he realised that he was in his underwear and had been under the influence of an illegal substance. "I don't think those tablets from the chiropodist agree with me…Where am I?" He was looking about him, bewildered and lost. In his hand he still clutched the fur jacket, which he now used to wipe his face.

"You're at my house" Alex explained. "It's quite a story."

"Would you like a cup of tea, Colin?"

"The lady with the dog! What are you doing here? What happened to the Wizard? And where's the green city? … I'm ever so thirsty. Can I have a glass of water please? And something to eat? I'm starving." He had sat himself down at the kitchen table in readiness. As he pulled his chair in closer towards the table, he noticed his state of undress, and burst into tears.

"Where are my clothes? Someone's taken my clothes!" Then he was staring at the contents of his hand. "Why have I got Barb's coat? … I don't understand… I want Mother."

His wailing, interspersed with capacious snotty sniffs was pitiful. Lisa handed him a large glass of water by way of diversion which he drank in one protracted draught, as a man who had just found the only oasis in a desert and wanted to drink it dry in case it turned out to be a mirage. After which he calmed down, gulped down snot and tears and waited expectantly for a meal to turn up and for the adults to tell him what to do. Shelley had sat down opposite him and as Colin looked longingly at the Aga where Lisa was frying bacon et al, all over again, even though she had cleared away the first sitting, the gentle interrogation began.

It was hard to make sense of what Colin said - it was too absurd. How could he possibly have seen Barb going into the back of the shop? Was he sure it was her? Perhaps he had imagined it? He had said he thought it was a vision…beautiful but, as Shelley said, rather improbable.

"He hadn't even ingested the marijuana at that stage" Alex mouthed over Colin's head to Shelley who nodded, as puzzled as he was. Then the killer blow.

"But I found her coat. Look! Here it is. I've still got it so she must have been there, mustn't she?" This was incontrovertible evidence and Colin beamed helpfully. He was right, wasn't he? Yes, he certainly was and they were all completely baffled.

"Why don't we hand it over to Davinia?" Alex suggested.

"No. Don't trust her." Shelley passed sentence, but then had an idea. Damascene. "Why don't we tell Nerinda? Let her deal with it?"

"Who's that?" It was Corpy, who had appeared in the doorway, recognisable but transformed after a sojourn in a hot bath, a shave (including his head) and wearing one of Alex's track suits, a little too large but pristine as it had been bought, with the others, for a brief flirtation with gym membership.

"Who? Nerinda?"

"No. Her." Corpy indicated Shelley who was sitting at the table watching Colin.

"That's Shelley. She's the one who chooses the books for you."

"Shelley?"

Now she looked up. "Yeah. That's me."

"Shelley …Walton?"

"How'd you know my surname?"

"Because it's the same as mine."

Shelley stared. "Do I know you?"

"Obviously not, which is my fault. …I think I'm your father."

Chapter Seventeen
It Gets Even Weirder

Even the dogs looked amazed. Colin stopped eating, for a moment, to participate in the general astonishment then returned to the task of clearing his plate. He was a bit grumpy - liked his bacon crispier and the toast was too brown but no one took much notice. Alex had told them he would be testy until his weed hangover had passed and then he would be fine. Lisa, now identified as Alex's wife, had found him a track suit, another of Alex's temporary gym uniforms, and he was now dressed like Corpy, while his own clothes joined the pile for the washing machine which was grunting and spinning with effort.

Shelley did not know what to think. She could hardly remember her dad who had removed himself from her life so long ago, abandoning her to a mother consumed by bitterness and rage. Why would she want to know him now? How could she be sure that he was who he said he was anyway? It was all too weird.

"You look just like your mother at that age" Corpy had said by way of explanation when she had asked how the hell could he recognise her after all this time? "When I first met her. Gorgeous. Couldn't wait to marry her."

"Then leave her" was Shelley's rejoinder.

Awkward did not begin to describe the moment but they were saved by the arrival of Fingers…or was it? No one could be quite sure and in the light of recent revelations it was not unsafe to assume that he could be someone entirely different, a changeling perhaps, swapped by faeries in the second guest bathroom. Only the fact that he too was wearing the last of Alex's ex-gym tracksuits confirmed the possibility that he was in fact the hairy bearded man who had disappeared upstairs about an hour ago.

"Corpy helped cut my hair" he said apologetically as he reluctantly presented himself for inspection, assuming that the air of bewilderment was down to his metamorphosis, "and I decided to shave off the beard. I think it needs doing again though." He was right; having cut off the length of his beard he had then attempted a close shave, resulting in a badly corrugated scrubland across the lower half of his face. His hair appeared to have been shaped around a pudding bowl so he looked like an ancient page boy, pink cheeked from the heat of the bathroom. He also stank of aftershave, but no one complained. It was a definite improvement, although both Troop and Dave began to sneeze.

"How shall we tell Nerinda?" Alex decided to change the subject and fixed his attention on Shelley, who was in turn fixed on Corpy. "Should we ring her, do you think?"

"No. Email. Now. You do it; keep it simple. There'll be enough explaining to do when she gets back to us; she's bound to want a meeting." Her unflinching gaze was fixed on he who claimed to be her father all the time that she was speaking; Corpy was visibly withering but determined not to fall away, not again. Lisa took Fingers on one side to explain what had happened while Colin valiantly stormed his way through the contents of his plate.

An uneasy silence descended.

"How's your toe, Colin?" Alex asked.

"My toe?" Colin leant over to look at his feet, still in their socks, masticating steadily. "Oh, yes, that toe. Fine. Can't feel a thing."

"That'll be the effect of the cannabis" announced Shelley, looking away from Corpy. "Great for pain relief - it should be legalised."

"Cannabis?" Colin stopped chewing. Alex suppressed a groan and threw Shelley one of those 'say that and you'll die' glances, which she completely ignored.

"Yeah. In the cellar. That you ate."

"Cannabis? Me?"

Lisa intervened. "Colin! Have you finished? Good. Straight back to sofa for you; you need to sleep. Alex, you send the email to Nerinda. Now. From the desktop in the study?" He knew it was not a question and that it would be fatal to disagree with his wife when she was in Mussolini mood. "Fingers. No offence to Corpy but that haircut is a brute. I think I can improve on it, if you will allow? I'm not a hairdresser but I've seen it done enough times to have a fair idea what to do. I can also have a go at the eyebrows." These seemed to tremor slightly, whether in fear or relief it was hard to say but Fingers was man enough to know when to hand over complete responsibility to the other sex, and nodded meekly. "Good. Upstairs. Bathroom. Dave, with me…You two need to talk." It was perhaps the last thing in the world they wanted to do, but father and daughter were left with little choice, not in someone else's kitchen.

Lisa shooed the others out like flapping hens, skipping and clucking and then the court was in session.

Neither side said a word. Avoided each other's gaze. Stared at the detritus of Colin's breakfast on the table before them. Shelley lethargically gathered some toast crumbs into a minute heap which she then flicked with thumb and index finger back across the table. They both watched the crumbs disperse and scatter and a thick quietness began to settle like dust across the room. Troop had been observing them from his billet on the floor, seeing all, but moving nothing. Timing was everything. He stood up, stretched languidly, a yoga-perfect downward dog with rear end high in the air, yawned until his jaw squeaked, then shook. Vigorously. The dust lifted, noise poured as from an overfilled jug and he wagged his tail exuberantly as he wandered straight over to Shelley and laid his head on her lap. She melted. Fell for it. Humans! Troop thought. This was just too easy.

"Hello. Who are you?" Had he been a cat (dog forbid), Troop would have been purring as she fondled his ears.

"That's Troop. My dog."

"Yours? I thought you didn't like dogs? That's what Mum's always said."

"She's right. I didn't, but this was different somehow. Sometimes I think he chose me…It's a long story and a bit sad."

"Tell me."

So, he did, and she listened. And the lifting dust began to clear. At which point Troop wandered nonchalantly around to Corpy, nuzzled his hand, then returned to billet and fell asleep. Properly.

When Alex was allowed to return to the kitchen with Lisa and a further transformed Fingers, sporting trimmed hedge eyebrows and a more normal short back and sides head of hair which had become soft and started to curl at the newly released edges, Corpy and Shelley were deep in discussion about books.

"*English Passengers* was so funny, but dark. I loved it. It was a great choice."

"Yes! Especially when they are in Tasmania! But you have to admit it doesn't compare to *Hamlet* or *Macbeth*. Nothing ever does."

Corpy could not disagree but he'd have to read them again. It had been years since he'd looked at a Shakespeare play. Shelley was stunned. She had had no idea that anyone in her family read anything other than magazines in waiting rooms or instructions for flat pack furniture.

"I'll lend you my copies if you like?" Yes please. He would like, immensely.

"You should go and see them in performance together" Lisa said from the kitchen doorway, unannounced and unnoticed. "We could make that happen, couldn't we Alex?"

Instead of answering, his phone rang, bouncing with impatience on the kitchen counter. It was Nerinda. She had just received his email and yes, she knew it was a Sunday and it was outside their usual remit but this was really rather important and couldn't wait; she wanted to speak to both he and Shelley as soon as possible. Preferably today.

They met in town at one of the innumerable coffee shops that never seemed to close. On the way, Alex had dropped off Corpy, Troop and Fingers who had all insisted, to a dog, that they wanted to go back to the street. No, it was very kind offer, thank you, but they were not going to abuse the Whiteley's hospitality by out-staying their welcome. Of course, they would be delighted to return for clean laundry and a bath, but the street was their life and yes, they did plan to change things, but until they did, that was where they would stay. However, yes, they would promise to make their way to the tree-lined avenue if the weather was particularly cold or dreadful. And… Fingers was a little embarrassed, would it be alright if he took the toothbrush and toothpaste with him? Cleaning his teeth was such a pleasure, the one thing on the street he really missed. Lisa was a wonderful, wonderful lady. Alex was a mate. Shelley explained after they had dropped the trio off at the non-hobo side of the railway bridge that being 'a mate' was about as good as it got. Theirs was an exclusive brotherhood, in its way, and matedom was an accolade afforded to very few, especially if you lived a normal residential life. His Community Service and brush with the law had helped though, if that meant anything to him. It did not, but Alex would take what he could get. They would discuss Corpy - he was her father, wasn't he? - and Fingers later. First, they had to deal with Nerinda.

Who turned out to be surprisingly understanding and, more importantly, extremely practical. They had agreed to tell her about everything except Davinia's private enterprise on eBay, which now seemed to be of little significance, especially as she would clearly never be doing it again. Nerinda had clocked the necessity for discretionary details. The role of Corpy and Fingers was to remain discreet, anonymous and at best, unspoken. Colin was undoubtably a victim and his inadvertent consumption of a banned substance would have to be overlooked. Shelley and Alex were also extremely nervous about being compromised by circumstances and did not want, at any price, their attempts to redeem themselves in the eyes of society to be sullied by events beyond their control. Nerinda got it all, and came up with a solution. She had a contact in the local constabulary, a female detective she had known for years and who had a particular interest in all things drug related. She was the one who had been involved in a particularly salacious local drugs bust a while ago when an international cartel had been found to be operating out of the city. Unfortunately, the main perpetrators - perps the police called them - had got away but the supply of drugs on their branch of the county line had dried up, at least for the moment. Alex and Shelley were fascinated - Nerinda seemed to know so much about it. It made them wonder what she might have done before she went into the Community Service business.

Nerinda would make contact with this detective. The police would almost certainly have to interview them but don't worry, she was sure that immunity from any wrong doing would be a given. No, she could not guarantee it, but she was as confident as she could be that there would be no negative fall out for either Shelley or Alex. What they were essentially doing was giving the police a tip off - not quite anonymous, but as good as.

"Do we have to involve the police? Couldn't we just report it to the Vet's Help Society Head Office and let them deal with it?" Alex wanted to know.

Nerinda looked at him before she answered.

"No. We don't know that Head Office is not involved."

Oh my God. They didn't; it had never occurred to them.

"Not Davinia, surely?" Even Shelley was shocked.

"No, probably not, but we don't know. I'm glad you came to me and not to her" Nerinda elucidated, "just in case…Think about it. The VHS is a national organisation with shops all over the country. How do we know that this is not just the tip of the iceberg?"

"I need more coffee. Double espresso at least." Alex had stood up and was furtively peering around the room, terrified now at having been overheard. They should never had had this conversation in such a public place. Nerinda saw him and grinned.

"Don't worry. Apart from the fact that it's virtually empty no one ever listens to others in coffee shops. How often have you ever overheard a conversation in one? There's too much noise from the cappuccino machines and the baristas. Look how we had to lean over the table to hear each other, never mind anyone else. I have quite a lot of my confidential client discussions in coffee shops; it looks so normal, puts my clients at ease and gets them away from the office where everyone knows what they are there for. Such a stigma. Regular skinny latte for me please". Shelley had a green tea for which she offered to pay, which Alex thought was sweet but adamantly refused. As he sat down again and prepared to fortify himself with excess caffeine, Nerinda posed a question,

"Who's Barb?"

And when it came to an answer, they had to admit that they really had no idea.

Chapter Eighteen
The Full Force of the Law

Colin was terrified of being interviewed by the police. When Alex and Shelley explained to him what was happening, he burst into searing tears. Lisa had helped him upstairs to the bathroom, soap and water so that when they returned from the meeting with Nerinda, they found a clean, fully dressed somewhat grumpy Colin whose hangover was still firing on all cylinders, exhibiting all the signs of drug induced paranoia and irrationality.

"How much of it did you eat, Colin?" Shelley asked, fascinated.

"I don't know. I was hungry. I thought it was spinach or something like that. Greens are supposed to be good for you." Here his sniffing and misery prevented further speech.

"You weren't to know - it wasn't your fault" Alex tried to soothe but terror intervened.

"I'm a criminal! I'm going to go to prison! What will Mother do? Who'll look after my fish? Oh, what'll Barb think of me? Do you think she'll visit me? Will she wait? I might be gone for years and years and years and she'll find somebody else…" he collapsed into hysteria. Lisa put her arms around him as he sobbed against her chest.

"It's Barb we wanted to ask you about…" began Alex but trailed off, waiting for calm. When it came, Colin having sobbed himself out and holding his head which he said felt like was looking at him from the other side of the room, the subject of Barb was resumed.

"The police will want to know more about her, Colin. That's all they'll be interested in, not you. You haven't done anything wrong."

"I'm a.. one of those, ..you know…flunkeys."

"Junkies. No, you're not, you're a victim. You didn't know what it was. You didn't even know it was there, did you?"

That was true, even Colin could see the wisdom of Shelley's words.

"I only went to find Barb. I thought the smell was from my sore toe." No one said anything, especially Alex, who had had the same thought more than once during the time leading up to the great weed farm revelation. Colin continued, calmer, caring, "Where is Barb?"

"That's what we'd all like to know. As well as other things, like how did her coat get there? How did she get into the shop? Who is she?"

Nerinda contacted the police as soon as she had left the coffee shop. Her liaison there was an ex-colleague, Catherine Scott, the large lady with vitiligo who had already made her debut VHS appearance after the snake episode. Catherine and Nerinda had been junior officers together which had been enough for Nerinda and she had bailed, first into social work and then into the Probation Service which kept her close in touch with her former life and friends. Catherine was an odd one, 'singular' in every sense of the word but the two women got on well and, perhaps what was more important, trusted each other. Nerinda knew that she could rely on Catherine to respect the somewhat nebulous nature of the 'tip off' and she was right, the detective did not ask the obvious, awkward questions but cut straight to the heart of the matter – the who, why and how of the cannabis factory.

Why was easy - it was hugely profitable at every level. The who and how were more complicated and the person of most immediate interest was, of course, the ubiquitous Barb.

"Find her and we'll find answers" Catherine told her team, whom she had assembled at short notice. Then she set off to interview Colin, not at his home but at the Whiteley's house in the tree-lined avenue - Nerinda's idea based upon what Alex and Shelley had told her about the hapless fish-loving pot head with the ingrowing toe nail. It would also enable Catherine to speak to the whistle blowers without compromising them or their co-conspirators. Shelley had also made it clear to Alex that Corpy and Troop and thereby Fingers, were not to be involved, in any way. She had her dad to think about.

Catherine's arrival at the house was heralded by a canine chorus of low growls on the part of Dave and a yappy duet from the interior of the detective's car. She never went anywhere, except her office when her boss was in a bad mood, without her dogs, her girls, Euclid and Pi: two Jack Russells of indeterminate origin, strong wills, decided tastes and almost no training. She declined Mrs Whiteley's more polite than enthusiastic offer to 'bring the dogs in, if you like' and entered the house without them. She patted Dave then got straight down to business. Once Colin had been reassured, convinced, promised and reassured several times more that he was not a criminal and no, definitely would not be going to prison, the discussion became much easier. Sadly however, not more helpful.

Colin could tell her nothing. He knew no more than they did about Barb, not her full name, her address, especially not her age. He could describe her appearance and tell them that she liked carrot cake, was beautiful and marvellous and just like the little mermaid on the rock she had given him for Christmas. Did he still have the wrapping, the bag she came in? No? That was a pity. So, they had met in Aquarium World and she had a nephew who brought her from the Forest of Dean? And he had a swanky car - could he describe it? Colin did what he could but was sorry, he did not drive and did not know much about cars but it was new looking and quite big and possibly navy blue, or black or something quite dark like that. He told the lady policeman every detail of his first meeting with Barb and all that he could remember about subsequent meetings thereafter. He showed her his tattoo and told her about his plan for Barb's, including his dilemma about whether or not to change the design to include a mermaid. It took a long time but Catherine learned very little of use. One thing she was particularly interested in though, was the timing of Barb's visits to the shop.

"She seems unlikely to have had independent access so I'm working on the premise that she was working with someone, or others, who are connected with the Veteran's Help Society. Is there anyone you can think of?"

"Not Davinia! Davinia wouldn't! She's marvellous." Colin was adamant and the others agreed, albeit for different reasons. Neither Alex nor Shelley could have justified why but they were both convinced that Davinia, for all her faults, would never have had the enterprise to start a cannabis farm on her own premises. Candy, aka Orange Pippin, an alias which took quite some explaining to the detective, was also above suspicion but both she and Davinia would be checked out anyway, as part of a process of elimination if nothing else.

"What other volunteers are there, or regular visitors to the shop?" Catherine wanted to know.

There was Anna, which made even Colin smile. No. Anna was out of the frame, literally; she would never be able to get up and down the cellar steps. Then there was Reg, but that was out of the question.

"Reg?"

"The regional manager."

"Regional manager – for the Veteran's Help Society? … Travelling around, visiting shops…by car?"

Yes, that was him, but surely not…? He was the regional manager. Davinia's boss! From Head Office.

"Exactly."

The following morning the shop had become a crime scene. Davinia had been informed the evening before and interviewed, as 'part of the ongoing investigation' by DCI Scott in the privacy of her own home, away at least from the embarrassment of having to visit a police station. Although the noise of those dreadful dogs in the back of the police officer's car parked outside her domain was a disgrace. No doubt it would have alerted all the neighbours about an unexpected guest at the private residence of a retail outlet manageress. Thank heavens it wasn't a police vehicle; that would have been altogether too humiliating. And surely selling a few items on eBay did not warrant an unsolicited visit by a Detective Chief Inspector? Davinia was mentally formulating a complaint about police insensitivity in which she was a most eloquent, convincing orator and the Chief Superintendent, or whoever was in charge, was utterly in her thrall, as she drove to work. Not that there was much work to be done. She had been permitted to enter the front of the shop and was dismayed beyond words to find the pavement outside the shop thronged with an eager crowd. The Vet's shop was at it again! The frisson of excitement was tangible, pulsing up and down the street like an athlete in training. When the blue and white police tape had been draped outside the premises, the word went out, and the people gathered. Interestingly, there were a great many undesirables evident among the increasing throng, those usually associated with loitering around in corners in sleeping bags and associated detritus of those of those on the street. On this occasion however, they were part of laundered society, components of the whole, united beyond the street by curiosity, gossip and an overwhelming stench.

Police access had been obtained via Head Office although Davinia had submitted her keys to the detective without demur. She had been shocked, deeply shocked, first that the police appeared to know nothing of her illicit trading on eBay and then, not just by the revelation that drugs were being farmed in her cellar but that a) she could have been suspected and b) she had not known. How could she not have known? It was mortifying. She had thought the smell was mould! That and Colin's foot - but here she blamed that bloody Alex man. He was a doctor, no, a surgeon, and he had said that unwashed feet and fungal infections gave off an aroma the same as a weed factory! She despaired for the NHS; she really did.

Such were her thoughts until she actually arrived at the shop, outraged that she could not park in her allotted space, which had been taped off and she was forced to use the public car park. The local council should be ashamed to charge so much money for such an essential facility. It was legalised extortion. Fine for those who drove expensive cars like the ridiculously over-sized 4 x 4 she had pulled in next to, they could afford it. But what about everybody else? No wonder the high street was in trouble. She would take it up with her MP, she really would. Then, forced to walk to her own place of employment like any ordinary employee, she was horrified to have to edge her way through a group of strangers, several layers thick, some of whom were even unwashed, to find herself on the wrong side of the police tape outside the premises of which she was the manageress. Then the police woman, who was patently too young to be fully qualified, refused to let her through, even though she explained exactly who she was. Apparently, it made no difference, her orders were not to let anyone in. As if she was 'anyone!' Fortunately, at that moment the female (certainly no lady) detective deigned to put in an appearance and said that she could be allowed into the front part of her own shop, but no further. There was some slight consolation in the importance of being assisted to cross beneath the tape, which was held up by the policewoman, then escorted into the shop by the officer in charge of the investigation although she hoped the enthralled spectators did not hear the comment about her 'helping with the enquiry' as she walked through the front door. At least she could still be seen through the double glazing; she sucked in her stomach and kept her smooth Botoxed face well within public view.

It was disappointing to find that her volunteers were already there, ostensibly also helping with enquiries but in reality, very much in the way and a pain for the police who simply wanted to examine the scene and clear out the cannabis. Davinia noticed that Colin seemed to be wearing a new track suit. Well, at least it wasn't a shell suit, and the shop was closed to customers, so she would let it pass on this occasion. She hoped he had not acquired it just because he was apparently the central player in this particular drama; she still did not know quite how he had become entrapped in the cellar or indeed, how the police had found about it. Nor how he had escaped. And what about Head Office? And Reg? How much did they know? Who had told them? Or was that yet more for her to worry about?

Once the shop floor had been checked and the office searched to ascertain that nothing had been taken and that the crime was, in fact, all about what had been added to the premises rather than removed, the staff were advised to leave – perhaps if they would like to go down to the station, where they could make their statements, where someone would bring them up to speed with what was happening? Yes, that suited very well and Alex offered to drive them there which suited Colin and Shelley even better. Orange Pippin wanted to know if he drove an environmentally friendly hybrid car but accepted the offer of a lift nevertheless, while Davinia preferred to make her own way thank you; things to do later; so little time, so much pressure, so much to accomplish. She was in the public car park today, most inconvenient. Oh! He was too? How nice. They could walk that way together. And when they all arrived at the same spot in the car park and Alex unlocked the 4 x4 beside which Davinia was parked, she wondered why she was even surprised. What was it? A Land Rover Discovery? She should have known. And all her suspicions about the NHS resurfaced and even the Botox could not hide the discontent on her face as she was forced to follow her deputy manageress, superannuated volunteer and two Community Service personnel all the way to the local police station.

At the police station it was no better. They were all herded in together and put in the same room to wait while, one by one, they gave their statements to the police in a little side room which was, thankfully, private. Colin went first which was ridiculous and was in there for far too long, followed by Alex who was quicker, but only just. Then Shelley, who could obviously barely read and write so goodness only knows what she managed to say, then, finally, herself. Orange Pippin was last but she did not count although they all wondered under which name she would sign her statement. So, there they were, for the best part of the day, sustained only by atrocious coffee from a machine and water from a cooler in the corner of the room. Colin was mesmerised by the water cooler; kept saying how the bubbles reminded him of his little mermaid on her rock and he drank gallons of it just so that he could see the bubbles activated as the water was extracted. Then he had to keep going to the 'little boy's room' so constantly slap-limped his despicable sandals and gruesome hand knitted socks up and down the corridor like Quasimodo, dressed for a visit to the gym. The waiting room was an abomination: so degrading. All Formica and plastic chairs screwed to the floor, chained like galley slaves, forever facing walls covered with posters about rape crisis with emergency numbers for every crime known to man, and some only to woman. And all the time Big Brother was staring out at them in the form of the desk sergeant from behind a perspex wall with a slot for engaging in conversation. No wonder the world was going to the dogs. Nasty hairy, smelly things. Colin was deeply affected by the 'are you suspicious about terrorism?' posters. At one point, Davinia had heard him whisper to Alex to ask if he had a piece of paper and a pen. Thankfully, he had not so Colin could not make a note of the number but then, before anyone could stop him, he had lumped his way over to the slot in the perspex and was asking the sergeant if he could have something to write on. Of course, the policeman, clearly past his sell by date, had jumped to the conclusion that Colin wanted to change his statement which made things extremely complicated and it really began to look as if they would be spending the night there. And she had so much to do! At least now she knew why her electricity bill had been so high and why Reg had said he would sort it. Traitor! Well, Head Office would have to deal with it; payment was not coming off her shop's bottom line. No way. Eventually it was ascertained that all Colin wanted was the number to call if he suspected terrorist activity so the desk sergeant gave him a flyer, with which he was exorbitantly thrilled and said he would put up in his kitchen. Then he divided his time between drinking water to the point of self-submersion and ostentatiously studying her Radley handbag in case it was a suspicious package. As if! She half hoped the little dog would take his hand off.

Just as Davinia had reached the point where another complaint about wasting valuable personal time had been devised, rehearsed and successfully executed in the privacy of her own mind, the woman detective wandered into the room, as if she had nothing else to do, and sat down.

"Thank you for your patience. I thought you'd like to know what's happening. I'll keep it brief. You've been here long enough and will want to get home I'm sure."

Vigorous nodding from Colin who was concerned about his fish, a frown from Davinia whose time was precious and irreplaceable and undisguised curiosity about what was going on, from the others.

"We've examined the premises, gathered evidence, lots of it, and are in the process of dismantling and removing the cannabis, which will be destroyed."

Orange Pippin looked righteously outraged and was sorely tempted to deliver a lecture about recycling; surely it could have been put to some good medicinal use? Her colleagues knew instinctively what she was thinking and prayed she would remain silent. Their prayers were heard. Catherine Scott continued, unaware of the narrowness of her escape.

"You'll be able to go back to work tomorrow but not for the rest of today I'm afraid. We've been in touch with the Veteran's Help Society

Head Office who have been most co-operative and our enquiries have been narrowed down to two people, possibly three.

Everyone who was innocent immediately assumed that they were guilty. Catherine had witnessed the same look before, on so many faces, and wanted to smile. But reassured instead.

"No one here is under any suspicion…but we are very anxious to trace the whereabouts of Reg Sutton, your regional manager, and his wife, Barbara Sutton, better known to you as …"

"Barb?" Colin wailed. "Barb! …. Oh, what have I done?... Barb is a married woman!"

"The least of her crimes" muttered Davinia.

"Oh, her most pernicious soul" misquoted Shelley.

"Married to Reg?" Alex disbelieved.

"Too much meat and dairy in their diet" judged Orange Pippin (Candy on her police statement).

"As yet we have not been able to find them, but rest assured that we will and then I think I can say, with confidence, that we will be able to conclude our investigation."

Davinia was in a state of shock but fortunately, not catatonic. She still had plenty to say. "I don't understand. How could Reg be involved? He's a regional manager – an excellent one, who takes his responsibilities very seriously. He's so meticulous and reliable."

"He certainly is" Catherine replied, "assiduous too. Especially where his personal interests appear to be concerned. It seems that in his capacity as the manager of a large area, he has been able to orchestrate a very successful drugs import and distribution system. Obviously, I cannot divulge details as yet but I will keep you informed; you have a right to know. It's unfortunate that you have been caught up in all this and I would like to thank you all, for your co-operation."

"Can I open the shop tomorrow?" Davinia wanted to know. Yes, of course; the VHS must carry on its excellent work. If the police had any further enquiries they would, of course, contact her.

"Is there anything else?" Davinia again, a little hesitantly. Everyone except Catherine knew perfectly well why.

"No, not at the moment. Thank you all."

Davinia had never been so grateful for her Botox investment; the relief she felt about her obviously unreported illicit trading would otherwise have rendered her akin to something Orange Pippin might drink as a smoothie. Davinia could depart in high spirits with a glad heart. Colin however, had a heart as broken as his gait. He shuffled miserably out of the police station, guided by Alex and Shelley, clutching his head with one hand and his tattoo with the other, moaning softly and muttering to himself. Back in the car, seated in the front for ease of access for his gammy toe, he let his grief flow. Unrestrained. Most of which, as it transpired, was the pain of mortification rather than irredeemably fractured passion.

"A married woman! I've been in love with a married woman! Oh, I'm so wicked. What will Mother say?"

"Don't tell her" Shelley advised from the back seat.

"You didn't know she was married. She didn't tell you." Alex consoled.

"But I should have asked! I should have known." Colin's wailing was getting louder; Alex considered turning on the radio.

"No, you shouldn't. She led you on. She's the wicked one." This was the first sensible thing Orange Pippin had said since before Christmas and it did not go unnoticed. "I always knew she was no good." This was less sensible, but no one argued; how could they?

Colin continued to wail, more quietly now; gradually it would reduce to a whimper then subside completely, by which time he would no longer be in love.

"Where are we going, Alex?" asked Shelley as they sailed past the shop in the 4 x 4.

"My house" he replied. "We need tea and cake – and fruit."

The next morning, they were all at the shop early, just in case. Who knew what might have happened overnight? And their punctuality paid off, first in the inevitable surge of customers that the latest thrilling VHS adventure had produced and second, of much greater excitement, the arrival of DCI Scott. She breezed in, dogs left to yap in the back of her car to Davinia's relief, and announced that there had been a development. It was the detective's suggestion that Colin should man the till - no one more capable she said which made him blush - while she updated the others in the privacy of the office. She particularly wanted to speak to Alex, Shelley and Davinia, of course, which made Davinia purr. Orange Pippin was determined to be in on the act so quietly installed herself in the most inaccessible corner of the room; if there was a fire, she would be the last out, but that was a risk worth taking.

The development concerned Reg and Barb, which was why Catherine had sent Colin off on detachment. Apparently, the runaways had booked a last-minute budget airline flight to Istanbul, with the intention of going to Georgia.

"But Georgia's in America!" Shelley had interrupted.

"Not the former Soviet Republic of" Catherine had explained. It seems that Barb had a sister and brother in law who lived in Tbilisi, so that was where they were headed, largely because it was outside the EU.

"Because of Brexit" Orange Pippin muttered glumly.

"No, because it's outside reciprocal EU extradition agreements. But don't worry, they didn't get there. In their hurry to get tickets Reg had omitted to book Priority Boarding so they were each restricted to one small bag on the plane. Barb had an oversize suitcase and a large designer handbag, both of which she refused to relinquish and this had led to a lively altercation with the airline staff at the departure gate. You know what budget airlines are like about cabin luggage. The police were summoned, Barb and Reg have been arrested and are now in custody."

They had been interviewed, separately. Reg was co-operating with the police but Barb was being most resistant, refusing to say anything except that it wasn't her fault and she didn't know anything about it. She had denied that the faux fur jacket was hers and robustly asserted that she had been deliberately framed by Colin, who had masterminded the whole scheme; she was just an innocent victim. Colin had led her on. Led her astray, deceived and duped her. It was all too much and she was traumatised, so she should be released immediately. At which point even Davinia yowled with as much mirth as her injections would permit. The detective manifestly failed to remain serious until she went on to describe what they had discovered. The network of VHS shops was being used as a two-way distribution system, focused on North Shields, which was not only the last stop for donated goods but the reception point for drugs coming into the UK from abroad. Bags of clothes were delivered to the end of the line discount outlet in North Shields where the illegal drugs were then collected, put into black bin bags and distributed across the country via the VHS shops. That was why coat hangers and rails were never used to move garments, only black bags.

"At Reg's insistence." Alex commented. "I suggested a better system and he was having none of it."

"That's why" Catherine replied. Davinia kept quiet; Alex did not look at her, nor she at him. "We've arrested one of the drivers who was in on it, but it does seem that growing their own, as it were, was a new initiative and largely experimental. Thankfully it was stopped before it started and, in the process, we have also been able to break an established chain of distribution. I would like to thank you for your assistance, which is very much appreciated."

It appeared that the briefing was over but no, not quite.

"I am also delighted to pass on to you the thanks of the Spanish police."

This caused quite a stir. Alex remembered Colin's Gift Aid debacle with discomfort but need not have worried. It seemed that Barb's sister and brother in law were wanted by the Spanish authorities for substantial unpaid fines deriving from illegal building across the Costa del Sol. They had fled the country after a court ruling had gone against them and vanished, obviously outside EU jurisdiction or they would have been traced. However, the apprehension of the Suttons meant that Interpol had been able to locate the fugitives in Tbilisi and arrangements with the Georgians were already underway for their return to Spain. Running away appeared to be built into Barb's DNA.

When the detective had left, speaking to Colin on her way out and thanking him personally for his important contribution to solving what was a most puzzling case, Alex was designated by the others to update Colin with the latest exciting instalment. It was agreed that it would be done in such a way that Colin's dignity would be preserved and there would be no further injury to his broken heart. Alex was a surgeon, used to difficult conversations, he must have acquired a suitable bedside manner by now, so no one better to do the job, was there? Davinia was clearly not taking no for an answer so it was with a heavy heart that Alex headed out towards the till while all the others, he noticed resentfully, appeared to have evaporated.

Colin was in ebullient mood. He could not wait to tell Mother how he had been so important, the detective said so, in helping to crack the case. Although he was not entirely sure what this meant it was obviously a very good thing. Gone was the ghastliness of the cellar, the headache, the pain in his toe, even the smell. He was the best man for working The Till - yes, the detective had actually said those words, and all was right with the world. He listened to what Alex said with sanguinity and then the Barb moment came. Gravely, quietly as if delivering news of a terminal illness to an unsuspecting patient, Alex began to describe, in the blandest possible way, Barb's role in the failed escape bid and her attempt to shift blame onto Colin. To his astonishment, Colin seemed entirely unmoved by the accusations of his renegade lady love and waited patiently for Alex to finish speaking, a benign expression on his face.

"It doesn't matter, Alex. It's all over."

"You don't mind?"

"No. It's been a deeply painful experience and I've suffered untold agony, but that's all behind me now."

Alex stared. Was this Colin he was hearing? What he could not know was that Colin, since he had been so unlucky in love, had been avidly reading Mother's magazines. All the answers were there on the problem pages, and so beautifully written; Colin had even memorised some of them, or thought he had. Whatever, his heart was well on the way to recovery and Alex did not need to worry. Kind of him to ask, but Colin was tickety boo. There was one thing that bothered him though. What was that? Alex enquired, fearing the worst: some sort of post-traumatic stress perhaps. Colin was crestfallen; serious and sombre. What was he to do with the little mermaid, bubbling innocently on her rock, still blonde, beautiful and doing an excellent job of oxygenating the fish tank? Should he keep her or should he return her to Barb? Wasn't it customary to return gifts when a love affair went sour?

Once it had been agreed that the little mermaid could remain in situ with a clear conscience and that returning her to Barb was possibly not the most appropriate or pressing action of the moment, Colin resumed his normal pre-Barb life, a cheerfully sorrier and wiser man. He was done with women, forever, and frankly, he told Alex, it was a relief. He had had no idea that love was so exhausting and stressful. It would be so nice to return to wearing clothes that were comfortable rather than dressing to impress (as described in one of Mother's magazines) and he had been alarmed at the amount of money he had had to spend on cake. His biggest worry now that the little mermaid had been taken care of, was his tattoo.

Yes, Alex had wondered what he was going to do about that. Maybe they should consult Shelley? Oh yes! That was a marvellous idea.

As Colin was being reintroduced and rehabilitated into a Barb free society, Davinia was in her office with the door firmly closed. Where those apart from the male staff talking *mano a mano* out at the till had gone, she had no idea, and cared even less. She had just opened an email from Head Office and was all in a flutter. The Man from Head Office was on his way to see them.

Chapter Nineteen
The Man from Head Office

Davinia was not sure what to expect but the slim man in trainers with the goatee beard and badly in need of a haircut was not it. He was not even carrying a briefcase but instead, what looked suspiciously like a backpack slung over one shoulder. No suit, no tie and wearing trainers! High end admittedly but she so hoped Colin would not notice; what had she always said about smart footwear? Their exalted guest crept in through the front door almost unnoticed and was to all intents and purposes a customer until he approached Colin and asked to see the manageress, who was expecting him.

"Davinia?"

The very same.

"She's awfully busy. The Man from Head Office is coming."

"I am indeed" he said comfortably. "You must be Colin, I think? You're quite a name at Head Office".

"I am?" Colin was choked with emotion. Mother would be so proud. He said nothing but beamed joyfully at the stranger who waited uncomplainingly, bathed in the light of Colin's glory, then gently broke the spell and reminded him about Davinia. Head Office should have waited just seconds longer.

"Colin! Is there any sign of him yet?" Davinia was calling from the back of the shop, something between a shout and a conspiratorial hiss.

Colin said nothing, still basking in his fame and merely pointed to the man at the till who had pushed himself forward and was now approaching. Davinia swallowed her shock and found her most professional Botox enhanced expression. They went into her office and shut the door. Colin could then revel in his notoriety and triumph and jiggle with excitement at the prospect of telling anyone who would listen.

The Man from H.O got straight to the point. What had happened had all been very distressing and potentially embarrassing for the Organisation, but he was happy to say that their legal team and PR department were all over it and what mattered now was damage limitation and moving forward. Reg would plead guilty and was no doubt looking forward to mitigating the severity of his punishment by co-operating fully with the police at every level. His wife however, had denied all involvement and was proving much less amenable. Colin was, of course, beyond suspicion despite her claims to the contrary but Mrs Sutton was proving to be something of a thorn in the side of the investigation and he understood that she was continuing to prove extremely troublesome at the remand centre where she was being held. Having just spoken to Colin he was reassured to see how well and maturely he was coping with what must have been a most distressing experience. Davinia nodded in agreement, wondering how a man with a goatee could be quite so efficient.

"Which leads me on to the present, Davinia." He could call her that, couldn't he? Good. So much more personal, particularly in view of what he was about to say. Her wonder shifted from his hairy chin to what was about to be said. Personal? She had only just met him.

"Head Office has been impressed by your handling of recent events as well as your record of sales and management. Very impressed. Your calm demeanour, capability and especially your relationship with your staff are exactly the qualities we require at a senior managerial level so, getting straight to the point – I don't believe in wasting time - we would like to offer you the position of Regional Sales Manager that has so recently become vacant." He stopped, she stared.

"Take over from Reg?"

"Exactly. With immediate effect. We need someone with your qualifications, who knows how we operate, as soon as possible – a seamless transition. What do you think?"

She was exhilarated, but wary. How much did Head Office know? Reg was singing like a bird but had he told them …everything?

"Have you spoken to Reg at all?"

"Only through his lawyer. It seems he has a very high opinion of you and, I may say, recommended you for the position. Between ourselves and his legal advisor, I understand that he is hoping that you will provide him with a statement testifying to his excellent character which will be used by his Defence to help reduce his sentence. He speaks very highly of your working relationship with him and I believe he is confident that you will be a valuable character witness."

I bet he is she thought, expressionless. So, nothing had been said about her online misdemeanours. Of course, she would be the new regional manager, delighted to accept, such an honour, a marvellous opportunity, they would not regret it, she would give it 110% and more, everything she had ever wanted, etc etc.

The Man from H.O. cut her short. Good, that was sorted then. Now, who should take over at the shop? He had an idea which he would like to share but first, he would like to speak to Mr Whiteley. He was there wasn't he? Excellent. They would use the office if she didn't mind – there must be so many other things she had to do. Thus, Alex was summoned and Davinia exiled to the shop floor and the steam-free steam room. The first thing I'm going to do as regional manager is get them a new steamer she resolved; that'll keep them out of trouble. Especially her.

The conversation was cordial and brief. Head Office would like to offer Alex the position of shop manager. They appreciated that he was from a completely different professional background but were confident that he had more than adequate transferable skills and, in the light of the medical, er, individualism, that had resulted in his Community Service, they wondered if, perhaps, this was an opportunity for him to change career? Man from H.O. stopped and like Davinia before him, Alex stared. Then unequivocally refused. No, he did not need to think about, thank you. he was flattered by the offer but could not possibly accept. Medicine was his life. However, he did have a suggestion.

"Shelley?"

"Yes."

"Community Service Shelley?"

"She would make an excellent manageress."

Head Office was now rummaging in its back pack and fetching out a very Smart Phone which was being rapidly jabbed and scrolled. Alex decided to press home his case.

"She's intelligent and well read, street wise, capable and excellent in a crisis. She was the one who dealt with the snake. She's also hard working and committed – I know, we've worked together all the time we've been here; she's a real team player."

Head Office was listening and reading, and liking the buzzwords. Now he began talking.

"Her reports from Davinia are not exactly complimentary."

"That was before they got to know each other. I think I can safely say that Davinia would not be so critical now, if you were to ask her. In fact, I'm sure she would be quite the opposite."

"Shelley was found guilty of shop lifting."

"Poacher turned gamekeeper. No one better to manage a shop in this day and age. Even charity shops get shop lifters."

There was a silence; both were thinking of the fur coat episode.

"You might have a point, Alex. It's certainly worth thinking about. I will have to discuss it with Head Office but it's something to bear in mind. And you are prepared to vouch for her?"

"I am. Absolutely. All Shelley needs is a chance to make something of herself. There is, of course, another aspect to this." Alex was appalled at himself – he was becoming as sly as Lisa, or, heaven forbid, Davinia, but all in a good cause.

"What's that?"

"It's an excellent publicity opportunity for the Veteran's Help Society. What you may not know, is that Shelley's father is himself a veteran who needs support, suffering from PTSD, on the street, that sort of thing. Additionally, it sends out exactly the right message about the VHS Community Service support project – not just helping people to rehabilitate and reform but actually taking them on, employing them, giving them responsibility. Believing in them."

The secret was knowing when to stop. Don't talk your way through the sale, Alex, he said to himself; shut up. But had he done enough?

He had. Head Office was intrigued, enthralled, on-side and already beginning to plan Press articles. Yes, it was a most interesting proposition and he liked it – a lot. Alex would not say anything to anyone about their discussion? Of course not, he never thought otherwise, but Head Office would have a think and a chat and would be in touch with Ms Walton, he was sure. And now he had to go – so much to do. It had been a pleasure, Mr Whiteley – Alex – and while he was sorry that they would not be working together in the future he hoped that they could keep in touch. The last Davinia saw of Head Office was the backpack disappearing out of the front door accompanied by poetic words in the draught promising 'to be in touch'.

***

It was dark, but the days were getting noticeably longer. Not warmer, but that would come.

"Something to look forward to" said Corpy.

Fingers nodded in agreement. The two men had been discussing what had brought them to the street. Neither had ever thought it would happen to them; no one ever did. At least Corpy had found his daughter though. Fingers bitterly regretted the loss of both his kids as well as the wife who had moved them 'out of harm's way' when booze had taken over his life. People often said they had lost everything, but in his case, it was true. He had gone from a lucrative position as head of security in a multi-national to nothing, a nobody, anonymous on the street and no, he would not tell even Corpy what his real name was. But yes, he was angry. The internal systems failure had not been his fault but he had had to take responsibility. He had been fired, was out of work, drank too much, lost his house, wife, kids, self-respect and hope. All he had left from that life was a suit jacket, dated, shapeless and soiled. He wore it as a hair shirt – his days of alcoholism were over but the jacket remained as a deterrent, a symbol of agony and loss.

"Better be getting along then" Fingers said, easing himself with damp limbs and stiff joints. "I might head over to the brazier. What about you?"

"We'll stay here, eh, Troop? Gotta good book to read."

"From Shelley?"

"Yeah."

"Nice… See you."

Corpy and Troop watched him fade into the dark night, intermittently lit up by the street lights as he passed beneath them; a Victorian slide show in slow motion. Then they settled themselves down in the VHS doorway on their cardboard with the sleeping bag and the blanket. Sleep came regularly and deeply to Corpy now, even when it was very cold. He no longer kept the SA80 at his side, cocked and ready to fire. It had been some time since he had needed it and besides, he had Troop. He switched on the LED torch that Shelley had given him for reading under the bedclothes, and opened her copy of *Hamlet.*

Printed in Great Britain
by Amazon

56400056R00133